Praise for Maryse Condé's
Who Slashed Celanire's Throat?

"Another great offering from one of our most gifted writers. Read and learn, but most of all, read and enjoy."

—Edwidge Danticat, author of *The Dew Breaker*

"Lush and lurid . . . sultry settings . . . seducing the reader with silken irony."

—*Kirkus Reviews*

"A fantastical tale of stunning survival and powerful revenge."

—*Elle Magazine*

"Mystical, magical, riveting, true. All these words apply to Maryse Condé's thought-provoking novel."

—Colin Channer, author of *Passing Through* and *Waiting in Vain*

"Maryse Condé is one of the most important novelists writing today. Her stories are both historical and present, in the moment, murmuring secrets flavored with a Caribbean language of swishing rhythms, sweet as nectar, and lyrical as the swooshing skirts of the Guadeloupean women who people her new novel."

—Quincy Troupe, author of *Transcircularities: New and Selected Poems* and *Miles: The Autobiography*

T0127535

Other books by Maryse Condé

Maryse Condé

Translated by Richard Philcox

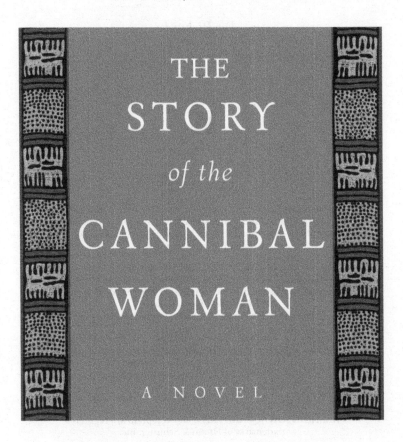

THE
STORY
of the
CANNIBAL
WOMAN

A NOVEL

"[Conde] demonstrates how one's entire sense of self gets swallowed up by trauma and its dislocating aftermath"
—*New York Times*

WASHINGTON SQUARE PRESS
New York London Toronto Sydney

For Richard

Washington Square Press
A Division of Simon & Schuster, Inc.
1230 Avenue of the Americas
New York, NY 10020

First Washington Square Press trade paperback edition April 2008

WASHINGTON SQUARE PRESS and colophon are registered
trademarks of Simon & Schuster, Inc.

For information about special discounts for bulk purchases,
please contact Simon & Schuster Special Sales at
1-800-456-6798 or business@simonandschuster.com

Manufactured in the United States of America

1 3 5 7 9 10 8 6 4 2

ISBN-13: 978-0-7432-7128-8
ISBN-10:   0-7432-7128-9
ISBN-13: 978-0-7432-7129-5 (pbk)
ISBN-10:   0-7432-7129-7 (pbk)

Imagine just thirty Englishmen
in the whole wide world.
Who would even notice them?

———

HENRI MICHAUX,
A Barbarian in Asia

ONE

Cape Town always slept in the same position, curled up in the muzzle of a gun. After hours of grim silence as heavy as a great fur coat of a former Soviet leader, the sound of engines began to sputter and roar throughout the city. In the distance, like the cries of cormorants, the horns of the first ferries split the clouds of mist grazing the sea as they left for Robben Island, once a concentration camp, now transformed into an international tourist attraction. Then the brakes of the overcrowded buses, arriving from the wretchedness of the shantytowns and converging on the splendors of the city center, screeched to a halt at the same stops. The feet of thousands of blacks in cheap shoes tramped toward the subaltern jobs that had always been their lot. All these sounds were preceded by the throbbing rounds of the police helicopters as their eyes pierced the dawn, searching to oust the criminals from their rat holes. For Cape Town at night oozed with all sorts of foulness and rottenness, a nightmare from which the city awoke completely drained, its storm channels churning bile and pus, its head of medlar trees and maritime pines bristling with fright.

Rosélie sat up in the bed she had now occupied alone for

the past three months, curled up in a fetal position, her face hard against the wall, terrified by the void behind her back. I couldn't sleep last night. I can't sleep anymore. Did I grind my teeth? Sometimes they clatter together like logs of wood on the raging waters of a river. I bite my lips: they bleed. I moan. I loll and I moan.

She stumbled across to the dressing table, with its three opaque mirrors blurred in places by green spots drifting like water lilies on an Indian lake, and contemplated with a morose fascination her close-cropped hair, yellowing in patches, the charcoal lines on her forehead the color of burnt sienna, the bags of flabby skin under her slanting eyes, her mouth wedged between two deep furrows—in other words a ravaged face showing signs of an already long passage that had been rough, so rough. Only the skin was not in keeping with the rest. As silky as when her mama, Rose, used to eat her up with kisses as a child:

"What a velvety, satiny skin!"

In Guadeloupe one usually exclaimed: "A skin as soft as a sapodilla!" But Rose loathed these Creole clichés and insisted on giving her own personal touch to things. That's how she forged the absurd name of Rosélie. Daughter of Rose and Elie. She worshiped her husband and wanted the whole world to know it. How far away those years seemed, almost as if they had never existed. It's true what they say, childhood is a myth, fabricated by senile grown-ups. As for me, I never was a child.

All around her the furniture chosen by Stephen shook itself and gradually cast off the disturbing animal shapes it took on in the dark, night after night. It had been her obsession ever since that weekend she had spent with Stephen two years earlier in the Kwa Maritane game park, close to the capital of a former Bantustan, Sun City, transformed into an international holiday resort including casino and hotels for stars. She hadn't expected the animals, so harmless during those three days, dozing in the shade of the bushes in the immensity of the veldt, to come alive at night as wild beasts and charge straight at her. What did frighten her were the men. White men. Guides, game wardens, local visitors, foreign tourists. All wearing boots and safari hats, sporting double-barreled guns, playing in a Western without a hint of a bison or Indian now massacred or defeated, herded toothless into their reservations. Stephen, on the contrary, loved dressing up in a bush jacket and canvas shorts in camouflage, a flask clipped to his waist and sunglasses perched on his nose.

"You don't know how to enjoy yourself," he reprimanded her, manly grabbing the wheel of a Land Rover.

Not her fault if she suffered from the complex of a victim and identified with those who are hunted.

Downstairs, the iron gate, armed with bolts, bars, and padlocks in an endeavor to keep out the ever-growing numbers of increasingly brazen nocturnal aggressors, creaked open. Deogratias, the night watchman, refreshed by six hours of sleep, was going home. Half an hour later, the gate creaked again. The hollow cough of a chain smoker, oblivious to the TV campaigns warning of the dangers of smoking, signaled the arrival of Dido, the coloured woman who cooked and did the housework, more friend in fact than servant, although paid a monthly wage. Soon she would climb the stairs to the bedroom, and in between the same old worries about her sleepless nights, her trials and tribulations—husband carried off by a heart attack, a son by AIDS—she would relate the agonies of the city down to the last detail. And it seemed to Rosélie she was imitating Rose, her mother, who, Lent come rainy season, conversed every morning with Meynalda, her servant, once a young girl from Anse-Bertrand who had never married but had grown up to be an old spinster alongside her. Both recounted their dreams and consulted *The Key to Your Dreams*, which Meynalda had inherited from one of her mother's employers (cooks ran in the family), translated from the Portuguese with an index and explanation of two hundred and fifty dreams.

"The shock woke me up," mused Rose. "It was in the gray hours of the dawn. Like the Good Samaritan, I was sitting on the edge of a well. People were hurrying past and throwing rocks at me. Gradually I was covered in blood."

"Blood means victory," Meynalda reassured her.

Victory over what? Certainly not over life. She had never been able to come to terms with life. She had never been able to get a firm grip on the reins of that wretched Arab stallion that rears and bucks as it likes. After six years of being madly in love, Elie, her husband, joined the ranks of womanizers and squandered his wages as clerk of the court on those *bòbò* women in the Carénage district. He had a good excuse. As soon as she was married Rose began to grow plump, no, rather inflate, no, rather swell up, and any diet, however strict, including the latest prescribed by a Greek dietician who had cured American movie stars, did as much good as a Band-Aid on a wooden leg. She had always been a "handsome Negress." In Guadeloupe the expression means what it means. It means a black woman, neither red nor quadroon nor yellow of skin, but black, with a full head of hair and thirty-two pearly teeth, tall, and buxom. Elie had fought to marry her—for you know how men are in our islands. He was what you'd call a mulatto, light-skinned in any case, with hair he flattened, oiled, and pomaded, making him look like Rudolph Valentino without the sheikh's headdress. Folks say that Rose bewitched him with her enchanting mezzo-soprano voice, for with a little training she could have made it as a professional singer. She had murmured in his ear the famous refrain from *Carmen*, preferring French melodies, even Spanish, over the Creole songs she considered too vulgar:

> *L'amour est enfant de Bohême*
> *Il n' a jamais, jamais connu de loi,*
> *Si tu ne m'aimes pas, je t'aime,*
> *Si je t'aime, prends garde à toi.*

Then on the birth of her daughter at the age of twenty-six, a perfidious sickness spread triumphant. Fat unrelentingly slid its adipose tissues between her and affection, love, and sex, all those things that humans desperately need in order not to end up going mad. Gradually her precious organ was reduced incongruously to a pathetic mouse's squeak. One scorching-hot day in March her voice finally gave up with a squawk while she was singing *Adios, pampas mias*. For sixteen years she was condemned to a wheelchair and for twenty-three to her bed from which her flesh seeped out like the uncontrollable floodwaters of a river. When deliverance finally came at the age of sixty-five, Roro Désir, of Doratour the undertakers ("Give us your departed and you'll have no regrets"), made a coffin four meters by four. Some people are not blessed by good fortune. At their birth comets zigzag furiously across the sky, collide, crash, and straddle each other. As a result this cosmic disorder influences their destiny and nothing goes right for them.

At seven in the morning the sun was well in control and came knocking stubbornly on the thick wooden shutters. Dido pushed open the door and tenderly kissed Rosélie, then set down the tray containing the newspaper and the first cups of coffee on the dressing table. In a rustle of paper she opened the *Cape Tribune* and went through it page by page, licking her lips, exclaiming greedily whenever a crime was much too juicy, while sipping her brew of "bull's blood," the jet-black coffee that she flavored with vanilla sugar and lemon peel.

Every morning therefore Rosélie wallowed in happiness at being served in bed like a sultana in a harem or a princess in a fairy tale:

"You can't call that coffee," she loved to grumble. "All that stuff you put in it loses the real taste, takes out the bitterness."

Raised on watered-down coffee, she then added:

"So I would like it less strong."

Used to her complaints, Dido made no reply and folded the paper. She was now ready for the day, cheered up by the coffee and her fill of horrors. A father had raped his daughter; a brother his younger sister; some intruders a chubby eight-month-old baby in its stroller. A man had slit his concubine's throat. Masked thieves had robbed four streets of houses. Dido tied a beige scarf around her salt-and-pepper mane of hair and slipped on a pair of shapeless gray overalls. But her mauve flowery skirt flared out a good ten inches underneath, her eyelids were daubed mauve and green, and her mouth dribbled with red lipstick. She looked like a transvestite, a drag queen! Out of the two women she was the one who corresponded most to people's idea of a pythoness, a sorceress, a soothsayer, or a healer, call her what you like.

"Rosélie Thibaudin, medium. A cure for the incurable," proclaimed the rainbow-colored cards printed at a discount on Kloof Street and distributed to the neighborhood shops.

Dido got the idea after cogitating furiously for a week. Once Stephen was gone, Rosélie was left without any means. All she knew how to do was paint. Painting is not like music, playing the piano, the violin, or the clarinet. A pianist, a violinist, a clarinetist can always give lessons to children and get paid by the hour. Painting is like literature. No immediate gain or utility. If the cards had read "Rosélie Thibaudin, painter" or "Rosélie Thibaudin, writer," nobody would have taken any notice. Whereas now the customers flocked in. She chose fifteen who seemed reliable. In order to make a good impression she had emptied the shelves of a nook upstairs and called it her consultation room. She had decorated it with an effigy of Erzulie Dantor, purchased during a voodoo exhibit in New York; an African fertility doll in dark wood, a souvenir of her six years spent at N'Dossou; and a reproduction by Jerome Bosch, one of her favorite painters. She had also hung one of her compositions on the wall. A pastel drawing without a title. She had great difficulties finding a title. She classified her canvases 1, 2, 3, 4 or A, B, C, D, leaving Stephen to find a name, something his imagination excelled at. During her séances she lit candles and perfumed the room with incense. Sometimes she topped off the atmosphere with a disc of Zen music bought in the Mitsukoshi department store in Tokyo. There are no inferior jobs. What could she have done besides being a medium? At least Stephen had bought the house in both their names, so nobody could evict her. She had disgraced the whole neighborhood. Imagine a Negress living on Faure Street! Parading on the wrought-iron balcony of a Victorian house, taking her meals on the patio between the traveler's tree and the bougainvillea, and luring a procession of clients of her color with her dubious commerce. As far as they could remember, pre- or post-apartheid, the only blacks spotted this side of Table Mountain were domestics. A few years earlier, when she had climbed out of the mover's truck with her white man, the neighbors had already been scandalized. They had found out that this newcomer, Stephen Stewart, was not one of their own. His father was English. His parents had divorced. His French mother had raised him over in France in Verberie. In a certain respect this aspect of his heredity explained their outrage. The French have tainted tastes, for their blood is tainted and over half are mongrels. All nature of people have climbed over their borders, pitched camp, and settled down in their midst.

Dido set down her cup and, looking important, exclaimed:

"I've found a client for you. A good one! He's French-speaking from one of those countries, Congo, Burundi, or Rwanda, in any case one of the three. His name's Faustin Rumiya or Roumaya or Roumimaya! You know me, I'm not much good with names. He's some important guy who got on the wrong side of his government. He is suspicious of everything and everyone. So for his first consultation you'll have to come to my place."

Yet another immigrant story! In this country everyone's got one up his sleeve; some are comical, others ridiculous or grotesque, each one more unlikely than the next. Deogratias the night watchman introduced himself as a former professor of political science from the state university in Rwanda. A miraculous survivor of the genocide in which his papa, his mama, his pregnant wife, and their three daughters had all perished. In fact, this lie might very well be true given his solemn expression, his liking for Greek and Latin words and overelaborate speeches. Zacharie the vegetable seller: PhD from Congo Brazza who had fled the civil war with his wife and seven children. Goretta the hairdresser, specializing in braids and weaving, was in fact the lead dancer in a traditional troupe from Zimbabwe. Warned beforehand by her lover, a minister who was crazy about her body, she had hid under a truck tarpaulin and traveled miles of laterite to escape the firing squad. What crime had she committed? We will never know. Rosélie inquired nonchalantly what this one was suffering from.

"He can't sleep!"

She had treated a good many cases of this sort. The ability to sleep, contrary to reason, is a faculty most unfairly meted out. For the slightest reason humans lose their sleep and agonize all night long, their eyes riveted on the hands of a clock. She walked over to the bathroom.

Her first appointment was at nine. She noted down everything in a spiral notebook in South Sea Blue, an ink she had been particularly fond of since school.

> *Patient No. 3*
> *Népoçumène Gbikpi*
> *Age: 34*
> *Nationality: Beninese*
> *Profession: Engineer*

Here was a tragic story that resembled her own. Népoçumène, a telecommunications engineer, had been away on business in Port Elizabeth. On his return home he had stumbled on his wife's lifeless body lying in a pool of blood at the door of their apartment. Perhaps raped. Murdered for a wretched handful of rand the couple kept deep in a chest of drawers.

As for Stephen, he had been working on his latest passion: a critical study of Yeats. At midnight he had gone out to the corner Pick 'n Pay store to buy a packet of Rothmans light in the red pack. Some thugs had murdered him for his wallet.

For some reason or other this version of the facts did not satisfy the police. In fact, Stephen's wallet had never left his back pocket. It had remained intact. There was no question of robbery.

"Perhaps the thieves had been disturbed before grabbing the wallet."

"Disturbed by whom?"

"Security guards. Pick 'n Pay customers. Other thieves. I don't know. Who's leading the investigation?"

"According to the cashier, Mr. Stewart did not enter the Pick 'n Pay. He was killed at the other end of the sidewalk."

Inspector Lewis Sithole, with the surprising slit eyes of an Asian, nodded his head. His opinion was that Mr. Stewart had not gone to the Pick 'n Pay to buy cigarettes but to meet somebody.

Who? What an imagination!

"Try to recall," he insisted, "whether you heard the telephone ring."

She had been asleep in the bedroom under the roof. Her studio occupied the entire second floor. They had taken down the inside walls to allow for more space and air. Stephen's study opened out onto the traveler's tree on the ground floor. In other words they were at opposite ends of the house. And then let's keep up with the times! Nowadays everyone has a cell phone. Stephen's didn't ring, it vibrated. Even if she had strained her ears, she wouldn't have heard anything.

And precisely, Inspector Sithole inquired, where was this cell phone?

The hospital hadn't given it back.

"Find it," he ordered. "It's an important piece of evidence!"

This was the second time a man had abandoned Rosélie with so little consideration. Twenty years ago, her flesh was still palatable! In despair she had resorted to another stratagem. The oldest profession in the world, so they say. It's not with a glad heart that a woman sells her body. She really must have nothing else up her sleeve. However much she tells herself and takes comfort in the feminists' point of view that even a legitimate wife, who has been blessed in white by the mayor and the priest and wears a ring on her finger, is nothing but a prostitute, something holds her back. In this case, however, Rosélie had no choice. Besides, it wasn't complicated: all you had to do was sit with your legs crossed at the Saigon bar along the seafront in N'Dossou. From six in the evening customers swarmed in like flies on a baby's eyes in Kaolack, Senegal. Tran Anh, the owner, was a Vietnamese whose hatred of communism had landed him in this corner of central Africa. He lived with Ana, a Fulani from Niger, driven by poverty to the same corner. The two of them had produced four boys with uncircumcised willies—much to their Muslim mother's grief—who squabbled naked under the tables. From outside, the Saigon didn't look like much. But it was always packed. Packed with civil servants who sipped their pastis while bemoaning their bank accounts. It was only the tenth of the month and they were already in debt! Not a franc left to pay for the daily ration of rice. They were polite and, in this AIDS-ridden age, strict users of condoms. Thank God there was not a single government minister, private secretary, or personal advisor among them, those who think they can get away with anything. At the most, some former division heads ejected on orders from the IMF. The height of luxury, the Saigon had its own generator, and oblivious to the power outages that were the plague of N'Dossou, the air inside was as fresh as an Algerian oasis. While waiting to be picked up Rosélie would read copies of *Elle* and *Femme d'Au-*

jourd'hui that Ana had kept for her. She liked to muse over the cooking recipes, strange for someone who never cooked. A well-written recipe makes your mouth water.

Stuffed Eggplant
Preparation: 30 min. + 30 min
Cooking time: 45 minutes
215 calories per person
For six helpings . . .

The bar also served a mysterious cocktail without alcohol called the Tsunami, invented by Tran Anh, sour as the bitterness of exile and green as tomorrow's promise despite the cold light of reality. One evening a white guy sat down at the bar with a Pilsner Urquell, that's a Czech beer. He looked around, got up, walked straight over to her table, and offered her a drink. His introduction was not very original, even conventional. It has worked ever since there have been bars, men, and women. He was no uglier than the rest. Somewhat better, even. She hesitated because she had never considered other partners in bed besides blacks. In her family nobody went in for mixed couples. The whites were terra incognita! The only exceptions were Great-uncle Elie, who left to work on the Panama Canal and ended his days with a Madrilenian, and cousin Altagras, whose name was erased from the family tree. Something attracted her to this white guy. They had walked out into the dusk as the red disk of the sun slipped untiringly into the ocean's watery deep. And passersby, numerous at this time of day, fired the first of those looks loaded with hostility and contempt that from then on would never leave them.

They had climbed into his red, somewhat flashy four-wheel drive, and navigating around the ruts and potholes that got deeper every rainy season, he had introduced himself. University professor. Taught Irish literature. Wilde, Joyce, Yeats, and Synge. His book on Joyce had been a mistake. Went completely unnoticed. Another on Seamus Heaney had been a critical success. He used to work in London. Listening to him, Rosélie was as fascinated as if an astronaut had described his days on the MIR space station. So people spend their time wallowing in fiction, getting worked up about lives they have never led, paper lives, lives in print, analyzing them and commenting on these fantasy worlds. By comparison she was ashamed of her own problems, so commonplace, so crude, so genuine.

What are you doing in N'Dossou?

Me? Nothing! A man has just left me high and dry. I've no work, I've no money. I've no roof over my head. I'm trying to survive and cure myself of my *lenbe*. Lovesick. Back home they call it *lenbe*.

He certainly could talk. Never a bore, though, full of unpretentious literary allusions and anecdotes about the countries he had visited.

Who was her favorite writer?

Mishima.

Found the name just in time. She wasn't going to say Victor Hugo or Alexandre Dumas, so obvious!

The Temple of the Golden Pavilion is magnificent, isn't it?

No, I prefer *Confessions of a Mask*.

Said confidently. Yet it was the only one she had read, in paperback in economy class from Paris to Pointe-à-Pitre, one

July when she was going back to spend her vacation with Rose and Elie. She had always been scolded for not reading. Ever since elementary school. Last in French composition. For her, the stories in books come nowhere near reality. Novelists are scared to invent the incredible, in other words life itself.

Did she like to travel?

There she felt obliged to tell the truth. She only knew a tiny portion, the tip of the iceberg, of the vast world around us: Guadeloupe, where she was born, Paris, where she had vaguely studied, and N'Dossou, where she had ended up three years earlier.

Three years of Africa! Do you like Africa?

Like! Does a prisoner awaiting his execution like being on death row? Now, now! Stop being facetious and witty! Africa hadn't always been a prison. She had been eager to make the journey, thinking she was about to launch on the great adventure. Despite her misfortunes she remained loyal to N'Dossou, an unattractive, unpretentious (how could it be anything else?) yet engaging city.

He had taken her home to his place, where they had slept in each other's arms until the following morning. This was unusual for Rosélie. Her civil servants usually climbed up to her studio apartment and didn't give her more than two hours of their time, watch in hand. As soon as they had finished with their well-oiled orgasm, they slipped on their clothes, awkwardly handed her a small commission, then limped back in their four-wheel-drives to their legitimate spouses. When she woke up, the houseboy, somewhat forward with a girl the boss had picked up on the cheap, served her coffee and a papaya that had seen better times. Stephen had already left for the university, leaving her an envelope stuffed with banknotes. He lived in the European quarter, with its crumbling buildings, its park and tree-lined avenues. Driving by a kindergarten, she had heard "Frère Jacques." A little farther on the off-key sounds of "Für Elise," which she too had murdered in her time to please Rose, floated out of a window.

Would she see him again? Did she want to see him again? She could find nothing wrong with him: perfectly groomed, smelling of Acqua de Giò, and good in bed. A lot of kissing, embracing, playing, and fondling, as if penetration was not the main issue.

That same evening he once more came through the door of the Saigon, where the civil servants recognized him and cast disapproving looks. A month later she moved in with him.

It was love with a capital *L*.

Rosélie put on the clothes carefully chosen by Dido. A dark brown boubou with a fitted yolk embroidered in golden yellow, and a matching head tie. She walked down the stairs in a regal manner befitting her role and entered her consulting room. Népoçumène was waiting for her, his face a little less haggard than usual. Was he sleeping now? Were his nightmares beginning to leave him in peace? Did he hear his wife's voice? She had told him over and over again he would hear her once he had forgiven her for having abandoned him. That was the most difficult part. She herself still couldn't hear Stephen's voice. All too often she was overwhelmed by bitterness and a kind of anger toward him.

Rosélie's gift became evident very early on. At the age of six all she had to do was place her little hands over Rose's eyelids for poor Rose to sleep like a baby until nine in the morning. Until then Rose had been tormented by Elie's absences; her body had begun to swell considerably, and as a result she could never get to sleep. At the age of ten Rosélie had made a pack of Creole dogs turn tail as they were about to attack her and her cousins on the road in Montebello just before Bois-Sergent, where her aunt had a house. On weekends, unbeknownst to the skeptics in the family, Papa Doudou, her grandfather on her father's side, took her to his property at Redoute, where the cows turned their backs on the bull and the mares refused to be mounted by the stud. She would look deep into their big gelatin eyes and the recalcitrant females would be completely transformed, as pliable as putty in your hands. Bad-mouthers, and there are some in every family, were skeptical and made no bones about it. Rosélie had been incapable of predicting that the same Papa Doudou would die of a hemorrhage from his testicles being ripped off by the horns of a small bull he was breaking in. And during Hurricane Deirdre she had been unable to foresee that a breadfruit tree would smash through Uncle Eliacin's house and flatten it like a cowpat, killing him outright as well as his wife and five children with the American TV names of Warner, Steve, Jessica, Kevin, and Randy. Okay, she had seen Deirdre coming. But you didn't need to be a rocket scientist to see a hurricane. Hurricanes are regular visitors. Year after year they arrive from the coast of Africa. What matters is their strength, and that is never the same.

As an adult she would have liked to turn her powers to good account. But astrology? Palmistry? Chiropractic? Osteopathy? Shiatsu? All that is not very serious. So she had got bogged down in her law studies. Elie had so admired the black robes around him that he dreamed of putting his daughter in one. Oh, let her tear the French language to pieces like lawyer Démosthène, the famous bard of independence! As for Rose, she regretted her daughter had not gone into politics. Her father had been a local hero whose full-length portrait occupied a place of honor in the living room.

If Dido hadn't been there, she would still be looking for herself.

She liked listening to the way Stephen relived their first meeting. It became fictional and poetical, as if it were a chapter in a novel, perhaps Irish, perhaps not.

"I landed up here a few months ago. Why, you ask? Because I realized I was becoming the spitting image of my father. I could no longer put up with London, its gray skies, my bedsitter, my teaching job, the boredom of the pubs and the Sunday papers. At least in N'Dossou everything seemed new under the sun. *Ex Africa semper aliquid novi.* One evening, after a scorching-hot day, I was searching for a cool breeze along the seafront, where the wind blows in from the ocean with occasional gusts and cools the sweat on your skin, when, out of breath and tired of tramping in the sand, I pushed open the door of a bar with a facade smeared in blue and a sign painted with palm trees: the Saigon. A stroke of luck.

The shadowy interior smelled of peppermint, reminding me of my childhood. On summer visits my aunt Chloé, my mother's sister, always used to give me a peppermint drink in a blue-stemmed glass. A view of the Mekong ran above the circular bar in bamboo. Another depicted the bay of Along with its extraordinary rocks like pieces in a game of chess. Ana was washing the glasses. Tran Anh, as usual, was idly blowing smoke rings into the air. You were sitting alone at your table, a little to the left. You were wearing a green dress with an orange pattern. [What was this about a green dress? He must have been dreaming. I loathe the color green.] I never accost women. Their cold eyes, their cruel teeth, and the way they have of sizing up and assessing men scares me. Will he be able to satisfy me? Black women were foreign, mysterious, a nebulous, unfathomable world. The other side of the moon. You looked so lost, so vulnerable that by comparison I felt serene and powerful. God Almighty. You were sitting behind a pile of magazines. You were leafing through one. Yet it was obvious you couldn't care less what was flicking past your eyes. Your mind was elsewhere."

Oh yes, my mind was elsewhere!

She was asking herself the same questions over and over again. What's going to become of me? How long can I last without a cent to my name? What is there left to sell? I've already sold for next to nothing my gold choker and chain, given me by Aunt Léna. The other jewels are from Rose. I could never part with them.

Dominique, a chance acquaintance who worked in real estate, had offered her a studio apartment. Never look a gift horse in the mouth. The apartment was badly situated in the

Ferbène district, a shantytown, sitting in the middle of a swamp that was supposed to have been drained during the public works projects at the time of independence. After forty years, the work had never been completed and the swamp had turned into a quagmire. Life there was not worth a dime. On the sidewalks garbage piled up higher than a man. But could they really be called sidewalks? The tangle of streets were flooded all year round with a brackish soup. La Liberté, the name of this rat- and vermin-infested building, housed the studio apartment generously loaned by Dominique. Ten stories high, elevator chronically in need of repair, cassava and plantain peelings as well as banana skins, green and yellow, littering the hallways, and raggedy clothes hung out to dry on the balconies. It overlooked a panorama of shacks. Beyond, a pallid and disheveled ocean regularly vomited up corpses. One never knew whether they were foolhardy fishermen, suicides tired of vegetating without love or money, or victims of revenge wreaked by parents or neighbors.

One morning Rosélie, plus two metal canteens of the type you never see now called cabin trunks, plus a plywood box, climbed out of one of Navitour's trucks.

NAVITOUR TRUCK RENTAL
WHEN YOU WANT IT, HOW YOU WANT IT!

The building's residents were stupefied. Okay, okay, Allah doesn't have to be merciful. But the least we can expect is that he hasn't gone off his rocker. In the glossy pages of *GuidArt* they had often drooled over the new tenant—that's her, I'm telling you, beside Salama Salama, the famous reggae singer, beloved by young and old alike. Salama Salama's real name was Sylvestre Urbain-Amélie. He had had to change his name for the stage, showbiz rules. Salama Salama sounds strange and exotic. What country was he from?

Devoured by curiosity, the tenants had dispatched Angéline, who got by in French after four years at school. Unfortunately, the door of apartment 4B was firmly closed to her. Rosélie had barricaded herself in together with the rest of her story. However hard the neighbors spied, the door of number 4B never opened an inch and they had had to wait another week for *GuidArt* to clarify matters. Salama Salama, the famous singer, beloved by young and old alike, had been appointed Minister for Culture, a position that had been cruelly lacking in the entourage of the president. In his magnanimity, the president had given his seventh daughter to go with the job. Seven, a magic number. He had seventeen biological and seven adopted daughters. This daughter was one of his own. Plus as many sons, making forty-eight children in all. A photo on page three showed Salama Salama on the arm of a teenage girl swathed in yards of Alençon lace, swollen by an early pregnancy, for they had put the cart before the horse, something quite common nowadays. He himself was wearing tails. The couple were to spend their honeymoon in Morocco with the crown prince, son of our late friend the king.

The story was becoming clear. Betrayal. Cruel disappointment. For the second time Angéline was dispatched to the fourth floor. She finally managed to get in and scolded Rosélie, who had collapsed on the bed, her two trunks and box lying unopened beside her. She forced open not only the door of Rosélie's apartment, but also her heart. She introduced her to Justine, Awu, Mandy, and Mariétou, and welcomed her into the band of women. Rosélie joined in the laughter, the repartee, pranks, and practical jokes that had been sorely missing in her solemn, solitary years as a young girl. Sometimes she thought of her family. Her father, who always thought himself the cat's whiskers. What would Elie say if he saw her abandoned by her second-rate Bob Marley (already the choice of this unknown African musician had been the subject of volumes of abuse), in this city at the end of the world, in the company of these illiterate women? And Rose? For whom nothing was good enough for her daughter. And her uncles? With their pencil-sharp mustaches. And her aunts? Especially Aunt Léna, wrapped in her Creole jewelry. During the course of imaginary dialogues she tried to plead her case in front of this tribunal, and getting no encouragement, she ended up eliminating it entirely from her memory.

All this merriment, joking, and secret talk ended at six in the evening. Angéline and the band of women scurried home, where, armed with brooms and sponge mops, they would scrub, wash, iron, and cook, in other words carry out all those jobs assigned the female species since the world began. For dusk brought home the creatures who had been absent all day long: the men. The men, embittered by their makeshift jobs at the other end of the city. As soon as they returned home they vented their frustration and disappointment, and the residence La Liberté echoed with shouts and recriminations, the screams of battered women and the cries of terrified children. It was then that Rosélie cowardly took refuge in the serenity of the Saigon, savoring with Tran Anh the smell of green papaya.

The day arrived when, finishing a game of cards, she made the announcement to her companions. She was going to live with an Englishman, a university professor. In order to avoid getting sentimental she tried her hand at being cynical, something she ventured from time to time. A stroke of luck, no? She not only got love, but a roof over her head and food on the table. Nobody laughed. Her words were met with a silence of disbelief. Mariétou demanded an explanation. English is not a nationality, it's a language. What was this all about? Rosélie explained, surprised deep down at her apologetic tone. Finally realizing what it actually meant, her girlfriends hurriedly withdrew, fleeing her like a leper. From that day on Rosélie found herself abandoned, her once inseparable companions now invisible, claiming they were too busy with their kids, their housework, or, even more unlikely, job hunting, for hoping and searching for a job in N'Dossou was like looking for a needle in a haystack. The day she left she was escorted by a cortege of children. They surrounded Stephen's four-by-four, as solemn as if they were coffining a body. The older teenagers, admirers of Pelé—at that time Zinedine Zidane, like the lamb in the fable, was still at his mother's breast or else swimming in the waters of her womb—stopped kicking their soccer ball to look daggers at her.

"What a place!" Stephen shivered.

As for Rosélie, she had tears in her eyes. A feeling of guilt was torturing her that was never to leave her in peace again. It was as if, irreversibly, she was cutting the ties of which she herself knew neither the nature nor the tenacity.

10:00 a.m.
Patient No. 7
Dawid Fagwela
Age: 73
Particularity: one of the few South African clients
Profession: retired miner

He was a former trade unionist who too had languished for years on Robben Island. The Ministry for Tourism had had the brilliant idea of retailoring his prison uniform and using him as a guide for the thousands of tourists who tramped through the concentration camp, heaving pitiful sighs at the sight of the tiny cell where Nelson Mandela, the exemplary hero, had been interned.

"How many years did he spend here?"

"Eighteen. He was then transferred to Pollsmoor to the south of Cape Town because he was a bad influence on the other prisoners."

"Can we visit that prison as well?"

That's all they thought about! Get as many pictures as possible for their photo albums. As for Dawid, the fact of reliving his abuse and torture day after day, and describing it down to the last detail to the inquisitive hordes in an endeavor to satisfy their curiosity, the poor guy was losing his head. It woke him up at night.

Was apartheid really over? Was he really free?

The hospital had kept him for several months and then diagnosed his case as incurable. His wife had refused this categorical diagnostic. Since Dido, her cousin, had spoken highly of Rosélie's talent, she came to consult her. At first

Rosélie hadn't known what to do. This case was different. It's not every day that a political prisoner turns into a tourist guide and travels from hell to paradise in a single lifetime. Then she got the idea of asking Dawid to record his memories on a tape recorder and write them down. Straightaway he plunged into the job from morning till night. No more time for the blues. Put his obsessions into words. Transform them into images. He planned on writing a book and had already found the title, the most difficult thing to find, according to Rosélie: "The True Confession of Lazarus, A Death Survivor." He had regained his smile and his sleep, and was eating and drinking again.

Proof that sometimes writing does serve some purpose.

TWO

Rosélie only ventured out at the end of the day. Now that Stephen was gone, she, like the Catholics on a pilgrimage to Lourdes, religiously headed for the Mount Nelson Hotel, where he loved to take afternoon tea. It was a magnificent colonnaded building, one of the last remnants of the British Empire, the colossus with clay feet that had crumbled into dust, a living example of "grandeur and decadence."

"Britannia rules the waves," they nevertheless proclaimed from India to Africa.

Right up to the early years of the twentieth century, it was filled with aristocrats fleeing the English winter and fog, for Cape Town is known for its bracing and energizing climate. Today the Mount Nelson is mainly a tourist attraction. Hordes of tourists in Nikes and T-shirts, leaving their all-inclusive deals at the Holiday Inn, invade the gardens and have their pictures taken as they walk up the drive of centuries-old oaks or pose smugly in front of the greenhouses of orchids from Thailand. In spite of this, the power and majesty of the place had such an effect that Stephen, who as a rule hated everything English in him, rediscovered the intonations of his childhood to address the waiters, those bearded, formidable Indians, tightly bound in their cummerbunds, who glided around like well-trained ghosts. Rosélie, less susceptible to the lost glories of a colonial past, liked the Mount Nelson for quite a different reason. The undesirables in Nikes and T-shirts never ventured onto the waxed parquet floors inside. Trained in the art of discretion, some would say hypocrisy, the personnel swept by, their eyes fixed on the horizon. Consequently, for the space of a few hours, gone were the inquisitive looks that ambushed Rosélie and Stephen, whatever they did and wherever they were. They slipped into anonymity as if resting in eternal peace. In the Churchill room they would sit facing a gossamery pianist wearing a dancer's headband who played "Smoke Gets in Your Eyes" and listen in silence as they filled their plates with scones and muffins, Stephen adding egg and cucumber sandwiches. They would drink gallons of Darjeeling tea. When outside in the garden it began to grow dark they would stroll home, making a detour by the Big Bazaar on Kloof Street, where they rummaged through everything and bought nothing, which gave the owner, an Afrikaner, an extra reason to be angry.

Rosélie thought she saw Stephen slip between the deep red chintz drapes. In the past, leaning against the piano, he would hum along in his nice, melodious voice. The Indian waiters knew all about the crime that had made headlines in every paper, even the very serious *Manchester and Guardian*, more geared to political analysis than brief news items. They never approached her, however, to present their condolences. Despite their reserve, something in their silence testified to their compassion.

One afternoon she was pouring herself a second cup of tea when a white man greeted her. Tall, with a slight paunch, a shock of black hair, gray eyes, and tanned cheeks. In answer to his polite request, she nodded that he could join her.

"My name is Manuel Desprez, but everyone calls me Manolo because I play the guitar. You don't recognize me, do you? I used to teach at the university with Stephen. We got on very well together. He told me so much about you I have the feeling I know you. What's more, I have spent several evenings at your place."

In Cape Town, like in N'Dossou and New York, Stephen would organize such lively and successful dinner parties, they never ended before dawn. Ever since an Australian, a Keats specialist, took her for the maid, Rosélie no longer attended them.

"You're making a lot of fuss about nothing," Stephen shrugged it off. "David is so absentminded he wouldn't recognize his own mother if she was standing in front of him."

She was by no means convinced and locked herself in her studio. Quite a few students came to these parties. Stephen assured her it was both a reward for the best in the department and a sure way of breaking the ice between professors and students, in other words between whites and blacks. When masters and disciples get drunk together, it's something they never forget. Rosélie bumped into these young things, awkward and embarrassed, as they came out of the toilet, and quickly withdrew so as not to embarrass them even more.

Manuel Desprez was still talking.

"I've been away in France on a sabbatical and when I got back at the beginning of the week I heard what had happened. I was about to come and see you."

She closed up. He was probably going to spout some commonplace remark, bemoan the absurdity of the crime, and find fault with the local police. It was true, in fact, that despite Inspector Lewis Sithole's constant visits and the notes he kept jotting down, Stephen's murderers seemed to have disappeared into thin air. But instead of uttering the predictable, his question was direct, even brutal:

"Aren't you going to return home?"

Home? If only I knew where home was.

Chance had it I was born in Guadeloupe. But nobody in my family is interested in me. Apart from that, I have lived in France. A man took me to Africa, then left me. Another took me to the United States, then brought me back to Africa, and he too left me stranded, this time in Cape Town. Oh, I forgot I've also lived in Japan. That makes for a fine charade, doesn't it? No, my only country was Stephen. I shall stay wherever he is.

Despite the insistence of his half brothers—his mother had passed away some months earlier—Rosélie had refused to take his body back to the family vault in Verberie. Stephen, who loathed Europe, would have certainly preferred to remain in the country he had chosen.

"South Africa is such a tough place," Manuel insisted.

The whole world is a tough place. They take potshots at you on the sidewalks of Manhattan as well as in London's Chelsea. You're not safe in the deadly Twin Towers, symbol of American capitalism. Almost three thousand dead, killed in a single morning. They rape old ladies in the east of Paris. They tell me that even my little Guadeloupe is keeping up with the times.

"I'm not talking just about violence."

About what, then? Racism? Let's talk about racism. I

could write volumes on the subject. If racism is more deadly than AIDs, it is also more widespread, more commonplace than flu in winter.

I've always dreamed of writing a book on racism. "Racism Explained to the Deaf and Hard of Hearing."

He became confused and changed the subject.

"They tell me you're a painter."

Rosélie stammered out a yes. This type of question always embarrassed her. As if she had been asked to put on a swimsuit, despite her cellulite, and pace up and down the stage of the Miss Guadeloupe contest. Manuel called a waiter, ordered a single malt, then went on to explain:

"My sister has a gallery on the rue du Bac in Paris. If I can help you in any way, I shall only be too pleased."

The tone was sincere. The things he must have heard at the university! Doris, the coloured secretary, entertained her audience with her hissing voice:

"They're not married, you know."

I was the one who refused. He proposed regularly. Without any real desire, in my opinion. Like a broker offering comprehensive car insurance.

"If something happens you'll be covered."

It's true that if I had listened to him I wouldn't be where I am today! Worrying about how to make ends meet.

"So of course she's not entitled to a pension," Doris hissed excitedly. "Since she can't do anything except paint ghastly pictures that nobody would want in their house, she's bought a crystal ball and calls herself a medium."

Split between hysterical laughter and commiseration, the circle of teachers gasped:

"No, you must be joking!"

The more generous-hearted proposed collecting donations. The idea didn't meet with general approval: giving
money or a check, it's humiliating. The gesture might hurt
her.

Before Stephen, few people had taken Rosélie's ambitions seriously. Elie would throw a fit whenever he saw her
wasting her time messing about with paint instead of revising
her math or science for the baccalaureate. If she couldn't be
a lawyer, he'd like her to be an economist. No Guadeloupean
can boast of a daughter as economist at the World Bank. As
for Rose, who was never short of compliments, she whined
for an explanation:

"What does that represent, darling? Is it a person, a tree,
or an animal?"

Those members of the family who had visited the Louvre
museum in Paris once or twice shook with hysterical laughter.
She thinks she's that painter who was fascinated by Tahiti and
also spent time in Martinique. What was his name?

In the eyes of Salama Salama, Rosélie's penchant for painting was incomprehensible and exasperated him. Stephen's
behavior was radically different. She hadn't been with him
for three months before he began to take charge of her affairs, as he did with everything else. She lacked technique because painting is like singing, cabinet making, or masonry:
it's not something you make up, it is governed by rules. So he
got her admitted to the National School of Beaux Arts, the
latest gift from France to N'Dossou, a place of extreme material poverty but spiritually very rich. The two are not incom-

patible. On the contrary. The Antillean proverb is mistaken when it claims: *Sak vid pa kienn doubout.* In other words, those who have an empty belly are only preoccupied with filling it. Not at all, they are devoted to the creation of Beauty and Spirituality. A French government minister had inaugurated the school in great pomp a few months earlier. The director was a friend. Stephen had no trouble whatsoever.

N'Dossou's entire population is no bigger than a district of Manhattan. Moreover, the entire country numbers fewer than a million inhabitants. The dense forest and fevers have got the better of it. The rumor quickly spread through the residential areas and suburbs that Rosélie had no business being where she was.

Favoritism! Favoritism!

Especially as she had no talent. Her paintings lacked that opacity generated by cultural authenticity. The professors, too busy saving up for their retirement, made no effort to defend her. Wounded by the criticism, Rosélie found no consolation in receiving her final diploma. Locked in her studio rented by Stephen in the Riviera IV district (everything an artist could wish for), next to the Afrika recording studios, she couldn't touch her brushes for weeks on end. Nobody could reassure her that she was anything but a conscientious student. She would have liked words of encouragement from painters as different as Modigliani, Wifredo Lam, and Roberto Matta to admit her into their magic circle.

Am I nothing more than one of those *tlacuilos*, Indians from Ixmiquilpan who filled the Spanish with so much admiration?

Stephen in no way influenced Rosélie. He merely expressed his approval. Why did she always get the feeling he behaved like a doting daddy?

You know, those parents who consider their little darling's daubings a masterpiece, frame it, and hang it on the wall.

He encouraged her to expose at the French Cultural Center, run by a friend of his, in between a sculptor from Niger and a watercolorist from Togo. The few visitors wrote admiring comments in the visitor's book on the creativity of Francophone artists. Stephen hosted a dinner for the only two journalists in the country who specialized in painting. Since the evening was devoted to the arts, he also invited his inseparable Fumio. Fumio was a Japanese artist who staged an avant-garde show in front of a stunned audience, more used to the singers of the National Instrumental Ensemble, fully clothed in ceremonial wrappers. His was a one-man show called *Ginza-Africa* (Ginza being a trendy district of Tokyo), during which he completely stripped and threw a full frontal into the bargain. Although Fumio was of not much use that particular evening, the two journalists were impressed by the dishes served up by the former cook of the Finnish embassy, the high point being the crabs stuffed with snails. They published articles as excellent as the meal. As a result, Rosélie sold two of her paintings to the owner of the Hotel Paradiso, on the seafront, who hung them in the lobby and forced his reluctant guests to enthuse over them.

The color of the air changed. Rosélie stood up, followed by Manuel Desprez. Nowhere was safe nowadays. Only the day before yesterday a group of tourists had been attacked outside the District Six Museum. He offered to escort her home. Deep down she knew only too well what the neighbors would say if, three months after the death of Stephen, she came home with a white man.

I'm telling you, they're all whores.

"Black and Asian women are alike, they're machines, they can't tell one man from another."

Cowardly, Rosélie declined his offer.

"Can I come and see you one of these days?" he insisted.

She thought she hadn't heard right. What type of Good Samaritan was this who took an interest in a morose, destitute widow of a left-handed marriage?

"I'd like to see your paintings," he stammered, taken aback by her look of surprise. "As I told you, my sister has a gallery. Sometimes I work as an art dealer for her."

Pity, nothing but pity!

As night fell a cool wind settled on their shoulders, a treacherous wind blowing in from the merciless Atlantic and Indian oceans, that swept through the streets, sending dust and grease papers flying. In the background, the massive Table Mountain, like an evil spirit, overshadowed the city.

Rosélie had been reluctant to move. She had sort of got used to New York. Why set off again? But Stephen was a stubborn man. Once he had something fixed in his mind, he was not afraid to make bold comparisons. After seven years in New York, he argued, to see South Africa after apartheid would be like going back in time. Going back to when the United States had just finished muzzling its police dogs and the fight for civil rights was over. They would have a front-row seat to observe how communities, once bitter enemies, learn how to live together. Apparently, in South Africa the experience was particularly remarkable. Not the slightest drop of blood spilled. But no agrarian reform either. No redistribution of land. No Africanization along the lines currently meant. In Durban, Jo'burg, and Cape Town the statues of the colonials remained firmly in place on horseback, just like in the good old days. Rosélie had been incapable of holding out against such an onslaught. She had laid her canvases, like recalcitrant schoolgirls, in boxes custom-made by a carpenter on 125th Street.

She hated Cape Town as soon as she left the airport, while sensing inside her a strange fascination. For towns are like humans. Their singular personality attracts, repels, or disconcerts. Cape Town possessed the brilliant sparkle and hardness of rock salt; its gardens and parks, the remarkable roughness of kelp. While Stephen admired pell-mell the mountains, the gnarled pines bent in two, the mass of flowers, the dazzling blue sky, and the endless expanse of ocean, she was blinded by both this splendor and the hideousness of the shacks that mushroomed all around her. No place had been more marked by its history. Never had she felt so denied, excluded, and relegated out of sight because of her color.

Outside the Victoria Cinema, the line was growing longer. A group of out-of-towners, recognizable by their antiquated dress, were chatting. Rosélie hurried on to avoid being struck down by their looks, then remembered with a start that she was alone. Stephen was no longer walking beside her, arm in arm, or ostentatiously placing an arm around her shoulder. They would not turn their heads in her direction. She no longer irritated, she no longer gave offense. She had become invisible. Sadly, she had to choose between being excluded or being invisible.

Invisible woman!

On Faure Street, Deogratias had already unrolled his mat at the foot of the traveler's tree, but was not lying in that favorite position of his, on his left side, his checkered flannel blanket drawn up to his eyes. Myths die hard. Most experts agree that Deogratias's ethnic group, the "descendants of a pastoral people," are not really Negroid. Look at their height, their slender figure. Look at their aquiline nose in particular. A nose says everything. Deogratias had a flat nose. This did not prevent him from undergoing the same fate as his brothers of taller stature. He was waiting for Rosélie with a piece of news that made his Adam's apple jump up and down. A fellow countryman had just arrived in Cape Town. A former government minister. What could he be up to? Rosélie ignored his excitability. Except for his speeches on the South Africans' xenophobia, his only subject of conversation was the need to hunt down those who had destroyed so many lives, bring them before the international court of justice in Arusha and organize trials that would echo round the world like those at Nuremberg. This was the price to pay for Africa's salvation. Together with Dido, Deogratias had been one of Rosélie's first patients, well before she had thought of setting up business on her own. When Stephen had hired him, Deogratias was suffering from terrible nightmares. At times, lying under the traveler's tree, he struggled with invisible torturers while his screams tore through the dark. Rosélie had taken care of him. She had been about to lose hope when his salvation came in the shape of Sylvaine, a young immigrant from the same ethnic group whom he had met at church. Sylvaine promptly gave him a daughter; the couple baptized her Hosannah in a shout of gratitude to the God who had reunited them. Although Rosélie had been extremely shocked, Stephen, as usual, had been more understanding.

"What do you expect him to do? Spend his life lamenting the dead? In the end, it's always life that wins."

After a quick look at the university housing, Stephen had dragged her on a house hunt. They both fell for the house on Faure Street. Of course, all those who knew Cape Town advised them not to live in the center of town. Much too dangerous! Worse than the Bronx! Worse than Harlem! But Harlem is no longer Harlem ever since Rudy Giuliani launched his trigger-happy police. To prove it, Magic Johnson has invested there. The center of town is worse than anything you've ever known. But Stephen was taken with so much space: ten rooms, a balcony, and a garage. Rosélie had fallen in love with the tree. With arms outstretched, it shouted to be let free in its little patch of lawn, and she got the impression the years had rolled back. A traveler's tree! A silent witness to her games at Papa Doudou's. She would huddle in its heart and the swarm of cousins would grouse they couldn't find her.

"Where on earth is she?"

The triangular trade had been reversed. Before arriving in Cape Town, the *Christ-Roi* had anchored at La Pointe, where it had replaced its ebony cargo with other species. The magic of the long-lost tree, of Nature, the smell of the mighty ocean parading as far as the eye could see, and the everlasting distress of her people like a canker in the midst of so much beauty cast a powerful, equivocal spell, a magical, perverse philter against which she was helpless. A frenzy of blood flooded through her heart, her head, her arms and legs, and she painted, painted for days on end, endeavoring to convey her conflicting feelings with her brushes. Rage. Repulsion. Seduction. Love. Hate. Stephen, who had been mortified by her lack of enthusiasm for New York, capital of the world in his eyes, was elated.

"You say you can't bear this city, this country. And yet it inspires you. You've never painted anything so original."

Without a moment's hesitation he bought the house, muttering that the estate agent was letting it go for a mere song. Something quite unlikely, since the center of Cape Town had recently been classified an historical area. But Rosélie didn't protest.

For three whole days a Congolese (there are forty thousand in the country) turned over the soil in the garden.

He planted canna lilies, gladioli, gerberas, and especially white flowered flag bushes, a fragile shrub with a liking for humidity.

Stephen was born in Hythe, a small coastal town in Kent. Cecil, his father, had been an engineer in charge of maintaining the military canal, a remnant of the Napoleonic wars. An unrewarding job he carried out dejectedly, dreaming of an Elsewhere, when he was offered a managerial position in Bangkok. Annie, however, his French wife and a former governess, was five months pregnant. Reluctant to leave her alone in her condition, he had given up the offer. Ever since, he had made the mother and child pay for his sacrifice.

"I never knew him to be anything else but irascible, furious with a rage that I understood much later when I began to feel it myself."

Stephen had grown up in a small, one-story brick house, three windows on the first floor, two on the second, so identical to the houses on either side along St. Nicholas Road that he had to check the two numbers over the front door before entering. After school, he was regularly beaten up in the public gardens by the little bullies who called him a sissy because of his pretty face. On Sundays his parents would have lunch in a pub, always the same one. While he sipped his lemonade they would glower at each other over their lager. The view from the pub looked out onto the gardens of the nearby castle where blond-haired little aristocrats pedaled hard on their bicycles. Finally Annie had the courage to divorce and took Stephen back to Verberie, her hometown, where the buildings and humans share the same grayness. A few years later she married again, this time a school principal, a childhood friend, like Cecil but gloomier. She had two boys.

In order to escape this horde of relatives—the mother, the mother's sisters, the stepfather, and the half brothers— Stephen got it into his head to return to university in England. Alas! Oxford and Cambridge thought his diction much too French! He'd lost his tonic accent, the rise in intonation and, especially, that distinguished stutter. So he had to make do with Reading. There, he had above all made his mark playing Chekhov with the university theater group. Since nobody claimed him—his father and mother having virtually forgotten him—Stephen began to travel the world. At the age of seventeen, he had almost got killed traveling through Italy and Greece on a scooter. At eighteen he lost his virginity in a bar in Houston where he had been raped by the owner and his wife in turn. At twenty, he dreamed of imitating Malraux. During a stay in Bangkok he had been content to photograph the bas-reliefs of the temples instead of looting them. At present, he proclaimed himself without a country and avoided Europe. Not entirely. He would spend a few days in the summer in Hythe, where he rented a car and drove along the coast, passing through the string of seaside resorts of Margate, Ramsgate, Sandgate, Greatstone, and Littlestone. Then a week in London.

Throughout his stay Stephen constantly called on Rosélie to bear witness.

"You can understand why I loathe this country."

She looked around her and failed to understand. She was rather charmed by the color of the sea, so different from the Caribbean you wondered whether it was made from the same substance, the white facades of the great hotels, somewhat worse for wear, the ill-dressed crowds munching fish and chips on the endless piers, the boutiques stuffed with cute, unnecessary objects, and the tea shops that closed at five o'clock, just when it was teatime. And then she adored London. She would wander aimlessly counting the mixed couples whom she alone noticed. She envied them; they looked so happy and carefree. How did they manage?

Stephen always lodged with his friend Andrew Spire. They had shared a room at Reading. During their university vacations they had discovered Europe together. Then they had gone through hard times in London, both of them dreaming of becoming an actor. Andrew was single, as finicky as an old bachelor, handsome and marmoreal like Michelangelo's *David*. Despite his frigid expression, he published unsavory, erotic poems dedicated to T in an avant-garde journal. Rosélie was convinced T was a man.

> *I would love to be the cigarette*
> *that your desire slowly consumes*
> *penis of fire that becomes smoke*
> *in your mouth.*

After years of walk-on parts with obscure theater companies, he had managed to get a teaching job at the Royal Academy of Dramatic Art, thanks to his connections in high-up places. The house he had inherited from his grandmother, widow of a senior civil servant in India, was furnished with marquetry-worked sideboards, canopied beds, rocking chairs, and copper-studded chests shipped back from Udaipur. Andrew had added half a dozen Siamese cats, meowing haughtily, who clawed and ran over the sofas as if they were perpetually in heat. After these weeks in London and Hythe, Stephen would cross the Channel and go to visit his mother alone, now widowed, and dumped in an institution for seniors by the sons from her second marriage, executives in a large private bank who were snowed under with work.

Rosélie preferred to drift idly through the streets of Paris. She was a regular guest of a hotel in the Marais because Cousin Altagras lived close by. Out of all the Thibaudins, and there were enough of them to populate an entire district of

Guadeloupe, all very prim and proper, Rosélie was the only member to frequent Cousin Altagras, daughter of one of Elie's half brothers, who had arrived in France after the Second World War supposedly to study art. It was not because she had married a white man. The Thibaudins were above such considerations. It was because Lucien Roubichou, that was the name of the husband, owed his fortune, his apartment on the Place des Vosges, and his Audi Quattro to a rather special kind of industry. In short, he was a porn merchant, responsible for a certain number of immortal masterpieces, well known in closed circles: *Lucy, Suck My Sushi; Don't Speak with Your Mouth Full;* and *Caress Me, Caress Me,* no connection with the famous song from Martinique. The family accused him of having used Altagras when she was a ravishing beauty and of now doing the same with their two daughters. Incidentally, he was a man of gentle manners, mad about cooking and Italian cinema. His specialty was vegetarian lasagna. His passion: Pier Paolo Pasolini, whose theorems he subtly analyzed. In spite of her diabolical reputation, Cousin Altagras was a disappointment for Rosélie. She had given up any artistic claims in order to cook beef stew for her litter of children. Marriage does that.

During the early years, however, Rosélie never missed an opportunity to accompany Stephen to Verberie. Vacations took her back to Guadeloupe less and less, for she could no longer bear the sight of Rose nailed to her bed, like a beached whale. Consequently, looking after her mother-in-law eased her conscience somewhat. And then at every street corner she bumped into Stephen as a child. Here was the school that looked like a prison where he had acquired his taste for literature. Here was the sports ground where he had contracted his loathing for games. Here was the academy where he had performed his first roles. Moved, she could see the likeness in his mother's worn-out face. He had inherited her somewhat prominent nose, her smoky gray eyes, and her resolutely feminine mouth. For this reason she could put up with Annie's constant harping. The old woman's memories revolved like a carousel around the Second World War. Southeast England had been particularly vulnerable. The children had been evacuated to the Midlands. Annie, just married, had left Cecil and joined the volunteers who escorted groups of little girls in tears. Since age stimulated the old woman's appetite, Rosélie forced herself to cook, consulting Aunt Léna's recipes she had jotted down in her favorite South Sea blue ink in her spiral notebook. *Féwos a zabocat. Soup Zabitan. Bélanjè au gwatin. Dombwés é pwa. Blaff.* Despite Stephen's warnings, the old lady had a tendency to drink too many rum punches. Flushed and giggling, she would be seized with an unusual exuberance. One day, following a sumptuous meal washed down with plenty of wine, a daughter-in-law came to show off her newborn baby, a pink, blond-haired little angel, the type people are so fond of. It was then that Annie, with flushed cheeks and slurred voice, turned to Stephen and begged him. No grandson. No grandson. Never, never could she hug a little half-caste in her arms.

These half-castes, aren't they the abomination of abominations?

Rosélie listened to her, flabbergasted. So all her patience, kindness, and Creole cooking had served no purpose whatsoever. Four centuries later the Code Noir was still a force of law:

"May our white subjects of either sex be prohibited from contracting marriage with the black population on pain of punishment or arbitrary penalty."

A leper and a plague victim she was. A leper and a plague victim she remained, carrying in her womb the germs capable of destroying civilization. From that day on she never set foot again in Verberie, where Annie whined for her, summer after summer. Stephen put the blame on her.

"A lot of fuss about nothing! How can you possibly pay attention to the ramblings of an old woman of seventy-five, slightly tipsy into the bargain? Whatever you may think, my mother likes you a lot!"

Yet a few words would have been enough to calm her mother-in-law's fears. Neither Rosélie nor Stephen had any intention of slipping on the uniform of a parent. Ever since she was little, Rosélie had been sickened by motherhood: those round bloated or bombshell-pointed bellies of her aunts, cousins, and relatives of every nature, constantly pregnant in their maternity smocks ordered straight from France. She loathed their smug expressions, rueful in their rocking chairs, demanding respect as if they were carrying the Holy of Holies. She especially loathed the newborn babies. In spite of their talcum powder and baby cologne, they stank. They stank, retaining the stench of uterus in the dimples of their pudgy flesh. These were the formidable times before the pill when only the good old Ogino method protected lovers. The terror of falling pregnant protected her, much more than Rose's tirades on the flower of maidenhood, which bloomed incongruously between her legs and should only be plucked on the night of the day when Mendelssohn's wedding march echoed through the church. Moreover, propositions were rare, lovers few and far between. She intimidated people, they whispered. Her mouth remained shut like a sharp-nosed puffer fish. She never smiled and always looked as if she were bored.

As for Stephen, his hatred of children was based on objective grounds. He had had to look after his sly and disobedient little half brothers, whom he was not exactly fond of, and they had no particular liking for him either. When he was not listening to them recite the fable of the crow and the fox, when he was not supervising their French homework, he took them to play in the park and read them *The Adventures of Babar*. He got up in the night to take them to piss. It was their fault he hadn't been able to browse through *Les Cahiers du Cinéma* or admire *Ascenseur pour l'échafaud* or *A bout de souffle*. He never had to choose between the Beatles and the Rolling Stones: "I want to hold your hand" or "I can't get no satisfaction."

His teenage years had been swallowed up by thankless jobs. As he grew older he became preoccupied with less selfish considerations: the hole in the ozone, the greenhouse effect, fast food, mad cow disease, bioterrorism, global warming, and the ugliness of a globalized world.

Rosélie and Stephen also agreed on this last point, a major consideration for a couple. They weren't interested in leaving a son and heir. Stephen elaborated on the subject with brio, claiming that the only valid creations are those of the imagination. Obviously, he had his books in mind, of which he was very proud. Especially the one on Seamus Heaney. At present he was preoccupied with his critical study of Yeats. He would start discussing it at breakfast, as if nothing else mattered, describing a thousand research possibilities.

"And what if I compared Yeats and Césaire? That's a bold move! What do you think?"

Nothing. Absolutely nothing. Because I don't know anything about it. I know nothing about anything. All I know is how to paint.

She would run and lock herself in her studio. Once the blinds had been opened, the impatient sun streamed into the room, daubing the walls with yellow. It playfully took the liberty of hanging its cheerful reflections on the canvases, which were in desperate need of them.

Sad, such sad canvases.

A lot of red. Not a bright red like the blood that soaks a birth, but dark and curdled like the blood that nurtures death. This color had always haunted her. When she was a little girl, Meynalda would buy gallons of blood from the butchers at the Saint-Antoine market in order to treat her chronic anemia. She would make it coagulate by throwing in handfuls of cooking salt. Then she would cut it into slices and fry it with chives and lard. It was her favorite dish for someone who only nibbled at her food, to Rose's great despair. The daughter was carved in bone, whereas the mother was kneaded in soft wax.

She also painted in dark brown, gray, black, and white.

Stephen didn't interfere but expressed surprise. Why always such gruesome subjects? Dismembered bodies, stumps, gouged eyes, spleens, and burst livers.

I like horror. I think that in a previous life I must have belonged to a pack of vampires. My long, pointed canines sunk into my mother's breast.

While she worked Rosélie remembered Stephen's words: "The only valid creations are those of the imagination."

His words seemed to her increasingly arrogant. She didn't know whether her creations were valid. How could she know for certain? Simply, she could not help painting. Like a convict in a chain gang. A convict whose bondage knows no end. When, exhausted, she went down to the kitchen, she would find Dido, her complaints, her gossip, and her newspapers, and the entire place smelling of lamb stew with spinach, a specialty of Rajasthan.

But Rosélie was never hungry. No more now than in the past. On her plate the green of the spinach, the saffron brown of the lamb, and the white perfumed rice from Thailand formed a still life. And she couldn't wait to go back up and lock herself in her studio.

THREE

Rosélie never went out because she didn't have any friends. In fact, even from an early age she never had any friends, cosseted by her jealous and possessive mother, and mixing with the family only because she had to. The conversations of her teenage cousins obsessed with their first kiss, or cousins now grown into womanhood obsessed with the performance or, alas, nonperformance in bed of their husbands and lovers, bored her. Ever since Simone Bazin des Roseraies, née Folle-Follette, had left Cape Town to follow her husband and consul to Somalia, she had no one but Dido to keep her company, and she treasured those moments. It's only normal. The popular saying goes that a woman needs another woman to talk to. Men are from Mars, women from Venus, and I didn't invent the expression. But enough of that.

Simone and Rosélie first met at the French Cultural Center. The French Cultural Center was guarded like Fort Knox ever since its wine cellar and stock of foie gras had been raided one Christmas Eve. Despite its cafeteria, which, until that terrible raid, had served excellent wines and delicious sandwiches, the center was always deserted. Charlotte Gainsbourg and Mathieu Kassovitz were doing their best. But how could you rival Bruce Willis and Arnold Schwarzenegger, who could be seen strutting across every movie screen in Cape Town?

One evening Rosélie found herself sitting not far from the lovely, golden-skinned Simone, who positively glowed, during a showing of Euzhan Palcy's *Sugar Cane Alley*. She had seen the film again and again in Paris, N'Dossou, and New York. She never missed a showing, not merely for its merits as a movie but because Euzhan Palcy's miserere each time empowered her with the reality she did not possess. For an hour and a half she could stand up and shout to the disbelievers:

"Look! I'm tired of telling you. Guadeloupe and Martinique actually exist! People live and die there. They make babies who in turn reproduce. They claim to possess a culture unlike any other: Creole culture."

Question: How do you recognize a compatriot? The Caribbean people have an instinct, like any other endangered species. That evening Simone was sitting with her children. As soon as the sepia-colored opening sequences started to roll the children began whispering in her ear. She likewise whispered her answers so as not to disturb the other spectators, pathetically trying to authenticate this far-off land that they had only seen depicted as fiction.

Kod yanm ka mawé yanm. Friendship binds those who are far from their shores.

From that day on, Rosélie and Simone became inseparable. Yet their personalities were strict opposites. Rosélie was attached to nothing, perhaps because nothing belonged to her. Simone was pathologically attached to those thousands of facets some people call traditions: Christmas carols, mandarin pips, and polka-dot dresses at New Year's, coconut sorbet at four in the afternoon, codfish fritters, crab *matoutou*, and red snapper stew for lunch. She would go for miles to buy blood and pig's intestines to make her black pudding. But above all, unlike Rosélie, she had an opinion on politics and just about everything else: underdevelopment, dictatorship, democracy, Kofi Annan, Muslim fundamentalism, homosexuality, terrorism, and the India-Pakistan conflict. Belonging to the same people as Aimé Césaire, the inspiration of Caribbean consciousness, she naturally had the right to teach everyone a thing or two. She dared make negative comments about Nelson Mandela, the untouchable. She believed his influence had not allowed the South African people to purge their frustration and be born again in a baptism of blood under the sun. See Fanon: "On Violence."

"One day all hell's going to break loose," she liked to say, rubbing her hands as if overjoyed at the prospect. "It'll explode like at Saint-Pierre. The whites will hurl themselves on the blacks, and the blacks on the whites."

For those who might not understand the comparison, she was alluding to the eruption of the Montagne Pelée and the total destruction of the town of Saint-Pierre in Martinique. Only one person escaped—a prisoner by the name of Cyparis . . . Oh, I'm sorry, that's another story.

What upset Simone the most as a devoted mother of five was the government's disregard for children. Didn't they know they were the future of the nation?

The child is the future of man.

In her opinion, kindergartens and nursery schools should be under government control and not left to individuals, who were only intent on making a profit. Having investigated several of these places, she had seen for herself how these innocent children were left to macerate in filth, urine, and fecal matter. No intellectual stimulation. The lucky ones had a few cuddly toys, coloring crayons, and modeling clay. So at the end of December she begged Rosélie to play Santa Claus with her and accompany her on a toy distribution mission. Rosélie, who had the regrettable habit of being intimidated by anyone whose willpower was stronger than hers, gave in. One afternoon, then, they set off in the embassy's Peugeot to empty their sack of toys at strategic points. The way they were received at Bambinos as well as Sweet Mickey's as well as Tiny Tots' Palace filled Rosélie with dismay. Worse than intruders, veritable undesirables! The directors scarcely poked their heads out of their offices while their assistants grabbed the packages in such an offhand way, it was to be feared the cumbersome objects would end up in the garbage.

Why, for goodness' sake?

Simone hadn't always been a homemaker. She had been a brilliant student at the School for Political Science in Paris and read all the classics of decolonization. So the explanation she provided was inspired by her readings of years gone by.

"We're not white women. We are black. The whites, however, have brainwashed these people to such an extent that they not only loathe themselves but everything of the same color. What's more, it's the class struggle. Here we are in a luxury car. We don't live in the townships. We're bourgeois. They hate us for not living like them."

Bourgeois? Speak for yourself. I live like a parasite. I don't have a career. I don't have any money or own any material or spiritual goods. I have neither a present nor a future.

Simone had a short memory; she hadn't always been a bourgeois. She was born in one of the most destitute villages of Martinique. Her father was a cane worker who had been a regular customer at the company rum store. There was never any meat on the table. The family was lucky when the fig bananas were accompanied by a slice of codfish and a little olive oil. At the age of ten, though she had never worn anything else but sandals, her godmother, a bourgeois mulatto from Prêcheur, gave her a pair of shiny pumps that her third daughter had not quite worn out. At boarding school she washed and ironed the only two dresses she had, one for weekdays and the nice one for Sunday mass. Right up to graduation she "massacred" the French language, which made her classmates die laughing. When she met Antoine Bazin des Roseraies, a minor aristocrat, nothing more, an egghead and first in his class, she had not been impressed. He had won her over only after a persistent courtship. Then, like in Mira Nair's *Monsoon Wedding*, after a marriage of convenience, the buds of love had blossomed.

At the present time, Simone would have been perfectly happy with a faithful husband and a loving family, if her public life had not been a calvary. On the many occasions when she represented France at her husband's side, she was systematically ignored and snubbed. Under her own roof, at her own receptions, the guests never spoke to her. At other people's dinner parties she was relegated to the bottom of the table. Nobody would believe she had studied at the School for Political Science. At her children's school they took her for the maid. Unlike Rosélie, she was feisty. With the help of her husband, albeit discreetly because of his function, she founded an association, the DNA, the Defense of the Negress Association, her handbook being a work by the Senegalese author Awa Thiam, *La Parole aux Négresses*, which she had read while at university. To those who balked at the word "Negress" and its colonial connotations, and who proposed periphrases such as "women of African origin," "women of color," "women of the South," or even "women on the move," Simone retorted that, on the contrary, it was good to shock.

The DNA had a large membership, wives of diplomats and international civil servants, teachers, traders, owners of beauty shops, visiting nurses, the manager of a travel agency, and the director of a school for models, one of whom had been voted runner-up in the election of Miss Black Maracas.

The association was known for including French, English, and Portuguese speakers, irrespective of class or nationality. Simone had no trouble inviting a wide range of guest speakers, for on this planet there is no black woman who one day or another has not been doubly humiliated because of her sex and color.

Simone had the brilliant idea of making the young poet Bebe Sephuma honorary president, since she enjoyed a reputation throughout the country as dazzling as Léopold Sédar Senghor's in Senegal, Derek Walcott's in St. Lucia, or Max Rippon's in Guadeloupe. There is no equivalent in a Western country, where poets are generally ignored. Yet she had only written three flimsy collections, one of which was dedicated to the woman who brought her into this world before being carried off by AIDS when Bebe was three months old. She had been blessed with good fortune when, on the death of her mother, an English couple had adopted her and saved her from the Bantustan, where she would have surely wasted away with the rest of her family. They had taken her to London and sent her to the best schools. Nevertheless, she had never forgotten the hell she had escaped from. As soon as she could, she returned to settle in Cape Town, where she became the uncontested leader of arts and letters. She had her own cultural column and appeared regularly on television. Since she sponsored a string of art galleries, it was Simone's idea to drag her to Rosélie's studio, the plan being that Bebe would love her work and offer her an exhibition in a select gallery.

"She could give you the chance you've been waiting for."

Rosélie and Bebe had often met. But obviously Rosélie did not interest Bebe, who would hurriedly greet her with a superficial smile. As for Rosélie, she had to admit that Bebe scared her. Too young. Too pretty. Too witty. A wicked smile revealing sharp, carnassial teeth made for tearing great chunks out of life, and betraying her formidable desire to succeed.

But what does it mean to succeed?

But in our countries, nobody ever gets a unanimous vote. Bebe Sephuma was not lacking in detractors. "Is she a true African? What does she know about our traditions?" whispered some of the disgruntled who recalled she had spent her childhood and adolescence in Highgate before reading philosophy at Christ Church, Oxford. As a result, she could not speak any of the languages of South Africa. Not even Afrikaans.

Simone managed to introduce Rosélie to the intimate circle of friends who were celebrating Bebe's twenty-seventh birthday. Duly coached, Rosélie slipped on a black silk sheath dress and brought out her gold bead choker, the one she would never part with, for it was her mother's, and applied her makeup. It's incredible what a little penciling around the eyes and a good lipstick can do! Under her arms she soaked herself with Jaipur by Boucheron. But she had a great deal of trouble trying to convince Stephen to accompany her, usually so worldly and infatuated with high society. He considered Bebe's poetry atrocious, and what's more, she spoke English with a pretentious accent.

Bebe lived in a villa decorated in a futurist manner by a Brazilian designer who was the darling of the rich South Africans. He had designed interiors of a number of pop singers and artists living in Cape Town and Johannesburg.

The villa was situated in Constantia. This neighborhood, one of the smartest residential districts of Cape Town, was gradually being taken over by ambassadors, businessmen, and experts from sub-Saharan Africa, as the good old Black Africa was now called. Not only were blacks seen as uniformed chauffeurs, their white-gloved hands holding the wheel, but sacrilege of sacrileges, they were also sprawling in the back, their peppercorn heads resting on the leather cushions of their Mercedes 380 SLS. Children with the same skin color were pedaling their expensive mountain bikes along drives lined with pine trees and centuries-old oaks.

But what struck Rosélie was not the environment, the interior design, the walls decorated with brightly colored *azulejos* and glass insets, the white marble tiles, the monochrome leather furnishings, the eclecticism of the decoration, a No mask next to a Calder mobile, a Fang mask rubbing shoul-

ders with a tapestry from Ethiopia. Not even the sumptuous-
ness of the dinner table, where nothing was lacking—from
pink champagne and caviar to Scottish salmon. What struck
Rosélie was that the dinner guests were made up solely of
mixed couples, white men and black women, as if they con-
stituted a humanity all their own that on no pretext should
be mistaken for any other.

The most self-assured was Antoine, Simone's husband,
on whom the nature of his job and the assurance of future
promotion conferred an immense authority. When he spoke,
his words had the power of a private bill being read to the
National Assembly.

The handsomest was without doubt Bebe's partner, Piotr.
This Swede, who would not have been out of place in a film
by Ingmar Bergman (the early Bergman) shared and sup-
ported her enthusiasm. Like her, he knew that Art should be
brought to the people and not the reverse. Like her, he had a
different notion of Art than that found in school manuals.
Art is everywhere, in the street, in everyday objects. To explain his point Piotr had recently pulled off a major accom-
plishment. With the help of a photographer, he had plastered
over the buses in Cape Town giant pictures of the market in
Cocody before it went up in flames, a London double-decker
filled with turbaned Sikhs, the junks and floating restaurants
of Hong Kong, the mosque at Djenné, and a caravan of
camels crossing the desert on their way to the salt mines at
Taoudenni.

The most romantic was Peter, an Australian, a telecommunications engineer who had had to flee Sokoto after elop-
ing with Latifah, the only daughter of the sultan. Latifah

spoke only Hausa, Peter only English. The couple had three children. But Peter had still not learned a word of Hausa and Latifah not a word of English, which goes to prove that passion forges its own idiom.

The most captivating was Stephen, with his intellectual charisma, his somewhat obscure language, and his references to works of fiction that nobody had ever heard of but that he made you want to read. Once he was at Bebe's, as Rosélie had guessed, he seemed to forget his reservations and was determined to charm anyone who approached him.

The most average was an American high school teacher from Boston who boasted of being a WASP, on honeymoon with his Congolese wife from Brazzaville who taught at the same school. Together they had written in French a seven-hundred-page novel, extremely boring, *Les derniers jestes d'Anténor Biblos*, published by Gallimard.

But it was Patrick who stole the evening, a somewhat common-faced fifty-year-old who escorted his wife, a Congolese, this time from Kinshasa. Patrick was a former deep-sea diver. For years he had lived on offshore oil rigs from Indonesia to Gabon, from which he escaped every two weeks to blow his phenomenal wages plus danger money in the brothels. At the age of fifty, when the hour of retirement had sounded, he had decided to settle down in Cape Town, where the climate suited his arthritis of the knee, contracted in the ocean depths. During the meal he held his audience captive, recounting quite simply how he used to dive down over a thousand feet, brushing against the fish and the coral amid the silence and darkness of the ocean deep.

But at dessert, however, the conversation got bogged

down in inescapable terrain. Life as a mixed couple. In the ensuing brouhaha everyone had a story of prejudice, rejection, or exclusion to tell, and one's heart never knew whether to laugh or cry or do both at the same time. In fact, no society is prepared to accept the freedom to love.

The most spectacular tale was that of Peter and Latifah. To prevent this union, which he considered unnatural, the sultan Rachid al-Hassan had his daughter locked up in one of the wings of his palace, the Palace of the Wind. Here she was watched over day and night by four ferocious hounds and six old hags who fed her nothing but curds in order to incapacitate her. She had escaped with the help of a guard who had poisoned the hounds with meatballs and drugged the old hags with a sleeping potion. Up to this very day the radio in Sokoto is still broadcasting the description of Peter as a wanted person and public enemy of the sultanate. The sultan has never given up hope of jailing him after having first castrated him with a fine blade inset with ivory dating from the eighteenth century.

Stephen refused to give in to the general gloom. He began by cheering up his audience with his sardonic erudition. The mixed couple is a very old and honorable institution. Ca' da Mosto and Valentin Fernandes can testify to it. It dates back to 1510, when a group of Portuguese from Lisbon, including criminals fleeing the kingdom, settled at the mouth of the river Senegal and, adopting the African custom, took up with black women. Although they were held in contempt by their fellow countrymen, they were adored by the Africans and called themselves *lançados em terra*, those who are thrown onto the shore, or *tango mâos*, the tattooed traders. At the same time, 1512 to be exact, other Portuguese were washed up on the shores of Brazil, near São Paolo, one of whom was João Ramalho, who took as his wife the daughter of a Tamoia Indian chief. On June 14, 1874, Lafcadio Hearn married Alethea Foley, a woman of mixed race from Cincinnati. In the same humorous vein, Stephen then asked why we only take into account the biological element. Isn't the union between a Spaniard and a Belgian a mixed marriage? Between a German and an Italian? A Czech and a Romanian? An American and a French woman? And after all, aren't all couples mixed? Although they may belong to the same society, the spouses themselves come from different social and family backgrounds. Even if a brother married his sister it would be another case of mixed marriage. No individual is identical to another.

He brought out a sense of pride in the guests by painting in glowing colors the day when the entire world would follow their example. Yes, the mixed couple would conquer all! The greatest thinkers of our time are saying that the world is in a state of hybridization. You only need two eyes to see it for yourself. New York, London, cities of hybrids. Hybridized cities.

In their enthusiasm Piotr and Bebe proposed they join forces, and pursue and repeat the "Art for the People" operation. Could he select lines from poems or meaningful quotes by writers? They would be blown up into giant posters and displayed in the markets, the bus stations, the railroad stations, and bus shelters, everywhere where crowds gather. Stephen was only too pleased to accept. He believed the poets who are reputed to be the most difficult are in fact the most accessible.

Simone looked at Rosélie angrily, betraying what she thought. Incorrigible Stephen! Once again he had managed to make himself the center of attention. Me, me, me!

Antoine and Simone were resolutely hostile to Stephen. For Antoine, Stephen remained a son of perfidious Albion, despite his French upbringing. He had not learned "Frère Jacques" at nursery school. He preferred Alice in her Wonderland to General Dourakine, and had never caught himself humming a song by Edith Piaf in the shower. As for Simone, she kept quiet about her real reservations. At the most, she would go as far as accusing him of being a show-off, an actor who always wanted to be center stage.

Rosélie received the criticism leniently. A little like a mother allowing for her son's failings. Hadn't Stephen always dreamed of becoming an actor? He had never achieved his ambition. Instead of sending a thrill through an audience, facing the applause, the standing ovation, and receiving the bouquets of flowers from an enthusiastic crowd, he had to be content with his drawing-room successes.

The evening at Bebe's ended in disaster.

Around two in the morning, Arthur, the half-German, half-English photographer (a hybrid!) who had participated in Piotr's artistic campaign, turned up perfectly drunk, accompanied by an ebony-skinned whore with hair dyed red, wearing a low-cut dress open to her navel, whom he had picked up at the Green Dolphin, where such creatures guarantee bliss for a few rand. His slurred opinion on the sexuality of black women made everyone feel uncomfortable. While fondling the breasts of his trophy, Arthur claimed he was incapable of getting a hard-on with a white woman.

"White women," he shouted, "are like a meal without salt or spices. A dish without condiments! I never touch them!"

Everyone looked at one another in embarrassment. Wasn't it precisely these sorts of clichés they were fighting against? The love of a white man for a black woman is not simply a quest for exoticism or the urgent desire for an orgasm. Let us replace the words "erection," "blow job," and "orgasm" with "tenderness," "communication," and "respect."

Inevitably the operation "Art for the People" was shelved. The morning after Bebe's reception, Stephen, now sober, recalled the mediocrity of her poems and exclaimed he had no intention of working with her. As a regular client of the girls at the Green Dolphin, Arthur contracted the clap and went straight home to London for a cure. Worse, Piotr broke up with Bebe for a model from Eritrea who had been on the cover of *Vogue*. But Bebe soon dried her tears. Hardly had he emptied his closets than she moved in the personal belongings of an Australian tennis player, seeded thirtieth internationally but, in the opinion of his coach, destined for stardom.

This repeat performance of a mixed couple so enraged her detractors that they dared to write in a literary journal for the first time that her poetry was a load of crap.

FOUR

Once Simone was gone, Rosélie only had Dido.

As a Cape coloured, Dido had not experienced all the savagery of apartheid. She was born in Lievland, about twelve miles from Stellenbosch, in a picture-perfect landscape of rugged mountains, jagged-edged against an unchanging blue sky. A mass of flowers. Covered with the curly mop of vineyards. Her family descended from slaves from Madagascar come to work in the vineyards, which the de Louw family had purchased from a French Huguenot.

Nothing really justified Dido's familiarity with Stephen and Rosélie. Nevertheless she would say "us," meaning "us French," referring to the trio they formed, because in even Dido's eyes, though the color of their skin was identical, Rosélie had nothing in common with the South African kaffirs who had been excluded from working in the vineyards and dumped farther and farther from the white world she had learned to hate and despise. Since the words "Guadeloupe, overseas département" meant no more to Dido than to the rest of the world, she considered Rosélie to be French. Didn't she speak French to perfection? Hadn't she studied in Paris? Didn't she eat her steak raw and her Camembert runny? Dido, who had a mind of her own and was not afraid to speak it, would gladly contradict her.

"You, you see racism everywhere! That's not racism. It's

because you're a woman they treat you like that. Women—black, white, yellow, or coloured—they're the asshole of the world!"

Stephen's version:

"Not everything can be attributed to racism. A lot of things are due to your individual attitude."

Whatever.

Although apartheid had spared Dido to a certain degree, life had had no consideration for her. She had first landed herself a good match in the shape of Amishand, an Indian. The couple opened a restaurant named Jaipur, which soon made an excellent name for itself. With their earnings they had built a house in Mitchell Plains, the coloured district. If you didn't meddle in politics—the right to vote, to education, to health benefits, to justice for all, and other such nonsense—life in South Africa could be sweet. Amishand was saving up to realize his dream of ending his days in India at Varanasi. If he was going to go up in flames, it might as well be on the shore of the Ganges. His relatives would scatter his ashes in the waters of the sacred river close by, and he would only have to make one small heavenly step to reach nirvana. His bank account was flourishing when coronary thrombosis dealt a deadly blow. From one day to the next Dido had become the Widow Perchaud, mother of Manil, a seven-year-old son she had killed herself raising in the memory of his deserving father. Alas, the beloved Manil had been the dagger that pierced her heart. Drink, women, men, and drugs! She had ruined herself paying off his debts, then was forced to mortgage and finally sell the Jaipur, that jewel of Indian gastronomy. She had reached the depth of degradation when she had had to hire herself out as a cook by the month. Fortunately, in her misfortune, she had met Rosélie, to whom she had grown attached, like family.

After Manil had died from AIDS, Dido lost the desire to live. She had been overwhelmed by a feeling of guilt. All that had been her fault. She had treated her son like a treasure she took pride in, like a bracelet to flaunt, like a necklace clasped to her neck. She hadn't loved him for what he was. Neither her prayers to the God of the Christians nor her sacrifices to the Hindu deities could bring peace back to her heart. Only Rosélie had managed to do that. Through the laying on of hands and locating the pressure points of Dido's pain.

The car disappeared into the night. Rosélie remained standing on the sidewalk littered with garbage. She had been lucky a taxi had accepted to take her to her appointment at Dido's. Once the sun had gone down, no taxi driver ventured into the black townships: Langa, Nyanga, Guguletu, Khayelitsha, forbidden zones! And even Mitchell Plains, once a calm, hardworking district, was now eaten up with the wrath and fury of gang warfare.

Rosélie looked left and right like a cautious schoolgirl, then ran across the sinister, ill-lit street.

Just as she was furiously battling with fate, so Dido was fighting to make her surroundings a little more human. She was the president of an association that refused to let Mitchell Plains become like the hell of so many other neighborhoods. In her little garden she had planted not only the inevitable bougainvillea, but also hibiscus, azaleas, crotons, and magnificent orchids: green-spotted lady's slippers. She had even managed to grow a blue palm that was covered with ivory-colored buds, as bright as candles on a Christmas tree. She hurried to open the door and whispered:

"Look! That's his car over there."

It was obvious she was taking great delight in the mystery.

Rosélie turned her head and saw a Mercedes huddled in the shadows, its sidelights glowing in the dark like the eyes of a drunkard. Dido led her inside. The living room was like the garden. You never saw such a jumble! Too much heavy furniture: sofas overstuffed with cushions patterned with flowers, triangles, and rosettes; armchairs with round, square, and rectangle lace macassars; pouffes; pedestal tables; and glass and lacquered coffee tables jostled one another on flowery rugs. Under the reproduction of a group of apsaras draped in yellow there sat a man dressed in an alpaca safari jacket. So motionless you thought he was asleep. But when the two women went over to him, he immediately opened his eyes, whose flash was so piercing, that's all you could see in his face. He stood up. He was slim, well built, but disappointingly small. Much smaller than Rosélie and her five feet ten inches. She had always been as lanky as a pole, the tallest in her class, sitting in the back row. Such a look would have better suited someone of another stature. Once Dido had led them into the guest room, as cluttered as the living room, with walls plastered with an array of prints, such as Ganesh with his monstrous trunk, monkey-headed Hanuman, and the handsome bearded face of Jesus Christ, our Savior, he asked abruptly, betraying his embarrassment:

"What do I do?"

"Nothing!" Rosélie smiled. "Just relax!"

She lit the incense and candles. Then she helped him take off his safari jacket and undervest, he resisting a little the intimacy of such gestures. She made him lie down on the sofa bed, laid her hands on his head and ran them over his warm shoulders. He closed his eyes.

"Dido tells me you can't sleep," she said softly.

"I don't think I've slept since 1994. Night after night I stuff myself with sleeping pills. So I get thirty minutes or an hour's sleep. You know what happened in our country?"

Who do you take me for? Everyone's heard about the genocide in Rwanda. Eighty thousand Tutsis cut down to size in next to no time. But although Stephen had contributed to a collective work on the subject without ever having set foot in Kigali, and often discussed it with Deogratias, she avoided the issue out of fear of voyeurism. Moreover, she was unable to conceptualize such a massacre. It was impossible for her to imagine men, women, and children with their heads chopped off, breast-feeding babies sliced in two, fetuses ripped from their mothers' wombs, and the sickening smell of blood and corpses thrown into the rivers and lakes during the killing spree.

She rubbed her hands with oil and began to massage him.

Very soon, he slipped into a semiconsciousness while she received through her palms his inner turmoil and endeavored to control it. Every time she set about healing wounds, she thought of the two beings she had been unable to relieve. Her mother, whom she adored. During her final years, when she still had enough courage to return to Guadeloupe for the vacations, she took refuge with Aunt Léna at Redoute. When Papa Doudou died, Aunt Léna, who hated her job as a social worker, retired. She dressed in sack cloth, stuck a *bakoua* hat on her head, and played the role of planter, wearing out the workers in her banana grove. Rose never complained about how seldom her beloved daughter visited her. She no longer went out, not even to take communion at dawn mass. Father Restif, a Breton with blue eyes, gave her the comfort of the Sacrament at home. She now weighed over five hundred pounds and refused to show herself. She inched open the door to let in only three people— Father Restif, the loyal Meynalda, and good doctor Magne. No need to mention that she no longer sang. She performed in public for the last time at the birthday of a great-niece when everybody begged her to sing. Breaking with habit, she had sung in Spanish:

> *Bésame, bésame mucho,*
> *como si fuera esta noche*
> *la ltima vez.*

Some people said that her deformity was the work of one of Elie's mistresses, a certain Ginéta, whom he had promised to marry and then abandoned with her four little bastards and her two eyes to cry with—at that time they hadn't invented the expression "single mother." Most people refused to accept such a commonplace explanation. Abandoning women and children is nothing new under the sun, neither in Guadeloupe nor in the rest of the world. Elie was neither the first nor the last in his category. Yet, as far back as Guade-loupeans could remember, they had never seen such a sickness as the one that was ravaging Rose. They thought rather she was paying for her papa, Ebenezer Charlebois, the most corrupt of all the politicians, who, with the help of a Haitian obeahman and Nigerian *dibias,* practiced human sacrifice to ensure his reelection. At every All Saints Day, instead of candles, his grave was daubed with a mixture of excrement and tar in revenge; then the word "CUR" written in capital letters evened the score.

Two years before he died, Elie had finally separated from Rose. He kept to his routine, continuing to drink his thirty-year-old Feneteau les Grappes Blanches rum with his friends in the living room before lunch. At half past twelve he was the first at table to devour a plateful of fried fish and lentils cooked in lard by Meynalda. At six in the evening he would join other friends at their meeting place, named the Senate, on the Place de la Victoire. No connection with that of the Luxembourg Palace in Paris. But he had taken up his night quarters in one of the family's upstairs-downstairs houses on the rue Dugommier. There the *bòbò* women, not at all intimidated by his eighty years of age, rivaled in ardor and imagination to entertain and satisfy him. Yet Rosélie had no right to throw the first stone, she who was blissfully whiling away her days at the other end of the world with her white guy. Well, blissfully, in a manner of speaking! For the second person to whom she had never been able to offer peace of mind was herself. When you think about it, it's not surprising. The cancer specialist doesn't treat his own cancer. Nor the dentist his abscess. She had believed that Stephen would give her that strength of which he had more than enough to spare. Instead, his presence and protection had paradoxically sapped the little confidence she had in herself. Then, suddenly, he had left her on her own. The sly, insidious reproach embittered her heart.

Half conscious, Faustin tossed and turned and moaned. She tightened the pressure of her hands on his forehead and neck, and he relaxed.

In New York they had lived on Riverside Drive, steps away from the university where Stephen worked. An apartment with a view of the river. On the other shore of the Hudson they could see the high-rises of New Jersey, and in the evening, to their right, the luminous steel girders of the George Washington Bridge.

Nevertheless, Rosélie couldn't help regretting N'Dossou. And all those who had helped her. Dominique, first of all. Dominique, quadroon with a heart of gold, from Cayenne in French Guiana. When you are five thousand miles from home, the overseas departments merge into one. Guadeloupe and Guiana united! Dominique and Rosélie had been seated not far from each other at the annual banquet of the Overseas Départements Association. As a result of her many sentimental misfortunes, there was no love lost between Dominique and black men. She always ended her judgments with the same lethal phrase:

"They're all filthy machos!"

Not that she liked white men any better. She did not dare ask that question which constantly dances at the back of the eyes and haunts the mind:

"Let's get straight to the point. Musically speaking, one

white half note equals two black quarter notes. Sexually speaking, is one white guy equal to a black?"

Then she would take refuge behind a militant attitude and accuse Rosélie of betrayal. Betrayal? Of what? Rosélie asked angrily.

The Race, of course!

Cut to the quick, Rosélie retorted. She experimented with a weapon that in fact she was rather good at using: irony. So it was the unfortunate Stephen who had dealt in the lucrative traffic of prize slaves? He had been an absentee planter? It must have been he who whispered to Bonaparte to reinstate slavery? Since women always get the blame—*cherchez la femme*, they say—some had hastily accused the beautiful Creole, Josephine de Beauharnais. The reason why some hotheads had mutilated her statue on the Savane in Fort-de-France in Martinique. A statue with its throat slashed. A sun throat slashed. Celanire, throat slashed. And that's not all.

Without stopping, Dominique accumulated a thousand reasons for loathing Stephen.

"Too polite to be honest. He's two-faced, I can sense it. He's hiding something. And then, he's too full of himself."

Stephen, two-faced? On the contrary, he spoke his mind. He poked fun at people, always ready to contradict, mock, and criticize. Rosélie wondered by what miracle she found favor in his eyes. During the early years she used to tremble, like a dunce at an oral exam, convinced the examiner would tire of her. She had waited for that moment for twenty years. In vain. His indulgence and patience had never failed. They had kept her safe and warm, like a premature baby in its incubator.

Then came Tran Anh and Ana. Tran Anh, openhearted but intimidated, didn't dare manifest his poor French in front of this white university professor and never opened his mouth in his presence. Stephen complained that Ana's armpits smelled and bluntly called her a whore.

"If she's a whore, then I am too!" Rosélie protested.

"You," laughed Stephen, "you're a saint."

Under her hands, the nodules, which had represented Faustin's torment and tension, faded away. His breathing became more relaxed. She couldn't do any more for a first meeting.

"That's all for today," she said.

Then, as he glanced around him somewhat dejectedly, she added convincingly:

"Tonight you will sleep, believe me."

He sat up, and holding one of her hands between his palms, he asked:

"When will I see you again?"

His tone of voice was so urgent it was almost as if he were asking for a date. But that's how attached patients get to those who treat them. She pressed down on his neck for a last time.

"Next Friday. But I'm not coming back here. Mitchell Plains is too dangerous. Where do you live? Would you like me to come to your place? I can treat you at home."

He shook his head.

"I have no home. I'm living with friends."

He stared at her like a small boy who is burying the last of his family.

"Then come to my place," she offered. "The police regularly patrol the neighborhood."

They had done so ever since Stephen's murder. Every cloud has a silver lining. He made a face and began to get dressed.

"Does that prove it's less dangerous? The police work hand in hand with the crooks. They're as corrupt as they are in America. My God, who could have imagined that post-apartheid South Africa would become such a jungle?"

Rosélie refrained from making any comment; she refused to judge, condemn, or question.

In the ensuing silence, he continued:

"Why do you stay here? I mean why don't you go home? This is no place for a woman on her own."

What place on earth is made for a woman on her own?

Tell me so that I can take refuge with my sisters, abandoned like myself. We'll form a sisterhood of Amazons with neither bow nor arrow. In that way we'll keep our right breasts.

No doubt about it, without even knowing him, Manuel must have passed the word on. She began the usual explanation. For her, South Africa was not merely a political concept: the former country of apartheid, the former white bastion of southern Africa. Or a new El Dorado, a paradise for the enterprising. She was intimately linked to it, for here was the grave where a loved one lay.

He interrupted her and said disparagingly:

"I know. Dido told me the whole story . . . a white guy."

It was as if he had slapped her full in the face. She staggered from the force of the blow, then turned her back on him.

"That'll be eight hundred rand," she said, trying to calm down.

Money was no problem for him, that was obvious. Without a word of protest, he held out a handful of banknotes. She counted them ostentatiously, then headed toward the door with a curt thank-you. He ran after her and grabbed her sleeve, murmuring, embarrassed, like a child:

"I didn't mean to hurt you."

What were you trying to do, then? But hurt me you never will. Not now! I'm used to it, you know.

Since she still didn't respond, he repeated his question.

"Will I see you again?"

Why not? Your money doesn't have the color of your prejudice.

"I told you, on Friday," she said with a nod of the head.

Then she preceded him into the living room, where Dido was glued to the TV, watching Keanu Reeves, who was so like her dead son, she said. She reluctantly turned round and asked:

"How did it go?"

She sounded like a madam inquiring of one of her girls how it went taking the virginity of a young boy. Neither one responded. Without a word, the two women accompanied Faustin to the front gate. The Mercedes had now drawn up along the sidewalk. A hefty bodyguard, openly holding a gun, dashed to open the door and Faustin dived into the back. The car noisily drove back up the silent street, everyone holed up in his house with his fears. The only signs of life were a pack of dogs under a streetlamp, fighting over a garbage can.

The two women went back inside.

For safety reasons Rosélie did not go back to Faure Street. She stayed and had dinner at Dido's, then slept in the small room she had just used for her consultation.

Faustin's brutality had accentuated her moroseness. Day after day, under every sky, under every latitude, so much incomprehension! So many insults! So many snubs! She compared her life to one of those quilts she had bought during a visit to Amish country in Pennsylvania: a mosaic of different textures of a slightly dull coloring. Brown cotton: the years in N'Dossou; gray wool: the days in New York; mauve felt: life in Cape Town; and black velvet since the death of Stephen.

The only exception, the scarlet silk of the stay in Japan.

From the outset, New York had terrified her: its vastness, its shrillness, and its medley of colors. No skin had the same color. No voice the same accent. Which one was the New Yorker? The African? The Indian? The Arab? The Jew? The fair-haired WASP? All swam with the same ease in the aquarium of the city. The English language did not reign supreme. Spanish collided with Yiddish, Serbo-Croat, Urdu—and all this Babel composed an indescribable cacophony. She began by holing herself up for three months in the depths of her apartment. To the point where she aroused the compassion of Linda, the Peruvian cleaning lady, who thought she was sick and as a result forgot about her husband not having a green card and the worry it was causing. Every morning she would bring her native remedies of leaves, roots, worms, and insect larvae that she bought in a *botánica* on Amsterdam

Avenue, run by a Puerto Rican they called Pepo the Magician. Touched by her thoughtfulness, Rosélie stoically drank these vile concoctions. To her surprise they ended up having an effect. One day she woke up cured.

That night at Dido's she fell asleep amid the forgotten din of ambulance sirens, the screams of police cars, and the barking of fire trucks. In Times Square, above the idling crowds, the neon signs raped the darkness.

I am in a New York state of mind.

FIVE

Every time Rosélie spent the night at Dido's, not only did Dido keep her awake until the early hours of the morning, harping on life's misfortunes—Amishand and his coronary thrombosis, Manil and AIDS, and the Jaipur restaurant, gone with its reputation for good food—but she also woke her up a few hours later to comment on the *Cape Tribune* and other national dailies.

That morning, the news of a dark, horrific event was spread across the front page.

A woman was accused of murdering her husband, who had been missing for several weeks. According to her son-in-law, who had become suspicious of the meat packed in plastic bags on the refrigerator shelves, she had cut him up into little pieces and frozen them. Why would be anybody's guess.

While Dido lamented on the state of barbarity in which the country had fallen, Rosélie was fascinated by the photo of this Fiela.

Around fifty. No more diabolical-looking than any other. She even looked quite gentle, almost shy. As thin as a smoked herring, which emphasized her angular features. The only thing that stood out were her eyes. Despite the poor quality of the photo, you couldn't help looking at them. Elongated, they stretched up toward her temples, eyelids drooping like blinkers through which gleamed her pupils.

She's my age. She's not beautiful. She could be me.

The husband, the victim, was tall and thin with a pleasant face. Not ugly. Rather attractive. With a rounded forehead under a skullcap of peppercorn hair, and an intriguing smile.

Rosélie remembered a case that had made headlines while she was living in Paris. A Japanese student had murdered a twenty-one-year-old Dutch student. He had raped her dead body, cut it up, and eaten several pieces. Declared insane, he had been extradited to Japan.

With Dido still lamenting, this time about her knees swollen with osteoarthritis and the corns on her feet that had kept her awake all night, they made their way to the bus stop. In daylight Mitchell Plains seemed less sinister. Behind the hedges topped with barbed wire, the houses were pretty and the yards filled with flowers. The pattern of avenues had a certain harmony to them. The old wreck of a bus, repainted in orange to give it a new look, skirted the airport and rattled through the ring of shantytowns. As a rule, Rosélie found the sight harrowing. At the Liberty IV bus stop a woman with braided hair plastered with red mud like a Masai, was sitting on the street, surrounded by her rags and her hollow-eyed triplets. Who could have fathered them? Imagining this monstrous coupling made you shiver. The passengers threw coins into her lap to ward off the evil spells she was bound to make. That morning Rosélie took no notice, her only thoughts were for the mysterious Fiela.

Now facing Table Mountain, the indefatigable jailer, the bus crawled toward the center. Soon, it filled with men and women muffled up in harshly colored acrylic shawls and sweaters. For although a deceptive sun shone in the midst of a blue-lacquered sky, the wind, that pitiless wind that twisted the pines to its liking, tore at the lips until they bled, and seeped in just about everywhere. Rosélie had never got used to these European-style clothes, these crowds "so swayed from their own cry," who seemed to have lost their joie de vivre, together with their finery. Away with clichés! "We are the people of dance," claimed Senghor. *"Zouk-la, sé sel médika-men nou ni,"* shouted Kassav as an echo. Nothing is more debatable. Nevertheless, in N'Dossou distress didn't grab you by the throat as it did in Cape Town. It adorned itself with the shimmering colors of boubous and head ties. It seemed ethereal, light, echoing with the rhythms of obaka dancing.

The bus entered the city and stopped amid the confusion of Grand Parade: tourists hurrying toward the massive hulk of the Castle, the former administrative center, passing market sellers crying out their wares of cheap clothes and spices from Madagascar and the Indian Ocean—peppers, saffron, cardamom, and cumin—others advertising their South African oranges, potbellied as grapefruit, grapes swollen with mauve juice, and apples with varnished scarlet cheeks. Here Cape Town was embellished by the disorder and colors of an African city. However, on reaching the residential suburbs, they gradually vanished. It became rectilinear, cold, immaculate, a poisonous flower growing at the extreme tip of the black continent.

Leaving Dido, Rosélie made her way to the central police station along Strand Street, an austere building where, previously, political prisoners were kept while waiting to be allocated to other jails in the province. She walked along endless corridors leading to sparsely lit rooms where black and white police officers were interrogating the accused with the same brutality. The latter were uniformly black, on this point nothing had changed. Crime knows no age. Old men who looked too old to concoct a crime rubbed shoulders with adolescents who looked too juvenile to try. In a cubicle a group of children who couldn't have been more than twelve years old were crying hot tears while they waited.

The Inspector was scribbling in his cramped office, whose space was being eaten up by huge metal filing cabinets. On the wall hung the photo that had gone round the world: Nelson Mandela, smiling beside Winnie, as he walked out of prison victorious.

Inspector Lewis Sithole was no taller than a fourteen-year-old. Puny-looking, he wore a khaki uniform that was too big for him. An arid forest of overly long hair formed a halo around his head, on which was perched a baseball cap. His beard, however, was sparse. Inspector Lewis Sithole was not a handsome man.

On seeing Rosélie he jumped to his feet and hurriedly proposed they go out. They would be better off outside. Did she mind walking? They could walk as far as the Camelia, that café on Heritage Square.

At the corner of the street, two white men, two homeless derelicts, their pink skin blackened with filth, were sprawled on a bed of packing paper. They stared at Lewis and Rosélie with threatening looks, as if they held them personally responsible for their tumble from the top to the bottom of the social ladder. That summed up Cape Town! That hostility of the whites which poisoned the air like a miasma. This feeling of danger which could sweep down from anywhere. However hard the authorities over there in Pretoria reveled in big speeches about the duty of forgiveness, the need to live together, Truth and Reconciliation, there was nothing but tension, hatred, and desire for revenge in this patch of land. At the Camelia, once the coloured waitress, coloured and crestfallen, had taken their order, Lewis inquired about Stephen's cell phone.

To tell the truth, she hadn't looked for it, not understanding really what he hoped to find in it.

Armed with patience, he explained to her that cell phones can store the last ten numbers called. This way, they could find out who had called Stephen.

Rosélie shrugged her shoulders. Provided someone had called him!

Lewis Sithole leaned over, so close she could feel his warm breath. No man in his right mind would walk around the center of Cape Town unarmed past midnight. She persisted: Stephen had an excellent reason for going out. He wanted some cigarettes, for God's sake!

Stephen refused to be intimidated by violence. He had even elaborated a theory on the subject and had no intention of behaving differently whatever the circumstances. In New York he would walk around the Bronx in the middle of the night. In London he didn't let himself be intimidated by dangerous neighborhoods. In Paris he would prowl around the Sentier district at any time of the day or night.

"If he wanted cigarettes," Lewis Sithole continued with the same air of patience, "he would have sent the watchman. At least he had his spear to defend himself."

"Deogratias sleeps like a log," retorted Rosélie. "Sometimes we can hear him snoring from our bedroom under the roof. That particular night, he didn't even hear Stephen go out."

"Yet the watchman at a neighbor's house saw him walk past. He says he seemed to be in a hurry. Almost running. Where do you think he was going?"

To the Pick 'n Pay.

Stephen always walked briskly. Especially after midnight, when there was not a soul about and it was five degrees Celsius.

She relived with the same spasm of pain that moment when her life had been turned upside down and plunged her into solitude and fear. It was a group of young partygoers coming out of a fish restaurant on Kloof Street who had alerted the police. The latter had taken their time. They had taken over an hour to arrive at the crime scene and drive the victim to the hospital. There he had continued to bleed in a so-called emergency room. In the morning the hospital had called Rosélie, who was sick with worry, for Stephen never spent the night away from home. He knew she worried when he was away for too long, even during the daytime.

"What would you do if I worked at the other end of town until goodness knows what hour?" he complained.

Yet, beneath the reproach, she sensed he was pleased with his power.

She had spent an unpleasant fifteen minutes with the learned assembly of physicians and interns. They had lowered their masks, and above the squares of white gauze, they bored into her with their multicolored eyes. A real police interrogation.

You really want us to believe that you are the closest living relative? What relation are you to him? You, his wife? What perverse and degenerate tastes had this handsome Englishman? Where is his mother? His father? His sister? There's nobody else but you? Where are you from in Africa? Guadeloupe? Where's that? Why did you come to Cape Town? What do you do here? You, a painter? A Kaffir, a painter? And what next?

Having run out of words, they sent her to identify the deceased in the morgue. In a drawer, someone other than Stephen was waiting for her—eyes closed, pinched nose, as white as a sheet, wearing a skullcap of lifeless hair. The next morning they had delivered this stranger, as rigid as a corpse.

Barring a few exceptions, the neighbors had been beyond reproach, for Death being what it is, when it turns up on this earth, everyone bows down and respects it.

Besides, Stephen had thumbed his nose at them while he was alive, and had now got what was coming to him. His abject death on a sidewalk was proof of this. Forgetting their hostility, they invaded the territory that mourning had purified. One of them told the university, while another informed the family—the half brothers in Verberie, the father in Hythe. Or was it the other way round? This one arranged the flowers in vases, that one discussed arrangements with the undertakers, while another finalized details for the church ceremony. Yet, instead of touching Rosélie, their attentions merely accentuated her pain. Furtively, they eradicated her. They dismissed her to the margins of a life of which she thought she had been the center for twenty years.

It was as if Stephen had been repossessed by this world from which he had always kept his distance. As if he had become what he had never been either for her or for himself, that is, a white man.

She was not the only one to remark on this exclusion. Dido, who was no fool, did too. Around noon, she came to join Rosélie in her lair, the room where she was holed up, incapable of tears. Handing her the black clothes she had had the presence of mind to order from her dressmaker, Dido dictated:

"Get dressed. Come downstairs. He's your husband. You lived with him for twenty years. It's your house. You must make your presence felt."

Rosélie had obeyed and confronted this sea of faces, full of hate and contempt under their masks of compassion. They converged on her to haul her far from the dry land to which she was clinging, then push her under and drown her. Shaking, she tried to exorcise her fears by doing her best to mouth the Psalms:

> *The Lord is my rock, my fortress and my deliverer,*
> *My God, my rock in whom I take refuge*
> *My shield, and the horn of my salvation, my stronghold.*
> *I call on the Lord who is worthy to be praised.*

Unfortunately, they didn't mean anything, just words out of her mouth. In the afternoon at the church of St. Peter's, amid the funereal smell of wilting flowers, dying candles, and incense, she had collapsed on Deogratias's shoulder. My night watchman. My cook. Now my only friends.

And the ceremony had been recuperated by the university vice-chancellor—the first black South African to acquire the position, of which he was so proud—the dean, the head of the department, both white, the mainly white colleagues, hand-picked students, and students from the colleges who had re-hearsed their end-of-year theater performances with Stephen.

Inspector Lewis Sithole's voice pierced the thick fog of her pain.

"It's been really a pleasure talking to you. But I have to go back. We have a terrible case on our hands. The public pros-ecutor's office is under enormous pressure. They want us to bring it to trial as soon as possible and make an example out of it."

"Fiela?" she asked familiarly, as if it were a girl she had sat beside on the benches of the Dubouchage school or a cousin, the daughter of an aunt, she'd grown up with in the same family.

He nodded, then added:

"It's a pity I can't call on you. I have the firm conviction you could help me."

She stared at him, surprised he could joke about such a subject. He was only half joking.

"Ever since we arrested her, despite a stream of psycholo-gists, psychiatrists, and communications specialists of all kinds, she hasn't opened her mouth. I don't know what her voice sounds like. They assure me, however, that nobody can resist you. During your sessions people recount everything they have on their conscience."

Rosélie agreed, murmuring:

"Can you heal those whom you don't understand?"

Patient No. 20
Fiela
Age: 50
Nationality: South African
Profession: Housewife

Don't keep anything from me. You know full well when you say "I" you mean "us." Let's go back to when you were a girl. Your mother died when you were ten. Have you ever got over it? Do you still dream about her at night?

Can you see yourself playing horsey on her lap?

As they headed toward the door, the Inspector continued:

"Oddly enough, she formed with Adriaan, her husband, a very loving couple. They were married for twenty-five years; they didn't just live together. No, they were married. Legitimately married. Both very religious. They were regulars at the Church of the Resurrection in Guguletu. They didn't miss a service. Then, surprise, surprise, two years after their wedding, Adriaan had a child with a neighbor's daughter. But apparently it didn't affect their relationship. She took the boy in and raised him. The whole business remains a mystery."

SIX

Fiela, you've settled into my thoughts and dreams. No bother at all. As discreet as an alter ego. You hide behind everything I do, invisible, like the silk lining of a doublet. You must have been like me, a solitary child, a taciturn teenager. Your aunt who raised you said how ungrateful you were. You had no friends. You didn't attract attention. The boys walked past without a glance, without a thought as to what you were dying to give them.

Every weekend since she had been on her own, Rosélie had followed Dido to Lievland, where her old mother, Elsie, had stayed on. The open-air life and visiting places had never interested Rosélie. It was Stephen who, at the slightest day off, had dragged her, moodily, through the game parks, onto the beaches, into the mountains and campgrounds where they ate *braais* in the company of strangers—who were disconcerted by the presence of a black woman—and on excursions out to sea to spy for whales they never saw. If she had been left to herself, she would have stayed home on Faure Street, moping with her memories. But Dido insisted she should "enjoy" herself.

Now that gangs ransomed passengers, raped and molested women traveling alone, taking the train was like an adventure into the Wild West. So Rosélie rented Papa Koumbaya's car. Stephen had known Papa Koumbaya's three younger sons at the university where they taught music. During his frequent visits to the jazz clubs, he had become friends with the older sons, who also were musicians. They had all made him laugh when they told him the story of how they had clubbed together and given a Thunderbird as a token of their affection to their old parents, crippled by a life of hard labor under the suns of apartheid. The parents had thanked them warmly, but nevertheless found the car too beautiful, far too beautiful for a couple of old fogies!

They had kept it in a garage, and Papa Koumbaya brought it out in exchange for a fistful of rand for wedding processions. Being driven to the altar in Papa Koumbaya's Thunderbird was one of Cape Town's costlier attractions. Renting his car to Rosélie for mundane excursions showed the full extent of the feelings he had for Stephen.

Rosélie didn't know who she preferred—Papa Koumbaya or the Thunderbird, red the color of desire, hissing like a snake, which, alas, the old man, an extremely careful driver, reined in along the highway like a jockey curbing his thoroughbred. As for Dido, she complained that Papa Koumbaya stank like a billy goat. And then there was nothing original about his stories. They were so basically South African. As a result, she stuck ear plugs in her ears while Rosélie opened wide her own. Shriveled like a gnome behind the wheel, Papa Koumbaya set about telling them a different way each time, spicing them up in new guises, adding moving details or picturesque anecdotes. For forty years he had lived with six others to the room in a men's hostel in Guguletu. When his body cried out too much, he would relieve himself by masturbating in front of a photo of Barta, his wife. Then he would wash away his disgust with gallons of bad beer. In the meantime Barta had been relegated beyond the six-hundred-mile limit to a barren bantustan. They made love during his brief leaves. Year in, year out, however, Barta gave birth to a son. In order to cheer up his miserable life as a pariah, he had learned on his own how to play a number of musical instruments, and communicated his passion for music to his sons. The seven of them had formed an orchestra, which played at services in the churches of the Assembly of God. The Koumbaya Ensemble. Strangely enough, the end of apartheid had sounded its death knell. Too rustic, too folksy when all you had to do was switch on the television to get the handsome Lenny Kravitz or the Spice Girls!

Rosélie would have driven through Stellenbosch and its whitewashed houses, full of memories of apartheid, without stopping. But Dido always woke up on entering the town and demanded they have a coffee in the rose-covered patio of D'ouwe Werf.

"I can't believe I'm actually sitting here," she would say. "When I was small, we were barred from this place, like so many others. And I used to dream about it. So you can understand how I feel sitting here today!"

Although the waitresses in their ample aprons were polite, the tourists had no scruples, staring in hilarity at this unusual trio. Were they a father and his two daughters? A husband and his two wives? They had no idea they were a sight themselves. Tourists had always fascinated Rosélie. In Guadeloupe, most of the visitors were extremely average French families, both in bank account and physique, seeking cheap exoticism.

Canadian women have long gone. They now prefer the males in Saint Martin.

Whereas the whole world was streaming into Cape Town. But why do you see only the garish, the brash, the loud, the fat, the potbellied, and the big-bottomed? Where were the handsome, the slim, the polite and discreet? Don't they travel anymore?

Despite the slow pace of Papa Koumbaya's driving, they soon reached Lievland from Stellenbosch. Lievland boiled down to its homestead. Nestled in the foothills, amid a setting of oaks, it was a magnificent example of eighteenth century Cape Dutch architecture. Throughout the years, every owner had added his mark. One a stable, another a gable, and yet another a granary covered in fire-retardant material where they stored coffins and provisions side by side. The tourists, raising their heads to the gabled facade before dragging their sneakers through the series of rooms, had no idea of the drama being played out upstairs. In 1994, swearing he would never see his beloved country in the hands of a Kaffir, Jan de Louw had turned his back on his vineyards and locked himself in his bedroom, his eyes stubbornly fixed on his wardrobe from Batavia made from coromandel ebony. His wife, Sofie, had first tried to get him to go downstairs. Unable to do so, she had written to Willem, their only son, who, long ago, had taken refuge in Australia. There, at least, the aborigines stayed in their place. At the most, they won medals at the Olympic Games! Willem had refused to set foot in South Africa. So Sofie had tried to look after the vineyards herself. But that's a man's job! With an aching heart she had had to sell her land and put the estate house on the well-known tourist circuit of AfriCultural Tours. It had become a major point of interest, attracting busloads of admiring tourists. A Dutch photographer fell in love with the place and asked for permission to include it in a series of postcards entitled "Marvels of the World." A Norwegian had flown from Hammerfest to have his picture taken alongside his bride. There was a time when Dido had proposed opening a restaurant in the former slave quarters, beside the stables, opposite the animal park. But Sofie had firmly opposed it. She suffered enough seeing hordes of strangers stream over the de Louws' floor and considered it a comedown. She didn't want to see them. She didn't want to hear their stupid comments.

"Did you see that barometer? How old is it? How does it work?"

"And that wonderful clock! Look, it not only shows the days but also the phases of the moon."

"How extraordinary!"

Every day from nine-thirty to five o'clock she would hole herself up in the kitchen behind the door marked PRIVATE. By craning her neck, the curious visitor could see the stone hearth that stretched the whole width of the kitchen, and salivate at the thought of the meat that was once smoked there.

Dido and her mother lived in the former slave quarters, a long, low building to the side of the homestead under a heavy roof that would have delighted an amateur of local color. No heating. No hot water. A rudimentary shower. A makeshift WC. In order to counterbalance the lack of comfort, Dido had scattered colored rugs over the floor of beaten earth, laid lace crochet work on the back of shapeless pieces of furniture, and, above all, hung one of Rosélie's paintings, oil on wood, in the center room. With no title, of course. Despite her allegations, the weekends at Lievland were anything but "enjoyable." They would walk around the vineyards. They would eat a *bobotie* cooked by Dido's mother. They would take a siesta. They would take another walk, this time on the road, and pick wildflowers. They would dine on the rest of the *bobotie*. With Dido's mother rambling on in the background about the time she visited Maputo, describing the city like a Muslim the Garden of Allah. They would then watch films on the VCR; always the same ones, featuring Keanu Reeves from every possible angle. They would go to bed. They wouldn't sleep. Yet they always got up at the crack of dawn and started all over again, except the *bobotie* would be replaced by a lamb curry. At 6:00 p.m. on the dot, Papa Koumbaya's car would be waiting. They would drive back to Cape Town. They would go to bed. They wouldn't sleep.

But that weekend, the thirteenth since Stephen had died, was destined to be different.

When they arrived, Rosélie and Dido found Sofie deep in conversation with Elsie.

Sofie was a frail little woman. Wearing a white headscarf tied into a bonnet and a black dress, she looked like someone out of a painting by Vermeer. Despite the extraordinary difference in size—Sofie, a featherweight, weighed under sixty pounds—Sofie reminded Rosélie of Rose. Rose had finished her days the same way: alone in a house that was too big, neglected by her husband and deserted by her only child. At the back of their eyes you could read an identical tale of solitude and desertion, as if this were the lot of mothers and wives.

Sofie looked up as they came in and croaked:

"It's Jan. He's thrown himself out of bed and fractured his skull. The doctor says he hasn't got long to live."

As if to ward off ill fortune, Elsie made the sign of the cross.

Dido and Sofie hurried over to the estate house. Seeing Rosélie hesitate, Dido shouted to her:

"Come on! You could help him. You know you're worth more than all the doctors on earth."

Faith is the only saving factor!

The tour buses were now jostling into the parking lot, and some Germans were getting out. Sofie explained she hadn't been surprised by her husband's act. Recently, Jan had changed a lot. He who devoured the newspapers, rejoicing at the upward curve of AIDS and the increase in the number of child rapes and robberies, was no longer interested in anything. He dozed all day long. He would ask for his mother and brother, who had been laid to rest years ago. Rosélie was ashamed of her curiosity. It was as if the ogre's padlocked door were finally creaking open on its hinges. She had never been near Jan, around whom Dido had woven a thick mythology of tales and legends in which he had become a hairy, longhaired, one-eyed beast, evil personified, his personal stench lingering around the homestead like a decaying carcass. At last she was going to see him with her own two eyes. A troubled feeling of triumph mingled with her curiosity. She was going to see for herself his downfall. For this voluntary end to his life was a point of no return. At last he had admitted that this country, where he and his kin believed they could lay down their law, had escaped them for good. The Kaffirs in power were here to stay.

Sofie entered first, then Dido. Gripped by a kind of fear, Rosélie was the last to cross the threshold.

What was she expecting?

A hulking, menacing man with an arrogant, slightly protruding jaw. Instead, deep in the four-poster bed lay Jan, as frail as his wife, dressed in a nightshirt with a pleated yoke, with chalky-white skin and his forehead wrapped in an enormous, soiled bandage that made him look like a sick fakir. The room was painted dark brown and made even darker by the closed shutters, which let in a thin shaft of light. You would never have dreamed that outside it was broad daylight. Besides the wardrobe from Batavia, the room was furnished pell-mell with a marquetry chest of drawers, a rosewood table, and a camphor wood trunk. In a corner stood the child's cot on which Sofie had slept for years. Seeing this, Rosélie's forebodings were swept away in a wind of compassion that brought her to the verge of forgiveness. The final moment the old man was going to confront, Stephen had confronted alone. Alone like Rose a few years earlier. How could she soften the blow? Could her meager talents be of any use?

It was then that Jan opened his eyes and she received his gaze full in the face. A bluish green gaze, stained in places by fibrils of blood, floating on the white of his cornea like clumps of seaweed. Bluish green like the ocean at the farthest end of the earth, at the extreme tip of this cape they call Good Hope. Wrongly. For the dismal cargo from the East Indies, Madagascar, and Mozambique, the sight of these jagged, rugged cliffs signified in fact the end of all hope.

His gaze pinned her rigid against the wall. It seemed he

was sending her back to former places, to a previous role. Standing behind the master's chair, waving peacock-feather fans to drive away flies and cool the sweat on his shoulders. Lying, legs spread open, fodder for the master. Back bent, lacerated by the overseer's whiplashes. For Jan, time had stopped still. Today meant yesterday. There was no tomorrow.

Sofie and Dido vainly tried to get her to come closer, but the pitiless beam from Jan's eyes paralyzed Rosélie while a host of feelings welled up inside her. The rage to hurt him, even kill him; in any case to make him lower his eyes. Part of her was ashamed, another part terrified by such violence. As a result, she could no more move than if she had been changed into a rock. After a while she got control of herself and, regaining a semblance of calm, turned the door handle and slipped into the corridor.

Stephen would have minimized the incident.

"As usual, you imagined the whole business. But if it was true, you were asking for it. Your pity deserves to be put to better use; the townships are full of people you could heal. But you don't want to set foot in them."

In fact, since the debacle with Simone, Rosélie had made this decision and kept to it.

She had understood that the townships were out of bounds to her. They were an exclusive domain patrolled by minivans painted with mysterious letters, MNM, FDT, CRT or even KKK—not what you think; on the contrary, a Dutch charity. They could be compared to gigantic bordellos, closed to intruders. The Westerners, burning with desire to erase the loathsome image of the Afrikaners, made frenzied love with the blacks, who passionately surrendered to the embraces they had secretly dreamed of. Whatever their type of work, they never stopped praising their protégés' creativity and intelligence. Amazingly, the blacks never showed the slightest grudge against the whites. No trace of resentment in their behavior. Always ready to serve. Like Boy Scouts.

In N'Dossou, New York, and even Tokyo, thanks to Stephen, classes of youngsters had been introduced to the complexities of the Anglo-Irish repertory: Synge, Bernard Shaw, and Shakespeare. In South Africa, he worked for Arté, a religious association from Canada approved by the Ministry of Education. The idea was that culture would safeguard the young generation from the perils of modernity. Stephen was preparing the sophomores at the Steve Biko High School in Khayelitsha to perform *A Midsummer Night's Dream*, since Arté believed Shakespeare to be a powerful antidote to crack. One day, swayed by his constant panegyrics, Rosélie forgot Simone's analysis and accompanied him to a rehearsal. History repeated itself. Even though it was silent, the hostility of the teenagers toward her was palpable, as cutting as a razor blade. She got the impression she was tarnishing the image of their beloved professor, who spoke English with an inimitable accent and was the embodiment of Old World sophistication. What was the sordid connection between him and this descendant of cannibals?

Fiela, Fiela, you see, we are alike.

Stephen was too sharp not to perceive this hostility, but his explanation was quite different.

"They sense you're not interested in them. Worse, they sense you despise them. So they react."

Despise them? Why would I despise them? I've no right to despise other human beings.

"You deny it, but you're arrogant."

Me, arrogant? Whereas deep down I'm scared to death. I'm scared of other humans, of the world, of life and death. I'm scared of everything!

Dido's return interrupted the stream of memories.

Sofie regretted she had rushed away. Jan now seemed to be in a coma. The doctor, called back for the emergency, claimed he wouldn't make it through the night.

If she had had the means, Rosélie would have bade her farewells to South Africa that very evening. Alas! Besides the fact she was incapable of paying for a ticket, even the cheapest economy fare, she had no idea where to go. A notary had just written, informing her that Aunt Yaëlle, Elie's last remaining sister, an eccentric, who for a long time had lived in Santiago de Cuba with a drunken musician, addicted to ether, it was rumored, breaking with the family's general hostility, had left her the house in Barbotteau, high in the hills, surrounded by the rampart of mountains, where she had taken refuge in her old age. Rosélie had memories of birthdays, frantically racing over the lawn, green with the hope of those years, slices of marble cake, smooth to the palate, and coconut sorbet served with silver spoons.

What would happen if she accepted the offer?

"*Ola fanm-la sa sòti?*" Where did this woman come from? the neighbors would grumble.

Those who are born and live in metropolitan France

have been given a name. They call them Negropolitans or Negxagonals. To have a name means you already exist. Stones that roll around the world gathering no moss have no name. They call them nomads.

Unable to turn her back on South Africa, Rosélie decided to leave Lievland. Jan had opened her eyes for her. Having lived week after week in these former slave quarters beside the master's house meant that she closed her eyes to the past, that she endorsed it, that she absolved it. She had visited Monticelli, Thomas Jefferson's house in Virginia. The finishing touches to historical color had been the African-Americans ensconced in smocks selling souvenirs in the slave quarters' gift shop.

Come and buy an ashtray made from genuine shackles! Branding irons made into paperweights!

Read all about it in *The Tale of the Mulatto Girl*, the memoirs of Jane Johnson, whose mother hired her out at the age of fifteen and who bore ten mulatto bastards! She never got her freedom. Her master loved her too much to lose her.

Rosélie's behavior was no less shocking.

Unfortunately, Papa Koumbaya, whom they had called on his cell phone, another of his sons' generous gifts, was partying in Nyanga. Since he could never refuse her anything, he promised to be there as soon as he could.

He turned up around midnight, somewhat tipsy, and provoked the ire of Dido, who could already see the Thunderbird in a ditch. But the journey back went off without a hitch.

The moon, so round it could have been drawn with a pair of compasses, illuminated every corner of the sky, which the wind, still blowing briskly, had washed clean of the tiniest

cloud. Its rays lit up the tangled mop of oaks, the farms huddled among the vineyards, the ribbon of the road, and then
the ocean, the ocean dressed in amethyst, untamed, slipping
farther and farther away, as far as the eye could see. Never
had Rosélie felt so alone. Never had she struggled so much
with a feeling of bitterness toward Stephen. He had brought
her to this loathsome country against her will and then abandoned her here.

Back at Faure Street, draped in his dark brown quilted
blanket, Deogratias was already asleep, lying at the foot of the
traveler's tree.

SEVEN

Rosélie, who didn't have Dido's culinary talents, was finishing a meager meal when the bell at the front gate rang. Slightly alarmed, she sat up. Who could that possibly be? She wasn't expecting anyone, since she had no friends and therefore no visitors. In some neighborhoods the gangs worked brazenly in broad daylight. Fake movers would empty a house from the cellar to the attic, then neatly liquidate the owners. But they wouldn't ring to announce their arrival, she reasoned.

She cautiously approached, and was so amazed when she saw him standing on the sidewalk, his face pressed up against the gate like an Arab hawking rugs, that she lost all sense of civility and shouted at him:

"What are you doing here? I don't work on Sundays."

He smiled, by no means deterred.

"It's not that. I wanted to see you, Rosélie."

He had called her by her name. Even worse, however, no sooner had he said it than she realized the wish was mutual. These past days, this incongruous, inadmissible desire had lain hidden behind the bitterness, the grief, and the anxiety of daily routine. Her fingers, turned strangely numb, finally managed to find the key. She stepped aside to let him in and pointed to the chairs in the garden.

"Shall we sit outside?"

But he preferred to go in. Inside, while he looked her over with a critical eye, she was angry with herself for wearing a battered pair of corduroy trousers, a sweater with holes at the elbows, and no makeup. What man in his right senses could possibly be interested in her?

"You shouldn't stay locked up at home in this fine weather," he remarked. "Look at that sun! You ought to get out and—"

"—and enjoy myself, thank you, I've done that," she said, finishing his sentence in a gloomy mocking tone of voice.

She stood powerless while he seized her hand and covered it with kisses.

"Forgive me once again for last time. I don't know what came over me, I had the urge to hurt you. I suppose I was jealous."

Hold on! Where is this leading us?

In order to conduct an extramarital affair with all the lies, pretense, and hypocrisy it entails, you need a morale of iron that Rosélie didn't have. After drifting into troubled waters, sinking, and almost drowning during her terrifying days, at night she liked to come back to the firm, reassuring pontoon of Stephen's body anchored in the same place. Lovemaking was no longer a physical, bodily struggle from which they emerged exhausted and sweating. It was a pleasant, uneventful stroll in a familiar garden. Afterward, Stephen would uncork a bottle of Italian white wine, Lacrima Christi, read comic strips out loud, and dream of Yeats. Beneath her closed eyelids she could see Rose again, even hear her:

Amado mío,
Love me forever
And let forever begin tonight.

In twenty years she had had only one affair, only one, and the memory of it tucked away, far away, in the corner of her mind, had lost all reality. Had she really lived the madness of those days? Yet, three months after the death of her companion, here was a man whom she didn't know from Adam, a man she dominated by at least six inches, who was turning her on. She was not proud of it. At the same time, she was deeply distraught, experiencing such sensations and feelings, so long forgotten that she thought she had never felt them. Her life was not over, then?

"Let me take you out to Clifton," he proposed. " I know a place where they serve mussels and Mort Subite beer. It's just like being in Brussels."

If it was just to have a drink, she had gallons of white wine. Every week Dido brought back crates from Lievland. In the kitchen she almost broke two glasses and cut herself opening a bottle, she was so nervous. When she came back into the living room he was standing in front of one of her paintings. Turning round, he asked her the inevitable question.

"What does that represent?"
She smiled. "Whatever you like."
He seemed disconcerted, repeating:
"Whatever I like?"
Then he laughed, revealing his uneven, square teeth. He

came toward her, took both glasses from her hands, and set them down on a piece of furniture, as if he had wasted enough time with words, gestures, and smiles and now needed to get down to essentials. They made love with the frenzy of two high school students on the living room's dark red sofa.

Afterward, Rosélie was shattered. Years of fidelity wiped out in a single morning! Her fidelity had nothing binding about it. Stephen had never presented her with a parchment to sign:

Commandment No. 10: "Thou shalt covet no one but me." It was the fruit of a personal decision.

He jumped up, for, like Stephen, he seemed to possess that quality that was so cruelly lacking in her: he was at ease with himself, satisfied at being who he was.

"Get dressed!" he ordered with the authority conferred on him by the pleasure he had just given her. "I'm taking you to a club in the Malay district where they play music from Zaire."

"Music from Zaire?" she said, pulling a face.

"Well, from the Congo, since Zaire no longer exists."

Seeing little enthusiasm, he smiled.

"You must reintegrate; you've lived too long among white folk."

But this time he was joking.

Rosélie had been sleeping like she hadn't slept for three months when Dido entered with her tray and aroma of coffee. It was late. The sun's rays had filtered into the very middle of the bedroom. Dido had travestied herself as a domestic—headscarf, colorless blouse—but as usual sat down intimately on the bed as if she were at home. That morning she made no comments about the newspapers and announced in an excited voice:

"I have to go back to Lievland. Sofie called. Jan has just died."

But Rosélie no longer had time for Jan. She recounted the night's events. Dido listened without interrupting and first of all said by way of conclusion:

"It's done you a world of good. You were able to sleep. You look ten years younger."

But her approval was short-lived. She went and fetched a sheet of paper and sat down in front of the chest of drawers.

"Now let's see what type of person he is," she said severely.

"What type?"

Rosélie realized that she knew nothing about a man with whom she had performed one of the most secret and intimate acts imaginable.

Dido licked the end of her pencil.

"He took you out? Where did he take you?"

"To the Paradise," she said docilely. "In the Malay district."

The Bo-Kaap or Malay district, as the inhabitants of Cape Town call this fascinating and charming enclave of ocher, pink, and blue facades, is in fact a misnomer. Historians tell us that fewer than one percent of slaves actually came from Malaysia and, consequently, have left few traces in the region. They also call it the Muslim district. This seems more appropriate given the number of mosques in the area. Moreover, a religious leader by the name of Abu Bakr Effendi lived and founded a school there. Malay or Muslim, Bo-Kaap is one of the nicest areas of Cape Town because of its tangled network of alleys, its tiny restaurants smelling of ginger and curry; and it is also one of the safest, the only neighborhood in this city of living dangerously where you can stroll around on foot.

Dido pulled a face.

"He didn't go to much trouble. The Paradise is a very ordinary sort of place. Admission is a few rand. The club belongs to a Congolese refugee. It's where all the French-speaking Africans hang out."

In his eyes, I don't deserve any better. I'm not a prize conquest.

"At his age, he must have a wife and children. Where are they?"

Rosélie nodded.

"He's married to an African-American," she replied naturally, hiding how stunned she had been on hearing the news. (So he had a liking for foreign women.) "They have two daughters. When he lost his job, his wife went back to her family. They haven't seen each other in years."

Dido rolled her eyes.

"The usual story! They've always quarreled with their wives. Always separated or in the process of divorce. What's he doing in South Africa?"

Rosélie made a vague gesture.

"Like everyone else. He came to do business."

"My God!" Dido groaned. "The worst kind. The so-called African businessman. In that case, why isn't he in Johannesburg? That's where the business is!"

Rosélie confessed she didn't know. Dido continued her interrogation.

"I've heard he's a government minister?"

"He didn't mention it," Rosélie once again confessed.

"Then he can't be too proud of it," Dido concluded in a cutting tone. "Why does he drag around all those bodyguards with him?"

"It seems his enemies tried to assassinate him while he was living in Kinshasa, then again in Brazzaville."

Dido sniffed scornfully on hearing this story of hired killers. At that moment, Rosélie endeavored to reassure her and adopted a casual approach. What was she frightened of? What was she trying to protect her from? Whatever people might think, she wasn't born yesterday. The heart had nothing to do with it. Just a one-night stand, that's all it was. Dido put her harshly in her place.

"I've already heard that tune. You're wrong, women can't divorce sex from the heart. You least of all."

Thereupon she stuffed her paper in a drawer.

"Don't trust him. That Faustin tells me there's nothing good about him."

She sounded like Dominique ranting on against Stephen years earlier. Dido didn't like Stephen either, even though she hadn't dared admit it. At times Rosélie caught her looking at him, black with animosity. Good friends are always Cassandras.

Rosélie got dressed, then went downstairs to drink three

cups of coffee on the patio. She needed at least that to regain a semblance of equilibrium.

On the other side of the street, her hands protected by pink rubber gloves, her face behind a blue mica eyeshade, Mrs. Schipper, the neighbor, was trimming her roses. Snip snip snip. The branches fell around her like heads during the Reign of Terror. As usual, she looked straight through Rosélie. This voluntary blindness had lasted four years.

The night with Faustin gave Rosélie the courage she had lacked up till then. She pushed open the door to Stephen's lair. It was an oval room, "my oval office," Stephen liked to joke, the loveliest room in the house, evidently designed to be a living room, as the marquetry and moldings on the ceiling testified. His favorite picture, the third of a series he had named *Virgins, Monsters, and Witches*, had pride of place. Stephen's den was filled with an ill-assorted collection of furniture, the way he liked it, an armchair bought for next to nothing at the flea market standing next to an expensive roll desk in lemon wood. Stephen was very proud of his library filled with leather-bound first editions in French and English. What was she going to do with them, she who hated the opaque, oppressive presence of books? She decided to donate them to the university. She would call Doris the very next morning. Dido would love the extra flat, wide-screen Sony TV—Stephen adored the latest gadgets—which would set Keanu Reeves off to better advantage. As for the CD player, Deogratias, who was a lover of Gregorian chant, would be overjoyed with it. But all those CDs and videocassettes? Stephen's taste in music was totally opposite to hers, strictly jazz and Verdi operas, which she hated. She would give everything to Mrs. Hillster. Mrs. Hillster was a great friend of Stephen's. Twice or three times a week she would come and have tea, and sit and chat with him at the foot of the traveler's tree. Mrs. Hillster was an English lady, the widow of a senior civil servant who in the seventies had written a report, oh nothing too critical, against apartheid. This gave her the right to criticize the government and to fill everybody's head with "All they have to do is this" or "All they have to do is that."

Apart from that, she owned the most delightful shop imaginable, called the Threepenny Opera. Everything was shelved together in total disorder: Christmas carols with requiems, motets with oratorios, cello suites with raï music, and Cesaria Evora with Cheb Mami. Rummaging around, you came up with all sorts of things. That's how more than once Rosélie's heart had missed a beat. One day, in the middle of a collection of iscathamiya music, she had come across some old recordings of biguines by Stellio: Elie's favorite music, together with the Afro-Cubans. "Guantanamera," "Dos gardenias," and "tutti quanti." In his youth Elie had even tried his lips at clarinet playing. Together with his four brothers, Emeric, Eliacin, Evrard, and Emile, they had formed a group called the Musical Brothers. The band had made quite a name for itself playing at afternoon dances and quadrille balls. But in the long run music is not enough to feed a man on his own, let alone four strapping guys. The band had broken up. Whereas his brothers found jobs wherever they could—two emigrated to Paris, another to Canada—the valiant Elie sat for the civil service exam and spent the next forty years in a stuffy office on the second floor of the clerk's office in Pointe-à-Pitre. Another time Rosélie had discovered Salama Salama's gold record, *The Reggae of the Wretched*, that had sold over a million copies and whose music had no trouble feeding him comfortably. She had helped him compose the lyrics.

> *Dance, the wretched of the earth,*
> *Dance, the prisoners of hunger,*
> *Yes, dance, dance, dance to forget!*
> *Me rasta man, I urge you to love one another.*
> *If everyone loved each other*
> *Loved each other in the morning, loved each*
>   *other in the evening,*
> *Loved each other at noon, loved each other at*
>   *midnight,*
> *The world would be a better place.*

Her cheeks were still burning.

A young Nepalese, Bishupal Limbu, reigned over the Threepenny Opera. One customer would ask for the *Concerto for Violin* by Alan Berg, another for *Legend* by Bob Marley, and some woman the *Requiem* by Gilles. Despite the surrounding jumble, Bishupal would head straight for the recording. His musical knowledge was surprising. His literary knowledge too. During his rare spare moments, he always had his nose stuck in a book. He often came to Faure Street to borrow a book from Stephen. In three months he had read the complete works of Charles Dickens and Thomas Hardy and had begun to tackle William Faulkner. Taciturn and looking ill at ease, a fringe of jet-black hair caressing his slit eyes, he dreamed of becoming a poet. His poetry had been published in a journal in Johannesburg. Stephen had convinced him to take a correspondence course to prepare for English composition exams.

"To give him some basics. He massacres the English language and thinks his grammatical mistakes are poetic license."

Mrs. Hillster considered him a genius, pinning his poems to the shop walls, and treated him like a son and an exotic curio. But it so happened that one lunchtime while he was out, two masked boys stormed in and, brandishing a sawed-off shotgun, emptied the contents of a safe stuffed with rand, pounds sterling, and dollars that Mrs. Hillster kept in the shop out of her distrust of banks. For good measure, they had given the poor woman a thorough beating when she tried to intervene. They hadn't broken into the safe, so Bishupal, who knew both its contents and combination, was assumed to be an obvious accomplice. The police had therefore arrested him. But they were unable to prove a thing. Witnesses had seen him at the time these sad events had come to pass with his nose in *As I Lay Dying*, sitting at a table in the Pizzeria Napoletana. On her hospital bed, despite a jaw out of joint, broken ribs, and contusions, Mrs. Hillster swore he was innocent. According to her, Bishupal wouldn't hurt a fly. This incident had occurred a few days after Stephen's death, at a time when Rosélie had only her own misfortunes on her mind. To make a donation, even belatedly, of over two hundred CDs would be an excellent way of begging forgiveness.

She sat down behind the desk and stared at the murky eye of the computer. There was something troubling to the thought that now that Stephen was gone, the computer stored everything that had preoccupied him. All she need do to penetrate this artificial brain was press a few keys. Yet this would be a sacrilege. Without hesitating, she decided to destroy its memory and then donate the computer, a shell drained of its substance, to the Steve Biko High School. During the funeral a delegation of students and teachers had carried a wreath. Chris Nkosi, who had played Puck in *A Midsummer Night's Dream,* had read in tears one of his own poems. Without thinking, she tried to open the drawers. Locked except for two of them. The first was filled with those odds and ends you accumulate throughout life: business cards for people you will never do business with, blue erasable Waterman cartridges, matchbooks advertising Café Milano, Café Lalo, Café Mozart, felt-tip pens of every color, staplers without staples, and a small Chinese compass pointing feverishly toward the northeast. There was nothing worth keeping. Rosélie pulled the wastepaper basket toward her, and it was then she saw it, the cell phone they thought was lost. Nestling against one of the desk's legs, half hidden under the jute rug. A tiny, very expensive object, just a few inches wide, folded into its black leather case. She flipped it open and pressed a key and it lit up, evil-looking and green, like an emerald in the palm of her hand.

It's Inspector Lewis Sithole who will be happy.

In the other drawer there was a pile of photo albums. She opened one haphazardly. On the first page four people were smiling at the camera. Or rather three people were smiling at the camera, she was standing to one side, aloof and sulky. She turned the photo over: Lone Pine—1994—With Lisa and Richard—<u>Memorable Stay</u>. Stephen had underlined the last two words. The memorable stay fluttered, at first vague and uncertain in her memory, then settled motionless. She remembered. They had taken advantage of one of Stephen's leaves to visit Death Valley in California. After driving for several hours, they had arrived at a small town whose name foreshadowed what it had to offer. Lone Pine. A few houses huddled along a main street. A fast-food restaurant where individuals with faces of America's most wanted were swallowing platefuls of carbohydrates. A gas station where enormous trucks had come to a halt. Around a trailer park garlands of jeans, checkered shirts, and children's sleepsuits were fluttering in the breeze. All the moroseness of Middle America was gathered there. Plus something else, something frightening. It was as if the bestiality of the inhabitants hidden behind these commonplace facades, like an ogre in his lair, would pounce at the slightest pretext. The guidebook had graced the Beaver Inn with three stars even so. Going down to join Stephen at the bar, she saw him in deep conversation with a couple. Around forty. The woman: blond, smartly dressed, and pretty. The man: slightly overfed, a mop of hair, and a pleasant face. As she walked over, they watched her behind their what-a-wonderful-world smiles, switched on for the occasion, with a mixture of aloofness and anxiety. What was this black woman doing walking straight toward them? She reached the table, and it was then that Stephen introduced her, drawing her close with a possessive hug.

"My wife, Rosélie."

Every time, he never failed! She complained he was playing the conjurer pulling a lugubrious and surprising object
out of his hat. In front of his colleagues, his acquaintances,
the neighborhood shopkeepers, the newspaper seller, the cigarette merchant, and the florist. She would force a muttered
greeting. Every time, the other person would strain their
ears, on high alert. In her mouth the French accent that conjured up pell-mell Gay Paree, Chanel suits, Christian Dior,
Must de Cartier, and the white lace of the French cancan
sounded like an insufferable parody.

You mean to say you're French?

Oh no! I'm from Guadeloupe!

Where's that?

My God, what a mix-up!

She suspected Stephen of reveling in the reactions his introduction produced. Remembering them in bed was his life
buoy against their sexual shipwreck. Clinging to these memories gave a kick to an exercise that in the long run could have
ended up as a routine and endowed it with a taste for the
taboo, even perversity or vice.

Lisa and Richard stood up like robots and awkwardly
held out their hands.

The unexpected thing about America is that you can live
there for years without meeting the natives. Nor even speaking their language. Rosélie had ended up learning English,
but not without difficulty. But since she didn't have an outside job, the only Americans she knew were Stephen's colleagues. When they came for dinner at Riverside Drive, their
conversation revolved around literature or politics, subjects
that were foreign to her.

"What *are* you interested in?" Stephen would ask mockingly after every one of those dinners. "Next time we'll do our best to please you."

What am I interested in? Me, me, nothing but me.

In fact, besides Linda, the only people she spoke to were the day porter, a Pakistani in a dark blue uniform; the night porter, a Bulgarian in a brown uniform; and the security patrolmen in their light blue uniforms with gilded facings, swaggering along the neighborhood streets, all of them Latinos.

Lisa and Richard went far beyond her wildest imagination. Richard was a lawyer. Lisa worked for a television station. They were parents of three sons. Both divorced, they each had three daughters from their previous marriages. They didn't spare one detail recounting their first marriages, the tribulations of their divorces, the trouble with their parents, their quarrels with their in-laws, the problems with their children, their rivalry with brothers and sisters, their marital difficulties, their sexual boredom, the failed orgies, the successful affairs, and their futile sessions with their shrink, who, nevertheless, had cured Hillary Clinton of her depression. This outpouring was especially painful, as it was directed solely at Stephen. Products of centuries of racism and exclusion of blacks, Lisa and Richard were incapable of looking at Rosélie in the eye and treating her like any other human being. At the most they managed to grimace an inane smile, by half turning in her direction. In fact, Rosélie, used to invisibility, could have put up with it if she had been deaf as well. On day four, while Lisa and Richard were giving endless descriptions of their trip to Tuscany and their futile efforts to get the dark, curly-haired Italian gardener into bed with them, she couldn't take it any longer and fled. A taxi drove her to the Los Angeles Sheraton, from where she called Stephen. He soon joined her. She was waiting for him with some very precise questions. What enjoyment did he get from such company? Did he care about the ordeal it meant for her? Instead of giving an answer, he made love to her with unusual violence, gagging her with kisses.

"You don't know how to have fun," he complained yet again.

Have fun? Was that having fun? They didn't share the same sense of humor.

Back in New York, Stephen invited Lisa and Richard to one of his dinners. But at the last minute they canceled with a lame excuse and were never seen again.

Rosélie also gathered enough strength to climb up to her studio, open the windows, and gaze at her paintings. Since Stephen had gone she hadn't touched her brushes. Since the officiant was no longer there for the naming ceremonies, she no longer gave birth.

Oddly enough, in Cape Town she had sold a fair number of paintings. All it took was for Mrs. Hillster, while on a visit to her studio in the company of Stephen, now the official guide, to enthuse over *Devils, She-Devils, and Zombies* and buy it for her shop; as a result, a number of customers had made the detour to Faure Street to be the first to own a painting by this genius, who was still totally unknown but destined in the more or less long term for the spotlight of celebrity, as Mrs.

Hillster declared, duly coached. Since South Africa was a cauldron where all the world's nationalities were cooking, the Germans, Norwegians, Swiss, Indians, and the Mexicans, who remarked learnedly on the similarities with their very own Frida Kahlo—the blood, the entrails, the physical suffering—left with their treasures under their arm, looking very pleased with themselves.

Dido thought along the same lines as Simone.

"You know Bebe Sephuma. Couldn't she give a helping hand? That's what you need!"

How could she explain that Bebe Sephuma was not interested in her? Not *glamorous* enough for a magazine cover! Too awkward and self-conscious! And then she wasn't English-speaking. People who speak English feel a deep contempt for the rest of the world. The time is long gone when French was considered the language of culture. For serious minds it now seems nothing more than frivolous gibberish.

Once again she was seized with doubt. What were the fruits of her labor worth? As long as she was busy choosing, then mixing the colors, applying the paint with long or short brush strokes, savoring its vivifying smell, her eyes were fixed on this white square of canvas that her imagination slowly peopled and transformed. She heard nothing except for the hum of the outside world that mellowed inside her. She was inhabited by a happiness, no doubt comparable with that of a woman whose fetus moves in the very depths of her flesh. However, once she had lost her waters and given birth, she detached herself from her creation. Worse, she took a sudden dislike to it, like a cruel mother who dreams of throwing her newborn in a garbage dump, wrapped in a plastic bag. So why did she go on painting? Because she couldn't do otherwise.

But God in his mysterious ways had perhaps put an end to her agony. Now that Stephen was gone, she was no longer anything at all. A masseuse, a medium, a curandera, call it what you like.

"Rosélie Thibaudin, healer of incurable cases."

At the same time, illogically, the loss of her gift was destroying her.

Sometimes I feel like a motherless child.

EIGHT

C hange your man and you change your rhythm of life. With Stephen, Rosélie always played the same musical score. *Allegro ma non troppo.* She spent her days practically alone. As early as seven in the morning he would leave for the university with a colleague and neighbor, a Virginia Woolf specialist, author of a remarkable study on *Mrs. Dalloway.* In his absence she painted without taking note of the passing hours. Around one o'clock Dido called her from the bottom of the stairs, and Rosélie interrupted her work to watch her eat a usually copious lunch. Dido had what they call a hearty appetite. She spiced her meals with comments on the harshness of women's condition, the chaos of the world in general, and South Africa in particular, which didn't prevent her from eating up greedily and scraping her plate. Rosélie always felt slightly envious in front of this ravenous mouth and its masticating teeth. After a few cups of coffee on the patio, she went back up to her studio while Dido returned to the kitchen, where she noisily loaded the antediluvian dishwasher, bought secondhand at a university sale. Then she went and ironed in the living room while listening to Hugh Masekela. The music whirled, wafted up two flights of stairs, and joined Rosélie under the roof. Listening to it, in spite of herself, she ended up knowing every tune like she used to know her father's Afro-Cuban melodies, Rose's love songs, and Salama Salama's reggae music, and she caught herself humming them.

The end of the afternoon brightened up when Stephen came home in another colleague's car, this time a Chaucer specialist. Then tea at the Mount Nelson followed by dinner in a restaurant along the seafront. Always the same one, not because of the food—the fries were greasy and the chicken tasteless, rubbery hormone-fed meat—but because Ted, the owner, an Englishman, was living with Laurence, a black woman. Although Rosélie and Laurence sat coldly staring at each other, having absolutely nothing in common—Laurence working in a lingerie shop, preoccupied with thongs and frilly lace underwear, Rosélie preoccupied with her painting—Ted and Stephen, who had defied their society's taboo, found themselves drawn closer together like two war veterans back from the front line. As usual Stephen would chatter away. But with Ted he didn't talk about literature or politics. He would comment on the behavior of the royal family. According to him, Princess Diana had been a genuine antipersonnel mine that one of these days Buckingham Palace would step on. Besides, he declared, royalty was destined to be abolished. The prospect saddened Ted. He cherished the Queen and the Queen Mother, hats and handbags included. Neither Laurence nor Rosélie had an opinion on the question. Moreover, neither Stephen nor Ted asked them for one. In the distance Rosélie stared at the glow of Robben Island, which she had never visited and which was constantly calling her. A penal colony turned into a tourist attraction! Its lights winked in the distance, a reminder of a past that stubbornly refused to be transformed.

What do you do with the past? What a cumbersome

corpse! Should we embalm it, idealize it, and let it take over our destiny? Or should we hurriedly bury it as a disgrace and forget it altogether? Should we metamorphose it?

Rosélie seldom accompanied Stephen to the department's receptions. Cheese and cheap white wine in plastic cups. Very seldom to his colleagues' parties. *Braais* and better-quality white wine. Never to his rounds of the waterfront jazz clubs. Jack Daniel's and salted peanuts. She locked herself in her studio whenever he had guests. In short, her nocturnal activities boiled down to very little: evenings at the French Cultural Center and the DNA programs that had been severely trimmed since Simone left.

In fact, the DNA was dying.

They had hurriedly elected another Martinican woman as president who taught music theory at the French lycée. Whereas her students created mayhem in her classroom when they were not skipping class en masse, her husband was a sports idol whose picture, like Che Guevara's in the sixties, hung in every student's room. He coached a soccer team that had won the African Juniors Cup. They had hoped therefore that her appointment would arouse a competitive spirit in her and she would take the DNA to new heights. Nothing of the sort happened. She lacked savoir faire. In eight months she had only invited a relatively unknown Caribbean scholar, who happened to be in Cape Town for a conference on aesthetics.

Instead of a routine, Faustin established the unexpected and spelled disorder.

She waited for him in vain for days on end. He would turn up unexpectedly, stay for a few minutes, leave for some mysterious rendezvous, come back, leave again, then decide to stay. Each time, the Mercedes zoomed up peaceful Faure Street. When he spent the night, his bodyguards, playing *belote* in the garden and downing beer after beer, disturbed everyone's peace. Except for Deogratias, whom nothing could disturb. Rosélie trembled at the thought of the neighbors' hostility. This would be their excuse for evicting her from the neighborhood. Disturbing the peace at night.

As soon as he came in the front door, it was a hubbub of telephone conversations, CNN and BBC News, and commentaries from Radio France Internationale. Since he still couldn't sleep—on that point Rosélie had to admit she had been ineffective—he dragged her to nightclubs, not to dance (they were past the age, although in Guadeloupe arthritis doesn't stop the old and achy from shaking a leg) but to listen to music. He had a particular liking for the Dogon, owned by some Malians, because the singer, a Senegalese, could be mistaken for the voice of the Gabonese Pierre Akendengué. He reduced Cape Town to its French-speaking population, for in a certain way he despised South Africa. Not for the political reasons she had heard voiced over and over again by Stephen. Simply because it did not form part of the prestigious circle of countries that spoke French. For him, to speak French forty years after African independence remained an honor and a privilege.

Faustin provided no information about himself, as if introspection were banned. What sort of child, teenager, and student had he been? What did he think of the Eastern bloc, where he had studied for many years? Of the United States, where he had met his wife? This last point intrigued Rosélie. Retrospective jealousy? Not only that. She graced this stranger with the characteristics of the African-American women she had met, shivering as she remembered them, and realizing that they more than anyone had convinced her of her shortcomings by subtly setting her against a standard she could never achieve: that of matron, *poto-mitan*, of the civilizations of the diaspora. What had *she* accomplished in which the Race could glorify?

In short, Faustin's conversation was always superficial and insignificant. He described his grandparents' *rugo*, the peace that once enveloped the country of a thousand hills, and the village traditions of long ago. He showed no interest in her island, which he would have been unable to find on a map. He took no interest in her painting. The only time he had walked through her studio, he had emerged stunned:

"My God, it's Bluebeard's closet!"

He no longer alluded to Stephen as if it were better to forget this episode in Rosélie's life. Adult discussions on topics such as regional development, the future of the continent, and globalization he would reserve for Deogratias. After all, both men, originating from the same country, shared the same language, Rosélie told herself when these endless conversations drove her to distraction. He holed himself up to talk business with Raymond, his inseparable friend from Cameroon who had never lost the ways of ten years mistakenly spent in a seminary before giving in to his inordinate taste for women. On a courtesy visit to her studio he had been swept off his feet unexpectedly and surprisingly, like every infatuation, by a painting called *Tabaski*. A sheep with its throat slit, its scarlet blood draining into a blue enamel basin. He had questioned her. Did she think, like he did, that such sacrilegious practices should be banned, and that only the sacrifice by the Son of God counted? Did she hate Islam, like he did, the intolerance of the Muslims, their violence, and the dangers to the world they represented? Rosélie sharply defended her point of view. On the contrary, this religion that accompanied each of its rituals with a massacre of the innocents fascinated her. In N'Dossou the Muslims were mainly immigrants, Senegalese, Burkinabés, recognizable by their boubous and slippers they dragged through the filthy streets. Theirs was the Mossada district, huddled around a mosque. People in the neighborhood complained of the muezzin's call to prayer. But Rosélie adored this high-pitched, lugubrious voice whose call to prayer was like a summons to death.

From then on, weekends were spent at Constantia, where Raymond's villa stood not far from the home of Bebe Sephuma, who could be seen driving past at the wheel of her Porsche.

In actual fact, Raymond was the soul behind the association with Faustin. He was the one who had managed to sell as far as Pietersburg a type of garbage can called an Afri-bin. The huge orange ones took pride of place at crossroads. Smaller versions, green or blue, clung proudly to the backs of the garbage trucks. Raymond could talk forever on the subject.

"The major problem of Africa is that there is no public opinion. So a handful of crooks can systematically bleed the continent dry. So why isn't there a public opinion? Because people have no strength left. And why haven't they any strength left? Because of the garbage. They throw it anywhere. Walk into a popular district of Yaoundé or Madagascar, for instance, and you're swimming in garbage: on the

sidewalks, at street corners, in the gutters, everywhere! The
sun turns it into a terrible stench, but above all a powder keg
of germs that the stray dogs tote from one end of the city to
the other. So babies get sick; children's sores become in-
fected and fester. All sorts of epidemics spread among the
grown-ups. Since the sick, the helpless, and the feeble are too
poor to get treatment, the dictators take advantage of them
and lay down the law. With Afri-bin, that's history! Practical,
cheap, easy to handle, and airtight! Garbage smack into the
bin! People become healthy and, consequently, critical."

When he had finished boasting of his merchandise, he
clapped his hands and a cloud of domestics in dubious white
uniforms emerged from the kitchen. They poured pink
champagne into blue-stemmed flutes and served *koki* on silver gilt plates under the doleful eye of Thérèse. Thérèse was
as apathetic as her husband was bursting with energy. Every
day she leafed through *Divas* and *Amina.* Or else she watched
Egyptian and Indian films on her state-of-the-art DVD player.
She missed her children. Except for Berline, her latest little
girl, constantly clinging to her breast despite her twenty-four
months and her two rows of incisors, the five others lived in
Montreal with her sister—for their education, she explained.

Thérèse felt nothing but antipathy for South Africa.
Everything antagonized her: the crudeness of the Afrikaners,
the arrogance of the coloureds, and the xenophobia of the
blacks. Once she had gotten that out of her system, she con-
sented to forget about Rishi Kapoor and Neetu Singh in
Zahreela Insaan and join Rosélie to watch the adventures of
Jackie Chan in *Shanghai Kid.* Then she drank gallons of Rooi-
bos tea before returning to her two favorite subjects of con-

versation: her love for her children and her hatred of South Africa. When Rosélie withdrew with Faustin, Thérèse and Raymond gave them a smile of complicity, like lenient parents toward a couple of youngsters they had taken in.

"Good night!"

In this hurriedly furnished and badly maintained villa, Faustin had been given a studio apartment that opened out onto the rusty waters of a swimming pool. The domestics, busy doing nothing, seldom paid it a visit. Since the windows were never opened, the air was musty. Faustin changed the sheets himself. Making frenzied love in such a decor, on this uncomfortable, lumpy mattress, Rosélie regained the verve of those happy, younger days with Salama Salama when they used to hide from the concierge and the rent they owed. She got the impression that having come full circle, she had been brought back to square one.

At times she was crushed by a feeling of guilt. It had only been three months, and she was already cheating on Stephen, whose nails were still growing under the earth. If he could see her, how he would suffer! Fortunately, the dead see nothing. The worms are at work under their eyelids draining the eyeballs to the bone. Other times, her thoughts took a completely different direction. She asked herself on what unconfessed frustrations, on what bundles of dirty washing shoved day after day into a corner of her inner self she was taking revenge. In fact, had Stephen been her benefactor? Sharing his existence, living in his shadow had perhaps caused her enormous damage and prevented her from becoming an adult.

One year, Stephen, who never gave up, got it into his head to organize an exhibit at the Espace des Amériques, a gallery flanking the university. During a dinner party, he had placed her beside Fina Alvarez, the Venezuelan woman who ran the gallery. They had taken to each other, even more so because they had both been regular customers at a Brazilian restaurant in Paris, savoring the same *feijoada* during the same years.

"Can you believe how long it took for us to meet?" lamented Fina. "Perhaps we were sitting next to each other. Perhaps you got up to go to the rest room and said 'excuse me' to me."

Fina boasted of a black grandmother, a humble illiterate peasant, who had been a past master in the art of storytelling. The songs and tales she had heard when a child had been at the root of her artistic talent. Trembling at her judgment, Rosélie had invited her to her studio.

"You are a genius," she had assured her, smoking cigarette after cigarette as she strode past the canvases. "Believe me, it's not just talent you've got. It's *genius*. Sheer *genius!*"

In spite of these hyperboles, Rosélie had remained uncompromising. No exhibit at the gallery to comply with Stephen's schemes. Fina openly approved.

"You're right. One must succeed on one's own terms."

She knew what she was talking about. She had divorced two men who, she claimed, had upset her temperament by forcing her to cook for them twice a day. Apparently, the separation hadn't helped her, since after publishing three collections of poems and a novel by Actes Sud, she had given up and made do with a teaching job, which is the opposite of creativity. Fina was also a great walker. Every day, once she had finished striding through Riverside Park with Rosélie, she would accompany her back to 125th Street. But black grandmothers, although godmothers of creativity, are not a cure for bourgeois faintheartedness. Fina absolutely refused to venture any farther and left Rosélie to explore the forbidden territory of Harlem. Rosélie knew she would never be anything but an outsider. The articles in *Ebony* and *Essence* were not for her. Her name would never flash in neon lights in the pantheon of immortals. She would never be invited to those galas of self-celebration where the black creators take their revenge on centuries of Caucasian blindness. When nostalgia got the upper hand, she would go and eat grits and tripe at Sylvia's, breathing in the intimacy from which she would forever be excluded. Back at the Riverside apartment, she would lock herself in her studio, the only place that was actually hers in a place filled with Stephen's books, Stephen's CDs, Stephen's workout equipment, and his entire intrusive personality.

One day Fina introduced her to Jay Goldman. This former lover, still her good friend, as is the norm among intelligent people, dashed around Africa, squandering the fortune earned by the sweat of former generations on unusual artifacts. He was particularly proud of a collection of Luo water vessels in leather, calabash, wood, and tin; of Yoruba spinning tops, one of which was the size of a thimble; and of Pygmy bows and arrows, some of them still coated with their formidable poison. In a more serious vein, his collection included a number of Gauguins, Braques, and Picassos. Not only did Jay Goldman not spare his superlatives, but without bargaining he bought a series of paintings from Rosélie he named *Nocturnal Dogs*. He offered to organize a private exhibition for her in his loft, just steps away from the apartment of John-John Kennedy, who had not yet made his fatal dive into the icy waters of the Atlantic Ocean. He would take care of the publicity, the invitations, and the reception. He also mentioned he was the friend of a well-known producer of an arts program on TV.

Rosélie, who was in seventh heaven, couldn't remember how she came back to earth with a bump. How she had found out that although Jay had perhaps shared Fina's bed in the past, and neither of them could remember much about it, he was in fact an old friend of Stephen's. He had lived at his place in N'Dossou. Together with Fumio, the two men had started out on a search for Ashanti gold weights and driven in a jeep to Kumasi in Ghana. The tires had burst three times and they had slept two nights out in the open under the canopy of centuries-old silk cotton trees. At the end of their journey they were admitted to an audience with the Asantehene in his palace, and this visit had been worth all their tribulations.

In short, everything boiled down to a friendly plot behind her back. It dealt a serious blow to her friendship with Fina, and for the first time she thought of leaving Stephen. Lycées and colleges were mushrooming in Guadeloupe. Then there was France. She was bound to find some school where she could teach art. For weeks, Fina sent her delirious messages, as if they had had a homosexual affair.

Falvarez@hotmail.com
to
rthibaudin@aol.com
I've never stopped loving you. I didn't betray you.
Fina

As for Stephen, he poked fun at her hostile reaction.

"Why are you blaming us? Because we wanted to help you? We could have been open about it. It could have been done lightheartedly and enjoyably, but you are so proud you forced us to lie."

Proud?

Before slamming the door and running down the stairs, for he never took the elevator, exercise oblige, he concluded:

"You know, you'll never make it on your own!"

How right he was! She had stubbornly persisted. One year later, she had succeeded in organizing an exhibition in a seedy-looking gallery in Soho. A disaster! After three days, the owners, two first-rate crooks, cleared out. Notified by Stephen, who bore no ill feeling and was always ready to intervene in the event of a catastrophe, the police recovered three of her paintings. The others had vanished! Oh yes, she had sold one picture to a Spanish museum for their collection of primitive art of the Americas! Another to the museum of womankind in Coyoacán. The M2A2, nothing alarming, just the acronym for the Martinican Museum for the Arts of the Americas, sent her an urgent request for a contribution. In short, at the age of fifty, she found herself to be an illustrious unknown. Her canvases were gathering dust by the dozens in the attic. She had been washed up on a foreign shore and she had no idea whether she loved it or hated it.

NINE

Fiela, all this time I have neglected you in my thoughts. What was I thinking of? Love, pleasure, like a sixteen-year-old who has gone to bed for the first time. For me, perhaps it's the last. Soon it will be the day of your trial. Do you have a lawyer? Is he gifted? Good or bad, how can he manage to defend you if you don't tell him a thing? If you keep everything locked up inside?

One bright, peaceful morning when the sun was gamboling across the light wooden floor, Faustin suddenly announced he was leaving for the airport. She wouldn't see him for several days. He had to be in Johannesburg for a meeting of paramount importance concerning his nomination, he explained in a mysterious voice. Ah, the famous nomination. Nominated to what? Nominated by whom? Nominated for what? Rosélie knew nothing about it. Yet, hearing him constantly mention it, she had begun to wish it for Faustin, like you wish for rain on cracked, parched earth, crying out from drought.

Johannesburg was somewhat mythical, the forbidden city. Unlike Cape Town, clinging to its whiteness, it now belonged to the blacks. Businessmen, reputable and disreputable, crooks, small and big time, artists, real and alleged, and creators of all sorts streamed into the city. In came the jobless tired of being out of a job in the former bantustans, the miners tired of scraping the belly of the earth, and the farm workers tired of working themselves to the bone on the white man's farms. A hybrid and dangerous population had come into being. In Johannesburg life was no blue chip. Anything went.

Stephen went there every May to attend the annual conference of the James Joyce Association.

Oh yes, they discussed *Ulysses* and *Finnegans Wake* in Jo'burg!

Once the workshops were over, the international specialists barricaded themselves in their three-star hotels. One time Stephen had strayed from the beaten path and had only managed to escape with his life from four strapping muggers by handing over his wallet, his gold signet ring, a present from his father at the age of seventeen, his chain bracelet, and his watch, which, although purchased duty-free at Frankfurt Airport, had cost him a fortune. Despite these misadventures, Rosélie was convinced Stephen was only too glad to spend a few days alone. What did he do over there?

To make up for this unexpected departure, Faustin kissed her tenderly, claiming:

"I won't be away for more than a week."

Such an assurance didn't mean a thing. Unlike Stephen, whose every movement was programmed in advance, you could never predict Faustin's next move.

Life then resumed its former rhythm. Dido, who, in her possessiveness, had not taken kindly to being deprived of her morning conversations, set off again for the bedroom with her tray, her heady cups of coffee, and her newspapers. She opened the shutters triumphantly, then began reading the *Cape Tribune* and other dailies.

Fiela's trial had started. She still had not opened her mouth. Two young white defense lawyers, officially appointed

to the case, did not look like much, but were bravely struggling to do their best. They called to the stand a number of
witnesses who testified to the good works of their client. They
gave evidence, for example, that she cured hopeless cases
with the remedies she dispensed free of charge.

Curandera like me. When did you discover this gift of
healing? Did you put it to better use than me, safeguarding
your loved ones from misfortune?

One photo showed her on the bench of the accused. Sitting straight as an *i*. Her face impenetrable. Not in the least
aggressive. Her incomparable eyes sparkled. Over the rest of
her face there sat a mask of indifference, as if all this agita-
tion was none of her business. For the first time there was a
photo of her stepson, the accuser. A twenty-two-year-old unemployed with a mop of hair whom she had raised and
treated like her own son, all the witnesses agreed. What had
happened for him to turn against her in such a way? He
could only speak of her with words of hatred and bitterness.

Dido folded the paper and went on chattering. Willem,
come to bury his father, wanted to take his mother back to
Australia. He had made his money selling hardware in Sydney. Sofie refused to follow him: she couldn't abandon Jan
lying under the oaks at Lievland. So Rosélie was not the only
one to feel herself tied to a land because of a dead man.
What a grip the deceased have!

That week Rosélie paid more attention to her patients.

Like you, Fiela, I have neglected them. I ought to be
ashamed of myself. What can I expect of this man? I won't
get anything more than I've been getting. A little pleasure,
let's say even a lot. And that's all.

One morning, dressed in her magician's finery, carefully starched and ironed, she received Emma and Judith, her favorite patient, although she had put her off twice.

Patient No. 12
Judith Bartok
Age: 8 years old
Schoolgirl

Judith, daughter of Emma and cousin to Doris, was her mother's pride and joy, although life had been hard on both of them. Judith was all Emma had left from a man who, having sponged off her for ten years, had cleared off to Maputo. There he had found a job that paid well and a woman to spoil him. One afternoon when Judith was coming home from kindergarten, although she had been told never, ever talk to strangers, she had accepted a piece of chewing gum from a man. He had immediately piled her into a car with his accomplices and dragged her to a plot of waste ground where she was then raped half a dozen times. The police had never even traced, much less identified the gang. As a result, she had been struck mute. If you touched her, she would curl up like a sensitive plant and cry. Her calvary lasted a year. All on her own, Rosélie had returned her speech to her and brought back, at times, a semblance of a smile to her lips. Do we need compassion and love in order to heal? Are miracles made of that? When she ran her hands over the little abused body, endeavoring to establish an equilibrium, Rosélie relived the scene where the girl's childhood had been lost, and her eyes brimmed with tears.

How can we escape the circle of our hell?

We are broken and crushed and our hair turns white before its time.

Fiela, you had no friends. Like me. You made do with the herbs from your garden. You met Adriaan one Sunday at church. He was very different from you. Always joking. He made you laugh. He looked at your body. For the first time, a man took an interest in you. I know what it's like. You were in seventh heaven. Nevertheless, two years after your wedding he gave a belly to the neighbor's daughter. Martha, a girl of fifteen. You suffered the martyr, but you didn't show it. You took the baby in, baby Julian. You raised him. You made a man out of him to the best of your ability.

While Emma sat down in the kitchen with Dido for a cup of coffee, both berating the wickedness of life and its constant surprises, the session with Judith began. The allotted time never varied. While measuring by touch the flow of her energy and redistributing it where it was needed, Rosélie questioned her. About school and its daily ennui. About catechism and its weekly ennui. About piano lessons and the torture of scales. About dancing and the torture of points. At least she loved karate, which, according to Emma, taught you how to defend yourself. Halfway through she would regularly ask for a story in her acid-drop voice. Rosélie had already embroidered endlessly on the adventures of Rabbit and Zamba and Ti-Jan L'Orizon, which Rose used to recount to her in her childhood on those evenings when Elie, having deigned to dine at home, was getting ready to sleep in her bed and probably make love to her. At those moments, gone were the tears and instead, her voice soared up from the first floor to the attic, light and joyful:

You won't admit you love me and so
How am I ever to know.
You only tell me
Perhaps, perhaps, perhaps.

Rosélie would be lulled to sleep by this little night music.

She had prepared herself for any further requests by Judith by buying a simplified version of *The Arabian Nights*, which she practiced reciting: " 'Scheherazade stopped when the day began to brighten Shahryar's apartment. The following night she went on with her story . . .' " But that day Judith had something else in mind. She was carrying a satchel under her arm, which she opened mysteriously and from which she pulled out a bundle of large sheets of paper. Rosélie took them one by one, marveling at these bright drawings done with that freedom of form and color associated with the blitheness of childhood. What a miracle! What human ingenuity! These drawings signified that her imagination had been purified. She was cured. She had been able to survive her past with no trace of an indelible scar. While Rosélie was searching for words of encouragement and admiration, Judith drew her head close to hers, put her mouth against her ear, and whispered:

"Don't tell anyone. Especially Mummy. It's a secret. When I grow up I want to be a painter. Like you."

Life's like that. Sometimes it presents you with an innocent, spontaneous picture like those wildflowers growing on the side of the highway at the spot of a fatal accident. Rescuers take hours to cut the victims free from the wreckage and then lay the corpses among the buttercups, the poppies, and the cornflowers.

TEN

Like the distribution of toys with Simone a few years earlier, the distribution of Stephen's souvenirs were not what Rosélie expected. Her disillusionments began with her visit to Mrs. Hillster. In the space of a few months, Mrs. Hillster had aged considerably. A gash had left a scar on her forehead that disappeared amid her snow-white hair. She limped and leaned awkwardly on a cane. Above all, she bore the expression of those who have experienced injustice and demand reparation from society, society in general. Rosélie was treated to yet another telling of the day that had marked the end of Mrs. Hillster's peace of mind, dwelling at length on the misfortunes of her beloved Bishupal.

"Those police brutes treated him as if he were guilty. They beat him, they almost killed him."

Taking advantage of a moment when Mrs. Hillster stopped to catch her breath, Rosélie placed her offer. Would she accept the collection of Stephen's CDs? Mrs. Hillster seemed contrite.

"You haven't noticed, then?" she said, indicating a "For Sale" sign in the window.

"I'm selling everything. My house in Rondebosch, my shop. I've already had several offers, but nothing I like. I want to leave. I want to leave Cape Town. I'm too old for all this violence, I'm scared, I can't take it anymore. If I accepted your present, you would be giving it to someone else."

Rosélie remained speechless. Mrs. Hillster had been saying all along that South Africa had replaced England in her heart. She had arrived a blond twenty-year-old bride and followed her husband, Simon, from posting to posting. She waxed lyrical about her favorite region, KwaZulu-Natal, its sweltering natural parks, its lacy coastline, and the jewels of little towns strung along the shore. Politically speaking, there had been no shortage of difficulties given Simon's liberal views. He was on first-name terms with the ANC leaders, gave them shelter and money. They had been living in Johannesburg at the time of the Soweto and Sharpeville uprisings, and in Cape Town when it was the turn of the Crossroads squatters. Each time, the government accused Simon of colluding with the rioters and threatened to send him back to England. Rosélie was stupefied. Witness to the darkest hours of the country's history and to the most appalling events of injustice and inhumanity, Mrs. Hillster, now that two petty crooks had mugged her, was clearing off! How self-centered!

As if she could read Rosélie's thoughts, Mrs. Hillster explained:

"You see, I was not prepared for the victims to take their perpetrators' lessons to heart and that the blacks would learn to strike, kill, and rape so quickly."

Something they have always done. But you didn't want to admit it. You always thought them to be innocent, smiling angels, ready to proffer the other cheek. For better or for worse, they are showing you they are men, quite simply men. Neither devils nor angels.

"You're going back to England, then?" Rosélie merely asked.

Mrs. Hillster made a face.

"No, of course not! I'm going to live with Cecilia."

Good heavens! Cecilia, her only daughter, lived in Bermuda. Every time she came back from visiting her, Mrs. Hillster would rant about this Disneyfied England, as artificial as a dolls' kingdom with its little, white-roofed houses fit for Snow White's dwarves. One Christmas, Rosélie and Stephen had taken refuge there to escape the snow in New York, and she recalled her malaise. The island of Bermuda had deliberately transformed itself into a Garden of Eden for wealthy tourists. But at what a price! The restaurants dished up that tasteless cuisine called continental, capable of adapting to any palate. What continent? Atlantis? They had attended a cultural week, visibly designed for the clientele of American cruise ships. The highlight had been a gala evening when a local singer, who was black in skin only, sang a medley of Sinatra songs, vigorously applauded by the spectators.

Encore for "The Lady Is a Tramp"!

It's as if you need shantytowns, ghettos, and racial inequality to produce a specific culture. And that was where Mrs. Hillster was going to retire to after fifty years in a smoldering land where the most bitter of combats had been waged?

At that moment, Rosélie met the gaze of Bishupal as he looked at her while perched on a stool, a book between his hands. She was about to smile at him when a mask of hostility veiled his face. He lowered his head and ostensibly plunged back into his book. Surprised, she asked Mrs. Hillster:

"And what about him, what will he do if you leave?"

Rosélie noticed for the first time that Bishupal, whom she had seen a dozen times without paying him any attention, was handsome. He couldn't be more than eighteen.

"He doesn't want to stay here either," Mrs. Hillster replied sadly. "He wants to go to England."

"England!" exclaimed Rosélie.

"He's just spent his vacation there and claims he made friends," Mrs. Hillster said, even more sorrowfully. "I keep telling him London is one of the most difficult places to live, but Stephen convinced him it's paradise, that there's plenty of work and housing."

Stephen, who loathed England! Who every summer swore he would never set foot there again!

So everyone was going off on their own. Life is a carousel that never stops turning. Only those sleeping under the earth stay put.

"And what about yourself?" Mrs. Hillster asked softly.

Rosélie gave the usual answer.

"You know full well I couldn't think of leaving him alone."

It might be objected that she had no scruples about leaving her mother and father. It's true, but they were different. They were not alone. The family mounted guard around their graves. Elie had survived Rose by very little, scarcely six months, as if, unbeknownst to him, she alone made his life worth living. At present, husband and wife, united in death as the saying goes, lay in the Thibaudin vault, two stories of expensive black-and-white marble. At the Feast of All Saints the monument was scrubbed, polished, and covered with candles like a birthday cake. But if she left Cape Town, there would be nobody to take care of Stephen. He would be abandoned. Stephen Stewart, aged fifty-four, born in Hythe, England, lying under a bare tombstone, facing the immensity of the ocean and the infinity of time.

Mrs. Hillster shrugged her shoulders.

"I can't understand you. The dead are always alone. Think about yourself. You're still young. You could make a new life for yourself."

Me, still young? I get the impression I'm over a thousand years old. I am a tree whose branches have been broken by hurricanes, whose leaves have been ripped off by great gales. I am naked, I am stripped bare.

Mrs. Hillster lowered her voice as if she were broaching a sordid subject.

"But that's not what I wanted to know. Have the police got any further with their inquiry?"

Rosélie shook her head.

"My God!" Mrs. Hillster sighed. "It's awful! Despite his failings, Stephen didn't deserve to die like he did."

No, of course not! No man deserves to die, cut down like a dog on a filthy sidewalk between two rows of garbage cans. But what failings are you talking about?

Mrs. Hillster shrugged her shoulders.

"Who among us can boast of being perfect? Don't take exception to what I'm about to say. Stephen was too domineering. He made people do what he wanted; he manipulated them. Especially you."

This was the first time she had dared criticize Stephen. She had always been all smiles, all billing and cooing and flirting despite her nearly seventy years.

Distraught, Rosélie walked out into the glare and din of Buitengragt.

The street disappeared between antique shops with massive Dutch facades and shopping malls of the flashier and more fake American style. Nausea was welling up inside her. What had Mrs. Hillster meant? It's a fact she never contradicted Stephen. But to speak of manipulation!

She darted into a taxi and had herself driven to the Steve Biko High School.

It was midmorning and the driver made no objections.

Khayelitsha was one of the most monstrous legacies of apartheid. It loomed up out of the sands of False Bay like a formidable bantustan erected at the gates of Cape Town: the coveted, inaccessible, and forbidden city. It had been designed to place the workers under house arrest as far away as possible as well as detain the undesirables looking for a job. The long-term plan was for the population of Langa, Nyanga, and Guguletu to be uprooted and for all the blacks to be herded into Khayelitsha and kept there by force. Rosélie noted that the area had been somewhat humanized since her last visit with Stephen some two years earlier. The new regime had built entire districts of modular houses, painted garish orange, green, and blue like blocks of Lego. A cultural center looking like a fairground stall stood at one of the corners of Albert Luthuli Square. All the bric-a-brac of South African craftwork was on display there: spears, wall hangings, and plates decorated with multicolored pearls. In spite of everything, the overall sadness grabbed you by the throat.

Remodeled after apartheid, the Steve Biko High School was not exactly welcoming. Not surprising the kids try to set fire to their schools with such architecture! A watchtower straight out of an American prison film stood in the center of a quadrangle of grayish buildings encircling a bare playground. It was as if the shrubs and flowers that thrived in the residential districts of Cape Town refused to grow in Khayelitsha. It was recess time. The older pupils cramped into combat-style fatigues were jostling with the younger ones dressed in just as unattractive bottle green uniforms.

The principal's name was Olu Ogundipe. Years earlier, on the eve of his arrest for his political opinions, he had had to flee his native country of Nigeria and escape to Jamaica, his wife's home island. Alas! Jamaica was no longer the land of the maroons. Even the Rastas strumming their guitars amid the smell of ganja smoke have long ceased caring about Ras Tafari and Marcus Garvey. Olu realized this soon enough. His Marxist positions aroused the anger of the authorities and he was sent packing. So South Africa seemed to him to be the best place to stand up to capitalism and racism. But although he was a well-known figure throughout Cape Town and the provinces, it wasn't because of his political essays or commendable causes; it was because his scarred and bearded face appeared on advertisements for a mobile phone company. At crossroads and along the highway he proclaimed convincingly:

MARYSE CONDÉ

"Always keep in touch with a Nokia T193."

Or else:

"Nokia T193
Use it for pleasure, for thrills, and for the Internet.
Use it to telephone as well."

His office was the very image of a museum of the black world, with its dozens of photos stuck to the walls. Rosélie patiently endured a homily on the African renaissance that perhaps was taking its time, but would eventually strike the white world with the violence of a thunderbolt, the favorite instrument of Shango, the Yoruba god. Olu Ogundipe ventured a comparison: the South Africans after apartheid were like the Haitians after their independence in 1804. They needed time to build a nation. Then they would be an example to the world.

Like the Haitians?

He gestured with contempt at the *Cape Tribune,* spread out on his desk, Fiela's photo on the front page.

"Just look at that! Why do they make such a fuss over that woman. She's mad. They should bring back the death penalty for cases like hers. What image does she give our country? Our newspapers remain in the hands of those who want to demoralize the reader and discredit the government. If I were Minister for Information I'd close down the lot of them."

Straightaway he conveyed his condolences, for he had known the deceased very well, that she knew. But between the lines of praise and pity there crept a subtle denunciation that the honorable Stephen Stewart had deserved his sad end. Wasn't he a European and the worst of species? The English species. Some are fond of saying that the English were the first to abolish the slave trade, then slavery, the first to decolonize Africa and the Caribbean. Quite the opposite. If you thought about it, British foreign policy was one of the most devious and destructive there is. In between his anathematizing, Rosélie managed to convey the purpose of her visit. She wanted to present Stephen's computer as a gift to the school. Olu seemed distressed, like Mrs. Hillster a few hours earlier. To fight nepotism and corruption the Minister for Education had just decreed that school principals were forbidden to accept gifts from individuals. These should be deposited with a state bank, the CND, which would then allocate them to schools and colleges according to their needs. He could not personally accept this precious souvenir from the honorable Dr. Stewart. Furthermore, if she deposited it with the CND, it would probably fall into the wrong hands. Rosélie, truly paranoid, got the impression he was hiding behind an administrative pretext and he wanted nothing more to do with Stephen.

There was nothing else to say. She accepted a cup of coffee that triggered a speech on the comparative merits of the plant. He only drank Blue Mountain coffee from Jamaica. Nothing like the adulterated arabica used in electric coffeemakers. Then Olu broached a subject that was dear to his heart: the decline of South African literature by black writers. Some attributed their silence to the end of apartheid, which had deprived them of subject matter. He was of another opinion. South African writers persisted in flouting their mother tongues, wrongly called national languages, since nations held them in contempt. So what is a mother tongue? A language that expresses added meaning, a language that expresses secret places of the heart, a language that expresses the inexpressible! If she only knew how many masterpieces were produced annually in Nigeria in the vernacular!

"Don't you have the same problem with French and Creole?" he asked. "Aren't the genuine masterpieces written in Creole?"

Rosélie, whose only knowledge of French Caribbean writing was *The Bridge of Beyond*, read one very rainy season, knew nothing about these issues. Olu went on to inquire about Aimé Césaire. He had had the pleasure of meeting him during his exile in the Caribbean. With a simplicity that did him credit, the great man had received him at city hall and shown him his island. What an unforgettable memory! The poet knew every Latin name for every tree, plant, flower, and blade of grass. Rosélie was about to take her leave when an idea crossed her mind. Surely the Ministry of Education didn't forbid donations to private individuals. Where was Chris Nkosi?

Olu seemed troubled. It so happened he knew Chris Nkosi very well. Ever since he was a small boy. When he was four his father had vanished without notice. An association Olu ran called "Let Them Come unto Me" had taken care of the family, the wife left behind without a cent and seven children. Chris was a good boy. He had passed his certificate the previous year and left school. As luck would have it, a Catholic foundation had immediately offered him a job in one of its schools. Rosélie was surprised that Chris Nkosi had not continued a career in the theater, since according to Stephen he was so gifted. Theater? It was as if she had uttered an obscenity. Olu shook his head furiously. Chris Nkosi was now an elementary school teacher. He taught English grammar and the history of Africa. He was married. If Rosélie intended to give him the computer in memory of Stephen, he would certainly refuse it. They had quarreled. Quarreled? That's news to me! Rosélie recalled the young man crying hot tears at the funeral and stammering out his poem. Surely the quarrel couldn't have been very serious. On the contrary, Olu assured her. Stephen had tried to put pressure on Chris to force him to become an actor. Faced with his rebuff, he had insulted him, calling him a coward who was betraying his vocation. Chris couldn't put up with it. Olu stared at her with sudden hostility.

"You know as well as I do that the honorable professor couldn't tolerate contention. Everyone had to do things his way. As a European, he wanted to do good in Africa, but he had the wrong idea of going about it. The theater! The theater! I won't go so far as France in 1789 saying: 'The Revolution doesn't give a damn about artists!' But do we really need theater, especially Western theater, at this moment in time?"

Rosélie was dumbfounded. She couldn't possibly believe Olu. Stephen would have wanted to regiment Chris's future to the point of quarreling with him? They were hiding something from her.

Once outside the school, she was amazed to find the sun still in its place, sitting stupidly in the middle of the sky, and the day was radiant. Two buses cluttered up Albert Luthuli

Square. A crowd of laughing, enthusiastic tourists was piling into the craft center. Inside her the mood was darker. She had the feeling she had suffered the rebuffs on behalf of Stephen. It was as if he were no longer acceptable. Nobody wanted anything more to do with him.

Faure Street: Inspector Lewis Sithole was waiting for her, leaning against the traveler's tree, poring over the *Cape Tribune* that Olu had censured. He lost no time with polite conversation and, folding the paper, got straight to the point.

"I was right in thinking your husband didn't just go out to buy cigarettes. Thanks to your cooperation, by giving us his mobile phone, we have proof that he received a call at zero hours seventeen minutes."

Seventeen minutes past midnight?

Stephen would never let himself be disturbed in the middle of the night. It must have been a mistake, a wrong number. Things like that happen!

Inspector Lewis Sithole went on as if her interruption were not worth stopping for.

"We had no trouble finding where the call came from. A public telephone booth. This confirms our suspicions that the caller was not taking any chances and did not want to call from home."

What story was this he was imagining? Yet another one who had missed his calling! He should have been writing detective stories. And where was this famous telephone booth?

"In Green Point."

"Green Point?" Rosélie repeated, stunned.

Neither she nor Stephen had friends in this suburb, a paradise for students and backpackers, which had nothing to offer but cheap hotels. It regularly made front-page news because of its high crime rate. Nothing very sophisticated, however: muggings, burglaries, and passersby beaten up for a few rand.

Lewis Sithole stared at her.

"You know no one who lives in this neighborhood?"

She shook her head. He didn't push the matter and said in a strange voice, both reassuring and threatening:

"Never mind. We'll find him, this mysterious caller."

Who would want to kill Stephen? Though certainly no saint in a stained-glass window, he had been a dispenser of good works. He wrote hundreds of letters of recommendation for his students. He lent considerable sums of money to his young colleagues. He would involve himself and his time personally. In New York he paid daily visits to Mount Sinai hospital, where a Jane Austen specialist was dying from cancer of the larynx. He who hated children was prepared to take in the twins of an assistant who was trying to finish her thesis on Mary Wollstonecraft by the end of the year. He gave free English lessons to Haitian, Puerto Rican, and Senegalese associations.

Inspector Lewis Sithole had no sooner left than Dido arrived with her inevitable tray of coffee.

"What's he on about again?" she grumbled.

Rosélie didn't have the courage to repeat his wild imaginings and merely recounted her day's misadventures, then looked her straight in the eyes.

"You didn't like Stephen very much, did you?"

Dido rolled her hazel eyes and stared at a point in the distance.

"Me, not like Stephen? Oh, come on!" she protested.

After a few moments, since Rosélie's silence demanded an answer, she reluctantly confessed.

"No, I didn't like him. He was an egoist and a despot. He prevented you from being yourself."

Myself?

But who am I? What beast, what flesh-eating fish? My teeth are pointed and my tongue is forked. Sometimes I can be seen swallowing in one gulp the insects attracted to my sweet smell. The bats are my sisters: half rat, half bird; ill at ease in the glare of daylight. We spend our time hanging upside down, seeking the dark that will take us back to the womb that bore us.

Elie and Rose never stopped thanking the Good Lord for their kind, sweet daughter, their only consolation in the shipwreck of their marriage. Without Rosélie they would have separated a long time ago. But in our family there must be no child of a divorce. A little girl needs a papa and a maman in order to grow up, even if they do hurl insults at each other day in and day out. The quarrels of Elie and Rose took a Homeric turn. She accused him, a mulatto as poor as a church mouse, of marrying her for the hundred acres of land Ebenezer, her father, had sown with fruit trees under the sun in Gourbeyre and for the houses he rented out just about everywhere on the island. Elie retorted that Ebenezer had stolen the property from some poor wretch. Maybe his own family was poor, but at least it was honest.

Rosélie never raised her voice. Never disobeyed, never rebelled. No preadolescent crisis, much less an adolescent one. The family cited her as an example to the cousins who got into bad ways. The school mistresses were less enthusiastic: "In class, she dreams. She sleeps standing up." The art teacher in particular complained: "You should see her free compositions. Hideous! The other day she drew a woman with legs wide open spurting a stream of blood. I shouted: 'Good Lord, what's that?' 'It's a rape,' she replied. 'Have you ever seen a rape?' I asked her angrily. 'Those sorts of things don't happen around here.' She replied: 'I'm raped every day.' And when I shouted in anger: 'Don't say such things! Who rapes you?' She answered quite calmly: 'My papa, my maman, everyone.' "

ELEVEN

Fiela, what have they got against him? He has always been by my side. Thoughtful. Considerate. Patient to my moods.

Often Stephen used to say:

"You are the most wonderful woman on earth. An extraordinary gift, too precious for me, like the ones my grandmother used to give me. My father and mother were so fraught with hate for each other they had no time for me. I grew up amid their indifference. So every Christmas my grandmother would decorate a tree in which she nestled little trumpets, little violas, violins, guitars, and bagpipes. She would switch on garlands of electric lights. On the branches she hung silver and gold balls that sparkled from the light. Then underneath she placed my present, wrapped in festive paper that I tore open when we got home from Midnight Mass. I can remember one year it was a white clown almost as tall as I was. When you pulled the strings it smiled and croaked, waving its arms: "Hi, how are you?" My grandmother died when I was ten. Shortly afterward my parents divorced. I followed my mother to Verberie and life never again gave me anything. Except you!"

Or else he would say:

"If I were to lose you, my life would revert to the desolate existence I led before I met you. I had nothing that was mine. I lived thanks to other men. Like a Tupinamba Indian

I devoured their liver, their spleen, and their heart. But these bitter feasts left me even more despondent. Sated, I realized my baseness. You gave me everything."

For their first Christmas together, he had wanted to take her on a journey. A real one. Because he realized that traveling for Rosélie meant only two things.

Either the drive from La Pointe to Basse-Terre. This was the time when she was a little girl and Rose still showed herself in public, when they would get up at four in the morning. The sky glowed pale over the hill of Massabielle as Elie, helped by Meynalda, loaded the Citroën with bottles of water, Tupperware containers of codfish fritters and curried chicken. Then the family would confront the perilous fifty-mile journey to attend a christening or a wedding.

Or else the journey by plane from La Pointe to Paris for her studies, for the Thibaudins considered Paris nothing more than a city where you were likely to find work. Neither Elie nor Rose was one of those fanatics who count up their stays in the *metropole* year after year and return home starry-eyed. In fact, Rose had only traveled once to the capital for her honeymoon. Her head had been ringing with the carnival songs of Cuba, Rio de Janeiro, and Salvador da Bahia. But how do you get to those places? Elie had no idea. One of his brothers had recommended a cheap hotel in Paris with furnished rooms and a kitchenette where you could do your cooking. The Hotel des Deux-Mondes stood on the place Denfert-Rochereau, a busy shopping district. Rose would walk round the statue of the Lion of Belfort, green as the mirage of grass in the middle of the desert sands, and continue on to the narrow rue Daguerre, overflowing with food stalls.

There she would rub shoulders with other housewives and bargain for tuna, scorpion fish—similar to the red snapper—red peppers, and violet-colored eggplant. Madly in love with his young bride, who weighed no more than 130 pounds and whose voice rivaled that of the kiskadee bird from Dominica, Elie had not been mean with his money throughout their stay. He had taken her to see films starring Tino Rossi, whom she adored and whose hit songs she sang:

> *Marinella, oh reste encore dans mes bras,*
> *Avec toi, je veux jusqu'au jour*
> *Chanter cette chanson d'amour.*

He showed her the Folies Bergère and the Moulin Rouge, but she was shocked by the dancers and thought they were little better than the ladies of easy virtue back home, showing off their legs and their breasts. Once, he was in the mood for a bit of culture and bought orchestra seats to a matinee performance at the Théâtre de l'Odéon of Corneille's *Le Cid*, which they used to recite at school.

Rose was bored in Paris. She returned home to Guadeloupe, determined never to travel again, and with the help of her illness, she kept her word.

Stephen chose Italy. He was astounded that the only museum Rosélie had visited as a child on Saturday afternoons under the supervision of her French teacher was the Lherminier Museum, a pretty colonial house with wrought-iron balustrades. All it housed were collections of faded postcards, lace and mother-of-pearl fans, and children's spinning tops. But it was the only museum in La Pointe. Rosélie got to know the museums in Paris much later when she was a student. Stephen couldn't get over it.

"When did you feel you had a vocation?"

Vocation? Rosélie was incapable of giving an answer. A child does not have a vocation. She wants to paint. Period. It's her caprice and her freedom to choose. She had entered into painting like a novice enters into religion. Without suspecting what lay in wait for her. Uncertainty. Fear. Solitude. Exhausting work. Lack of money and self-esteem. The search for recognition.

"You're a miracle," Stephen marveled. "You've reinvented painting."

Florence and Rome appalled Rosélie. She thought Art was a delectation enjoyed by the happy few. An elitist and outmoded notion. It is fodder for senior citizens, corporate employees, and underprivileged children. White-haired tourists and schoolchildren elbowed one another around the Uffizi and crowded onto the Ponte Vecchio. Paper litter, African priests, and Indonesian nuns fluttered around the square in front of St. Peter's.

The brightly colored grotesques daubed on the ceilings of the convents and libraries in Parma, and Venice, especially Venice, despite its hordes, reconciled her to Italy. The city of the Doges drifted on the waters of a lagoon the color of the Sargasso Sea. Ocean liners, reviving the journeys of long ago, were escorted lazily out to sea. Rosélie dragged Stephen along alleyways off the beaten path, into obscure churches and hidden monasteries. And that's how she came across Antonio Vivaldi. One evening, out of curiosity, they followed a small crowd into a patio cluttered with chairs and benches open to an indigo sky.

They were giving a private concert, a common sight in the city. The concertgoers all knew one another and kissed and hugged with that Latin effusiveness. They made room for the strangers, turning round to whisper and stare. Yet this open display of curiosity was as vivifying as a hot bath. One man came up to them. Was the signorina from Ethiopia? Ignoring her negative answer, he began talking about Ethiopia. Or rather about himself in Ethiopia, since people only talk about themselves. For years he had worked with a team from Doctors Without Borders. He missed those isolated villages shivering in the icy mornings and the bitter breeze where he had treated the living as emaciated as the dead. Since his return to Italy, life had lost its meaning.

"And what about Art? And Culture?" Stephen asked in surprise. "You must have missed them in Ethiopia, you who are so blessed in this country."

Art? Culture? He shrugged his shoulders.

Obviously he shared the view of a contemporary writer who had twice failed to win the Goncourt Book Prize: "Art and culture are necessary compensations for the misfortune of our lives."

There was silence as the orchestra sat down. In the warm night air, thick with humidity from the nearby sea, Andreas Scholl began to sing the *Stabat Mater* by Vivaldi. Thus began the passion between Rosélie and the maestro of Venice. The passion for music differs from the passion you feel for a human being because it never disappoints you.

Domineering? Manipulating?

Stephen also watched over her and took her in his arms

on nights when remorse gripped her in its persistent and steadfast embrace like on the very first day. He was never tired or exasperated. He made her drink when she was feverish with remorse, sponging her forehead and kissing her hands.

"You have nothing to be ashamed of," he reassured her.

Nothing to be ashamed of? Judge for yourselves.

December was drawing to a close. Flanked by the inevitable Andrew, they had not only spent Christmas in Scotland and eaten haggis, but also relived the trip George Orwell made in the dangerous waters of the Gulf of Corryvreckan. Like Orwell's boat, theirs had capsized and they had almost drowned. They had scarcely recovered from their fright when there came the call from Aunt Léna.

They hurriedly flew to London. But Stephen had kissed Rosélie good-bye at Gatwick, giving a hundred reasons why he couldn't accompany her. She was no dupe. Nobody can confront the death of a mother.

Rose's condition had not worsened. Simply, the heart, her poor heart, prisoner of layers of fat, no longer had the strength to pump blood to her brain and vital organs, which were failing. One evening, Meynalda, who slept in Rose's room to check on her breathing, as reedy as a premature baby's, thought it had stopped. The room was deathly silent, as the saying goes. Dr. Magne was sent for and certified that, from all appearances, she was still alive. In the morning she was still hanging on. Obviously something was holding her back in her place of misfortune: she was waiting for her daughter before closing her eyes.

And Rosélie took fright, imagining her mother's long-suffering, obstinate gaze filtering through her swollen eyelids. How could she confront her? She hadn't been back for three years under the flimsiest of excuses: the move to New York, a study trip by Stephen to Hawaii, and a bout of flu. To make amends, she had spent a fortune at Interflora for every occasion, knowing full well that these expensive bouquets of flowers could not hide the real reason.

On arrival at Orly-Ouest, it was raining. It always rains in Paris. Where is the City of Lights?

I see a damp and melancholic city. Under the Mirabeau Bridge, the waters of the Seine churn our memories, gray and heavy like drowned corpses.

Suddenly, the little courage she had mustered melted away. Her legs went weak, her eyes blurred with tears, and her strength failed her. There was no way she was going to dash to Roissy to catch her plane to Guadeloupe. She dived into a taxi and drove to the Porte Saint-Martin, a district that for her always symbolized desolation.

Hotel du Roi-Soleil. Rooms by the month and by the day. "For how many days?"

I don't know, I don't know.

The room looked out onto a narrow street, a sort of dead end. The electric light, as glaring as an operating room's, lit up a reproduction by Vincent van Gogh. Rosélie ordered two bottles of scotch and, for a person who didn't drink, emptied both of them.

When she resurfaced it was night.

Through the window the neon signs for cheap hotels flashed red-green-green-red. A pneumatic drill was hammering her head while a plug of steel wool choked her mouth. She nevertheless managed to get up and leave the room. To call the elevator. To walk straight as she passed reception. To reach the sidewalk. It was still raining. The Ghanaian whores, feminine silhouettes lined up in the shadows of the sidewalk among the garbage cans, asked one another in Ewe:

"Where does the sister come from?"

"Don't she look like a Malian?"

She entered a café. Soon a man accosted her. Nothing macho, just a young, fair-haired boy, probably a soldier on leave who had smelled a weak, helpless individual. Not long afterward they were back in her room, where he undressed, revealing a white, milky skin with no hair, few muscles, and a limp sex of enormous length. She opened her mouth. He fondled her breasts. But when he was about to penetrate her she collapsed. Who says that men have only a one-track mind and take unfair advantage of women?

Not Lucien Degras. Twenty-four and unemployed since he had left technical college. Ah yes, such is the lot of the majority in our postmodern societies. He listened to this stranger and took pity on her. Three days and three nights she raged delirious in his arms. She left no subject untouched: Rose's mysterious illness, Elie's infidelities, her flight and her fears. On the morning of the fourth day, he managed to drag her to a travel agency—L'Agence Hirondelle, Wings Around the World.

By noon he had paid a taxi for her out of his own money, for he had just received his unemployment check. Direction Roissy.

Eight hours later she arrived in La Pointe. The journey had been a nightmare. Babies crying. Children running up and down the aisles. Mothers desperately trying to quiet things down. Fathers calmly reading their papers in the midst of the hubbub. The family had dispatched Aunt Léna to the airport, her face furrowed with reproach. She kissed Rosélie on the forehead without saying a word and took the wheel of an old car she had inherited from Papa Doudou. During the bumper-to-bumper drive to the rue du Commandant Mortenol—there are too many cars on this wretched island!—they didn't exchange a word. Not one question, such as where were you? Not one reproach, such as she's been waiting for you for four days. Oh yes, she's waiting for you.

Rose was lying on her bed, her eyes half open.

When Rosélie entered they widened, stared at her, letting fly those darts, those arrows that would bore into her heart, her mind and soul, rainy season come dry season, at any hour of the day or night; then they rolled upward and glazed over.

Forever.

Meanwhile, fraught with worry, Stephen had moved heaven and earth, including his mother's retirement home in Verberie, his half brothers, the Hotel du Mont Parnasse in Paris, Cousin Altagras, Lucien Roubichou, and their numerous kids, the airline, and, as a last resort, the central police station.

"Fill in this form with your last name, first name, and address."

"You're not French?"

"She's not your wife? When did she disappear?"

"Did you quarrel?"

In despair, he ended up in La Pointe about the same

time as Rosélie. When he found her he hugged her in his arms in an embrace straight out of *Gone with the Wind,* reported a facetious nephew who was fond of movies.

"It was my fault," he said, shouldering the blame. "I should never have left you on your own."

Fearful all this fat would rapidly decompose, the undertakers had invented an ingenious system of refrigeration. They placed an insulated icebox at the bottom of the coffin that needed to be changed only every four hours. The family was dismayed by the stream of strangers filing in front of Rose's body. They came from all over to get a last look at the recluse, confined to her room for thirty years like a monstrous Gregor Samsa. They elbowed their way into the funeral home, hastily sweeping their breasts with the sign of the cross and getting an eyeful of the horrible sight.

Following these painful events, Rosélie symbolized the ingratitude of children that kills the hearts of so many parents. Worse, she gave no explanation for being inadmissibly late.

"If she had gone via the North Pole she would have got here quicker," as one uncle put it.

Rosélie walked behind the coffin like a zombie, or rather a junkie. Besides, she took drugs, it was whispered around in the family. This was not an entirely false rumor. Rosélie had tried marijuana in Salama Salama's time.

As for Stephen, his preppy looks were reassuring. The women especially appreciated them. It's sad, really, to think that white men make the best husbands. They don't chase around. They stay at home and watch game shows and the news on television before climbing into bed with their wedded wives. The good-for-nothing husbands, those who come home to snore at four in the morning, drained by their exploits with their ladyloves, sneered:

"All that glitters is not gold! In bed, a black is worth at least two whites."

True or false? They only had to ask Rosélie. But no one dared.

As for the politically minded cousins, they first found themselves in a predicament. For years Rosélie, who had never read a line of Fanon or Gramsci, had been their bête noire. The fact she was living with a white man and chose to live in the empire of evil didn't surprise them. But here was her white man, who was not French (only the naive can't tell the difference), proving to be the opposite of what they loathed. Not only was he always prepared to criticize France, Jacobin and colonialist at the dawn of the twenty-first century, but he professed he had no interest in rum punch or the beach.

"All that sand makes me sick," he claimed. "I didn't come here for that."

This favorable opinion changed to negative when he announced he was leaving the rue du Commandant Mortenol and taking his wife to St. Barts. St. Barts! Now he was showing his true face. In the end, for him and others of his color, the Caribbean was nothing more than a tray of exotic fruit for the tasting.

It was true that Stephen hated these tourist paradises. But although he was suffocating in La Pointe, this was not the real reason. He had trouble adapting to the Guadeloupean way of life. In other words, the constant stream of visitors, wave upon wave of friends, uncles, aunts, cousins, nephews, nieces, greatnephews, and great-nieces; the telephone calls without rhyme or reason, preferably at dawn or bang in the middle of siesta; lunches for christenings, first communions, engagements, weddings, silver, gold, or, more rarely, diamond anniversaries that lasted from noon to seven in the evening, and the everlasting discussions on the political status of the island.

"Do we need a single Assembly?"

Elected by universal suffrage, by proportional representation according to the principle of the current regional reforms.

Above all, he wanted to remove Rosélie, who lent herself only too well, from the grip of death: the mass and ceremony of the ninth day, the fifteenth day, the thirtieth day, the daily collective prayers and the annotated reading of *L'Imitation de Jésus-Christ*. Finally, quite simply, he believed that nothing would be better than the luxury of a five-star hotel to give her a new lease on life.

To a certain extent, they didn't feel out of place in St. Barts. Where were the natives hiding out? The island was swarming with Americans, Caucasians, and a handful of African-Americans. None of your university bookworm types, dressed any old how. None of the obese proletariat either. These were people with money, recognizable, despite the required look of jogging suits and Nikes, by their slim figures, their tan, and their assurance. On the beaches at Les Salines and l'Anse du Gouverneur the men showed off their tanned skins and flat stomachs while the women unraveled their hair like Rita Hayworth in *Gilda*. They politely grimaced a smile at Rosélie and made small talk, nothing intellectual:

"Beautiful weather, isn't it?"

"The water's great this morning."

"I hear the East Coast is snowed under!"

Stephen had somewhat miscalculated. Rosélie accompanied him to the beach, the pool, the restaurant, and the bar, swimming, eating, and drinking three or five cocktails an evening. But it was obvious she was not drinking in the luxury, blinded as she was by her own grief. So she was unaware that the hotel staff were eating her up with their eyes. Those who kept the books at reception had passed the information on: she was not married to Stephen. So the verdict of the men, from the gardeners and the pool boys to the servers of planter punches in their tight-fitting white pants, bulging back and front, was final. She was nothing more than a *bòbò* picked up in the airport in Guadeloupe or Martinique together with a gift package of aged rum, a jar of hot peppers, and three sticks of vanilla and cinnamon. The population of chambermaids wavered between rage and envy. What did she have that was so special to hook a white man and wallow at his side in painless opulence at the five-star Palm Beach, safe from the sun, AIDS, and underdevelopment? Not that beautiful. Not that light-skinned. Not that young. And bad hair.

Grief is a marathon runner that sets its own pace.

On their return to New York, Stephen took Rosélie to Carnegie Hall to listen to Vivaldi, and to Brooklyn to admire the Bartabas horses, and, on the advice of some colleagues, consulted Orin Sherman, a respected psychotherapist who treated half the university, but there was nothing doing. Zombie she was, and zombie she stayed, creeping blindfolded through the glare of her days and the shadows of the night. This lasted almost a year.

One morning her nostrils filled with the delightful aroma

of Linda's coffee—Linda, whose magic potions bought in a botanica on 110th Street had been having no effect. She felt the desire for Stephen's body, forgotten for so long on the other side of the king-size bed. Her hands burned to pick up her brushes again. Life had reasserted itself.

Shortly afterward, Aunt Léna, decidedly the messenger of misfortune, called to announce the death of Elie.

Elie had died while Carmen, his favorite *bòbò*, was giving him a blow job during the blissful hours of siesta. His member, on the point of bursting, had suddenly gone limp. She had looked up and there was the old man prostrate in his rocking chair, his eyes rolled upward and his mouth gaping wide open. Sealing the quarrel with the family, Rosélie refused to go to Guadeloupe to attend the funeral. Her time for mourning was over! She had finished eating her heart out. Above all, she confessed her father had never meant anything to her. She could not forgive him his infidelities toward her mother and the rivers of water his humiliations had made her cry.

It had all started when some good souls had reported to Rose he was complaining to his group of friends.

"Man, soon I'll need a ladder to climb up onto that woman!"

"Man, she's not the Aegean Sea, but the Sea of Grease."

"Man, that woman's a nightingale locked up in a demijohn."

He was a useless individual, devoid of dreams, utopia, and ambitions. A Creole-style dandy. He took himself to be the center of the world when he walked on his crooked legs to the clerk's office to scribble his mumbo jumbo, dressed in a white drill suit, his bunions pinched into button boots.

TWELVE

Fiela, he always forgave me, I who was not beyond reproach, who, I confess, had been unfaithful before. Did you ever cheat on Adriaan?

For it was at the very moment when Stephen had shown her so much indulgence and kindness that she had cruelly wounded him. At the very moment when, thanks to him, she ventured out once again into life without crutches. As if she had wanted to assess the strength she had regained by hitting the person dearest to her heart.

One evening, she was fed up with eating out of a tray on her knees in her room in front of a dreary television, despite its 126 channels, and decided to join the guests in the living room. She was amazed at their warm welcome. As if they were glad she was healed and back on earth. As if Stephen had been right when he claimed they loved her but never dared show it. It was the usual clique: specialists from the English and Comparative Literature Departments, with or without their spouses—at the mercy of that frightful species, the babysitter—favorite students, and Fina. Not only had Fina and Rosélie made up, but during those dark days Fina had proved to be her most loyal friend, wrapping her in tenderness and consideration. Stephen was fluttering around a stranger, obviously trying to charm him and include him in his crowd of admirers. When she came up, he hurriedly introduced her in his usual way:

"My wife, Rosélie."

Smiles. Handshakes.

Love at first sight seems to belong to the outmoded props of melodrama. Today, most adults no longer believe in it any more than children believe in Father Christmas. Yet, that evening, Rosélie discovered its vitality and its powers.

Born and raised in Manhattan, Ariel was the son of a mestizo father, whose parents were an Amerindian from Colombia and a Japanese woman from Hawaii. His mother was the daughter of a Haitian and a Polish Jew whose parents had narrowly escaped the uprising in the Warsaw ghetto. He spoke five languages fluently, each with the same foreign accent. He had so much mixed blood in him that he was unable to say which race he belonged to. What's more, he was handsome. A handsomeness that was not particular to any one people, as if every category of human had harmoniously combined to create him. His skin was copper-colored, his thick hair curly black, and his full eyebrows perfect arcs above his eyes. Oh, the eyes, those windows of the soul, large and luminous, though somewhat languishing.

After a while, Ariel and Rosélie felt the need to get away from the hubbub of these irksome individuals desperately discussing Ridley Scott's latest film, the tribulations of the Palestinians, and the famine in Ethiopia. To be alone together! The only refuge left was Rosélie's studio, where only close friends were admitted. Yet, here she was letting in this man she had only just met.

Ariel inspected each canvas as a connoisseur and delivered his verdict. In his opinion, she was influenced by the German neo-Expressionists. Her painting was so violent, somber, and virile whereas she appeared so feminine and gentle. So she too liked monkeys, those miniature humans with the eyes of a clairvoyant. Did she know the story of that señora in Cuba who housed all sorts of chimpanzees in her palace? Had she ever visited Frida Kahlo's Casa Azul in Mexico City? No? The power of art that forges a dialogue through time and space!

In fact, he was a friend of Fina's. He ran a community arts center in the Bronx called La América in honor of José Marti, his hero. La América was unlike any other center. First of all, classes and supplies were free. Knowledge should not have to be paid for. Second, it had as its motto the phrase by Montaigne "An honest man is a many-sided man." Although the center was mainly frequented by Latinos, given its location, it also attracted a fair number of young African-Americans, Caribbeans, and Asians. In fact, there was a bit of everything: old people of both sexes and every color who, after a life of hard work, were indulging in the delights of creativity, junkies endeavoring to replace one passion with another, the idle rich wanting to invent an occupation, the destitute trying to forget their destitution, atheists, and religious fanatics. All of them learned the essential truth, which may sound simplistic, that Art is the only language on the surface of the planet that can be shared without distinction of race or nationality, the two scourges preventing communication among men. At the end of the year Ariel would organize an exhibition and sale of his students' work, the only materialistic activity permitted in this temple of spirituality where profit was spurned. Connoisseurs came from every country in South America. One year a group arrived from

Japan, and another year some Senegalese traveled from Kao-lack. The Spoleto Festival regularly bought several paintings. A few months earlier *The New York Times* had devoted an entire page to him: "Ariel Echevarriá, a man of globality, not globalization."

Ariel ardently begged her to join him in this major project of his and teach painting (free) at La América.

Normally Rosélie would have rejected such an offer, with or without payment. The prospect of dealing with thirty undisciplined and quarrelsome students would have scared her off. But the times were not normal. It was the dawn of a new life.

Elie, the model husband, had gone to fetch the midwife. The baby girl presented well. Soon she would emerge from Rose's womb, not as a pale, skinny newborn that only her mother's milk and devotion would keep on this side of the world, but as a strong, beautiful child, ready for life's adventures. Rose sang to her the barcarolle from *The Tales of Hoffmann:*

Belle nuit, succède au jour,
A nos douleurs, fais trêve.

Confused, Rosélie had trouble finding her words. Yet Ariel, who could already read her thoughts, knew that her silence meant she accepted. He then asked her when she could come to La América to meet the students and begin her mission.

On the other side of the bay windows, the slow procession of cars streamed along Riverside Drive while the mosaic

of illuminated skyscrapers glittered in the distance. Nobody
could say how this tête-à-tête would have ended if Fina, out of
curiosity, hadn't pushed open the door. She clapped her
hands when she heard of Rosélie's plans. Wasn't this what she
had been hoping for all these years? By breaking her depen-
dence on Stephen, she would be able to prove to herself and
everyone else her unusual talent. At the same time the expression in her dark eyes, almond-shaped beneath the knot
of Frida Kahlo–like eyebrows, indicated she was not fooled as
to the nature of Rosélie's feelings, that she was overjoyed and
offered her complicity.

Once the guests had left, however, Stephen ridiculed her
plans with his usual verve. He was not venal. But why would
she work for nothing? This volunteer work masked the regrettable exploitation of man by man, glorified in the name
of Art. Did she realize the boredom and exhaustion involved
in teaching? Besides, she wasn't qualified to teach. Every man
to his trade and there'll be no complaints. As for this Ariel,
he was an ambiguous individual. It was rumored he swung
both ways. Where did the money he invested in the center
come from? Some people accused him of having close ties
with the drug world. More seriously, though, La América was
based on an absurd utopia, a childish premise straight out of
one of John Lennon's songs.

And the world will be one.

Men, women, and children of every country, of every
color, workers or not, unite under the banner of Art. To
think that we all have a budding talent just waiting to be
tapped, how naive can you get! Some are born talented.
Some are geniuses. Others are nobody at all. He had gone

with Fina to an exhibition of the students' work at La
América. Pathetic! But nobody dared tell the truth to the
Bronx. Tell the truth and run.

Rosélie did not contradict Stephen but did as she
pleased. The next morning, no sooner had he turned his
back than she went out, much to Linda's dismay. For months
she hadn't breathed in the smells of New York. The city was
in a festive spring mood and Nature was singing like Charles
Trenet:

> *Y a de la joie!*
> *Partout, y a de la joie!*

The sun was laughing at the blue corners of the sky. All
along Broadway the cherry trees were budding, waist deep in
a splash of forsythia blooms. She took her seat in a bus that,
cleaving the city, climbed up and up toward the Bronx, taking on an increasingly somber, increasingly humble, and increasingly hospitable humanity as it slowly progressed. When
a black kid sitting next to her placed his hand on her knee in
a friendly gesture, she felt that the contact that had been broken, through no fault of her own, had been renewed again
after all these years.

To tell the truth, La América was a nondescript place. It
was a former lunatic asylum, a two-story brick house topped
by a small tower called the Turret of the Raving Mad where
they used to lock up patients in straitjackets. It now housed
Ariel's apartment. The Center was located in a secluded
alley, behind a shabby plot of grass, cluttered with various
transportation devices used by teachers and students alike,

such as bicycles, roller skates, and skateboards, for they loathed technology and gas pollutants as much as they hated material gain. Rosélie soon noticed that at La América Art and Politics made strange bedfellows. The teachers, most of them refugees disowned by their governments, felt no gratitude toward their American savior. They constantly criticized U.S. foreign policy, and at the slightest pretext would demonstrate in the street, brandishing banners and defying the police. A march against the U.S. intervention in Somalia emptied the Pottery and Sculpture Department for weeks on end.

Professionally speaking, Stephen was right. Rosélie had no qualifications to teach. A classroom is a bit like a circus arena in which the lion tamer risks being devoured by his cubs at any moment. Rosélie, however, had no intention of taming anyone. She tolerated everything, imposed nothing, and thus liberated their creativity. Furthermore, as she had never known how to use words, she listened. For hours on end, sitting in her tiny office after class, she was almost carried away by the torrent of students' stories. Mothers battered by depraved husbands. Sisters drawn and quartered. Brothers robbing, raping, and murdering. Cousins dead from an overdose. Or else their bodies riddled with bullets by the police or rival gangs. Young boys and girls just out of prison or detoxification centers. Orphans killing themselves to feed their siblings. A fifteen-year-old taking care of her handicapped parents all on her own. By comparison her life seemed privileged. Even the quarrels between Rose and her Don Juan of a husband paled in comparison. Insipid. Despite her low regard for literature, she was dying to put these dramatic tales on paper and submit them to a major publishing house on the Left Bank, thus revealing the other side of the American Dream, the distress and abject misery hidden under the clichés: "the most powerful nation in the world" or "the triumph of democracy." But they would accuse her of exaggerating and lapsing into pessimism and despair.

People prefer schmaltzy stories. Exotic tales from the Caribbean. Once-upon-a-time stories. Spicy perfumes.

Life is marvelous. If you haven't noticed, you haven't hung your plow upon a star. Arab proverb!

In short, it wasn't long before the students at La América, like its director, were conquered by their new mistress.

"Love, the only love that exists," wrote André Breton. "Carnal love, I adore, I've never stopped adoring your poisonous shadow, your fatal shadow."

Rosélie and Ariel made love every day after classes in the Turret of the Raving Mad. I leave it up to you to imagine the scene.

This lasted a month, six months, perhaps a year. They lost track of time.

One morning—the memory of it shut out by her conscience still haunted her—this guilty happiness came to an end. Very suddenly. It was winter: a winter of ice and frost common to New York. The voracious beast had blown down from Canada, leaving a whirlwind of snow in its wake. It had frozen at dawn and the slippery crust on the sidewalks glistened in the timid morning sun. Wrapped up to their eyes, passersby groped their way along. At La América, students and teachers were crowded in the yard. The amazing news was on everyone's lips: Ariel had been arrested.

The pigs had picked him up at dawn. They accused him of having ties with drug dealers and laundering money on their behalf. La América was closed. Classes suspended.

Rosélie collapsed into the arms of Stephen, who once again said not a word of reproach.

What can passion be compared to? To a hurricane, David, Hugo, or Belinda, that swoops down on the island and ravages it entirely. There is nothing you can do about a hurricane except wait for its fury to pass. And that's what he had done. He had tried to warn her, to whisper that Ariel was a shady character. But had she been listening? Rosélie's chagrin was mixed with a feeling of humiliation. So she had fallen for a crook, one of those petty criminals that America produces by the thousand, a crony of Manuel Noriega's. The papers are full of their pitiful exploits. Because of him, she had hurt the best of men, the most perfect of companions. For although Stephen hadn't breathed a word, it was obvious he had suffered. He who was so fussy about his appearance, maniacal to the point of ironing his shirts himself and sending a suit back to the cleaners three times because of a crease in the trousers, now wore a shapeless pullover and a wrinkled pair of jeans. His hair curled down over his collar. His face was gaunt and haggard. He hadn't written one line or given a paper for months. He skipped through his classes.

Fina asserted just the opposite. While struggling to keep her weight down along the frozen paths of Riverside Park, she maintained that Ariel was an idealist, crazy about Art, with his head in the clouds. It basically boiled down to a political conspiracy. The State Department had wanted to destroy La América, a den of subversion. As for his swinging both ways, that was pure slander. Dozens of beauties could honestly swear that Ariel was a lover of women. Despite all her efforts, she couldn't manage to convince Rosélie to take the train to a prison in upstate New York. It's in B movies that lovers exchange tearful looks through the glass of the visiting room.

Ariel was freed after three months. No charge could be held against him. La América's books were in order. Its respected donors included a Saudi prince, a Kuwaiti, and a descendant of Winston Churchill.

The Center reopened its doors. But the enthusiasm had gone. Teachers and students alike had fled. In the empty classrooms there remained only a dozen students and two teachers: a Spanish anarchist, master in the technique of *azulejos*, and a Japanese communist, enamored of Gothic painting.

Using Fina as a go-between, Ariel sent Rosélie a series of enigmatic and passionate letters begging her not to confuse those who adored her with those who used her as a screen. She didn't answer. Not that she didn't love him anymore. On the contrary, when she thought of him, her entire being melted. Water poured from every part and every orifice of her body. And then she couldn't stop dreaming of the world they had hoped to build at La América. A world enamored of Art, diversity, and tolerance. Nobody would have to shoulder a prefabricated identity any longer, like a deadly garrote strangling the neck. A black woman could curl up in peace beside her white man. But the idea of hurting Stephen was unbearable. Never again. She'd rather die.

This enraged Fina.

"You're sacrificing yourself for nothing! For nothing!" she maintained.

For nothing?

"Is it Stephen you're calling nothing?" she choked each time Fina said it.

Fina was seething, but didn't answer.

One afternoon, beside herself, she stopped dead in the middle of the park and began yelling at all the echoes:

"Yes! Your Stephen is *de la mierda*. Do you hear me? *De la mierda!*"

As a good Latina, Fina had accustomed Rosélie to cut-and-dried expressions such as *coño, carajo,* and other curse words. But the friendship between the two women was unable to survive this one. They stopped seeing each other. Shortly afterward, Fina slammed the door on the university and went back to Venezuela, where she made a name for herself as a moviemaker. She made an autobiographical film of her childhood as an alienated bourgeois. Her only link with the people was her black grandmother, who was a magician and storyteller. About the same time, Ariel, in a more somber mood, retired to a plot of land inherited from his parents in Jérémie. The only access was by boat. It was an arid and bare piece of land where only columnar and hedge cactus grew. At night their gangling shapes could be taken for silhouettes of the dead who often wandered around in the dark. In Haiti, such things surprise no one. They call it marvelous realism. See René Depestre. Ariel tried to re-create an art school on the lines of La América. Unfortunately, in this famished country, people are ravenous for dollars. Unable to muster any volunteer teachers, he had to close the school. He ended up marrying Anthénor, pet name Sonore, the peasant woman who cooked him his pork *griot* and sweet potato bread. He gave her nine children, three of whom died as infants.

THIRTEEN

Every couple who goes through a crisis imagines that travel will provide a miracle cure. That's what they call an *idée reçue*. They believe that seeing new landscapes, meeting new people, and learning a foreign language is an infallible cure for their distress. Stephen and Rosélie were no different. In early summer, Stephen proposed they leave. Europe? Africa? Asia? He himself was in favor of Japan. For a long time Fumio had given him the desire to know this country, a little more than by the sushi bars in Soho or the *Empire of Signs* by Roland Barthes, which he had read dozens of times.

Rosélie refused, still smarting from her wounds to risk curious or racist looks flung full in her face or as a stab in the back. Despite Stephen's loathing for the beach, a stay in Montauk on Long Island had to make do. Montauk is what the East Coast has that is closest to a village. No movie theater. A drugstore where sleeping pills are shelved side by side with Kellogg's Corn Flakes. Wooden houses strung out along miles of beach. The ocean and the sky stretching to infinity. In Rosélie's eyes, the sea at Montauk, like the English Channel, had nothing in common with that coquette with green eyes who, picking up her lace petticoats, sashays into the bays of Guadeloupe or seethes against its reefs. It was dull and lifeless, strewn here and there with tufts of foam clinging to her colorless garb. Nothing elating. Swimming was anything but exhilarating.

Whereas she had trouble getting over Ariel, La América, and the sound and fury of adultery, Stephen recovered extremely quickly and extremely well. He had become friends with a group of rugged men wearing yellow oilskins and sou'westers who initiated him in deep-sea fishing. Every morning he would get up at dawn and return in the evening loaded with swordfish and marlin that slowly decomposed in the fridge, since Rosélie had always loathed fish and its tasteless, anemic, strong-smelling flesh. When he was not out at sea, he would go and drink mugs of beer at the local tavern with his newfound friends. We must admit that, to his credit, unlike his companions he never got drunk, and came home around midnight, fully sober and not bawling "My Funny Valentine."

One day a brunette, her pretty face crowned by a powder puff of curly hair, called out to Rosélie over the hedge and proposed they go for a swim. The invitation stunned her, especially as the other holidaymakers carefully avoided her. At the supermarket they would go out of their way not to find themselves in front of the basmati rice shelf at the same time as her. The stranger was called Amy Cohen, her husband, Caleb. They had three sons. They were Jews.

What is a Jew? Jean-Paul Sartre posed the question in *Anti-Semite and Jew.* Did he answer the question? Like every teenager, Rosélie had received *The Diary of Anne Frank* as a birthday present together with *Wuthering Heights.* She had read Emily Brontë's tale over and over again, much to Rose's surprise, since she could never get Rosélie interested in a novel, but she had never opened the Anne Frank. During endless discussions by Stephen and his colleagues, she had heard some maintain the Jews were victims turned perpetrators, while others claimed they were victims fighting for their survival. She was certain of one thing, though: they wore the yellow star as a mark of their singularity and exclusion, like her. Amy described to her journeys that, although they hadn't taken place in the hold of a slave ship, were nevertheless wrenching experiences. Fleeing fires and pogroms, hunted from one Central European country to another, her family had stopped in Vienna long enough for her grandfather, who was a violinist, to play in *Aïda* for the inauguration of the Wiener Staatsoper. Then they were on the run again. This time, for safety's sake, they had crossed the ocean and taken refuge in America. But that was where any resemblance to the naked migrants Rosélie knew, stopped. Amy's father had invented a fake mother-of-pearl for making shirt buttons that had made him rich. In a just twist of fortune his sons preferred music to shirt buttons, and the five boys played in the various city orchestras. Only Amy had decided to devote her life to her family. She left university without graduating, and ever since, her days were reduced to mashing vegetables into puree, filling babies' bottles with bottled water, and getting rid of foul-smelling diapers.

"Motherhood is the noblest of functions," she would say, up to her eyes in poop. "Alas, ever since the feminists, it has been discredited. It makes me furious!"

Rosélie, usually not very bold, was bold enough to come out with Stephen's famous axiom: "The most beautiful creations are those of the imagination." Amy's children, in fact, scared her. Three famished, howling children like vultures gorging on their mother's liver and entrails. Unperturbed, Amy smiled.

"If I'm going to be devoured, I prefer it to be by my children."

Did she mean Rosélie was being devoured by Stephen?

On weekends the men did not set out to sea. Grandparents, parents, and friends streamed in from New York. The city dwellers' cars jammed the streets while the tavern was always full. One Sunday Amy invited Rosélie and Stephen to lunch. Aaron, her youngest brother, with a mane of hair like Beethoven on the box sets of his complete symphonies, had just played Gustav Mahler in Paris and, together with his wife, Rebecca, had been horrified by the anti-Semitism of the French. What a terrible lot! Not surprising they produced a Drieu La Rochelle, Brasillach, Vichy, and Papon! Everyone had an anecdote to tell. The atmosphere became openly Francophobe.

"During the last war, guess what all the French soldiers wanted to learn in German?" Aaron asked.

". . . ."

" 'I surrender!' They all wanted to say 'I surrender!' "

As a rule, Stephen was the first to jeer at the French, but he liked nothing better than to sow dissension. In the midst of a chorus of laughter, he declared:

"I could turn Sartre's phrase round at you. Instead of 'It's the anti-Semite who makes the Jew,' 'It's the Jew who makes the anti-Semite.' "

Following a deathly silence, there was a general outcry. Stephen reveled in the effect he had produced and persisted.

"It's the same with Rosélie. Her individualistic behavior provokes a reaction. She then interprets it from a perspective she has fixed in advance."

Even Caleb, an overworked obstetrician, who only turned up at Montauk on weekends, stopped dozing in the sun beside his sons and came to join in the conversation. Amy was the shrillest of them all.

"Do you mean to say that racism doesn't exist?" she exclaimed.

His eyes gleaming, a stray lock of hair across his forehead, Stephen was in his element.

"That's not what I mean. Because American society is segregated, still today, even in New York, whatever they like to say, most whites, without being racist, feel a deep malaise in the company of a black person, and are extremely uncomfortable in their presence. The black has to be reassuring . . ."

The outcry turned into a racket. Everyone protested at the same time.

"Reassuring!" Amy shouted. "You're asking the victims to reassure the perpetrators!"

"Reassuring! What are they afraid of?" Caleb asked.

"You have just given the exact definition of racism!" screamed Aaron. "For the white man, the black is not a human being like himself."

Rosélie had been hearing this from Stephen for years. Every time she complained about his colleagues, the waiters in a restaurant, or the local shopkeepers, he made an excuse for their behavior and put the blame on her. She intimidated them by her aloofness, she disconcerted them by her silences. She didn't laugh at their jokes.

"Smile!" he begged her. "You are so lovely when you smile. They'll be so charmed they'll be eating out of your hand."

How can you smile at someone who doesn't see you? *Invisible woman.*

The discussion was interrupted for lunch to sample the pièce de résistance, the goulash. It smoldered again over Mocha Java coffee, then flared up with the liqueurs, a Poire Williams and a Courvoisier cognac Aaron had brought back from Paris. For although France was a haven for anti-Semites, it still remained a paradise for fine eating. It finally went out when the visitors got back in their cars and left for New York. The next morning, lying beside her on the beach, Amy let slip her first criticism of Stephen, a prelude to many others.

"I don't know how you can put up with such an insensitive man!"

Stephen, insensitive? Provocative, yes. He loved being politically incorrect.

During that particular vacation Rosélie did an oil painting, six feet by nine, that she called quite simply *The Sea at Montauk.* It was an infinite variety of grays. Caleb and Amy fell in love with it and bought it from her for several hundred dollars.

The reader who merely recites from a geography manual that New York is divided into five boroughs hasn't a clue that Brooklyn, in fact, is another country, a continent in miniature. You reach it across a bridge, a lasso thrown from the high towers of finance, making a perfect arc over the barges on the river, finally anchoring onto the pillars of a freeway. The nature lover can lose himself in its miles of parks; the art lover can visit its museums. The visitor who is tired of eating beef, cheese, and other burgers, the unsavory culinary inventions of Caucasians without a palate, can burn his tongue in the cheap Jamaican eating houses and exchange his pints of insipid beer for a Bacardi or, even better, a five-star Barbancourt rum. You will find Latino-Americans, Caribbean-Americans, Korean-Americans, Japanese-Americans, and Filipino-Americans. Few Americans without a hyphen. It is the realm of the Haitians and the Hassidic Jews.

The Cohens lived in Crown Heights in an old twelve-room house, surrounded by a garden, a genuine park of rare trees, inherited from Caleb's father, a wealthy trader gone home to confront the suicide attacks in Israel. The relaxed atmosphere of the neighborhood, where in the summer Amy would jog without a bra in a tiny pair of shorts and the children would play unsupervised in the garden and Caleb would walk back from the hospital at any hour of the night, had been dearly won. A few years earlier it had been the scene of some of the worst racial rioting. As a result, New York, even the entire country, had been almost swallowed up in an apocalypse of hatred. Then they had buried the dead. Wept. The purification of mourning had restored peace. Back to being themselves, everyone tried to live in harmony with their black, Jewish, or Asian neighbors.

Twice a week, Rosélie took the subway to Brooklyn.

It's a well-known fact that the New York subway is unlike any other. It's an Ali Baba's treasure trove of violence and stench. Those whose heart is hanging on by a thread should

be warned not to venture down there! Nutcases shove unsus-
pecting passengers under trains entering the station in a rattle of iron loud enough to deafen the deaf. Weirdos playing
with knives can slash your face. Bums, junkies, and perverts
have set up home there. Some of them beg in a tone of voice
once used by criminals when they demanded your money or
your life. Others exhibit sores and other disabilities to turn
your stomach. Yet others shout the end of America is nigh,
collapsing under the weight of its mortal sins. The reason
why Rosélie braved so many dangers was that Amy's company
brought her infinite happiness. In her presence she rediscovered the forgotten sensation of being a person, a human
being, unique, remarkable, perhaps created in God's image.
She was no longer an invisible woman. Amy showed interest
in her, in her painting, her hopes, and her failings. When
they were running together in the park, Rosélie revealed her
wounds: those that endure forever, those that fester, and
those that never heal. Amy, who had just admitted her incon-
tinent and bedridden mother to a home for the elderly and
hadn't the courage to visit her, could understand Rosélie,
since she was living the torment she herself had once lived.

"We haven't abandoned them," Amy asserted. "It's because we love them too much to watch them deteriorate. I
envy Caleb. He lost his mother when he was five. He hardly
remembers her and has built a myth around her. Young,
beautiful, and eternal. As for your father, fathers are made to
be admired and respected. Yours made a bad job of it. It's his
fault if you felt nothing for him."

Amy and Caleb's house, with its ornate rooms, its heavy,
old-fashioned furniture, and portraits of aunts and uncles,

was a bit like the house she had grown up in. It was also like La América, minus the presence of Ariel.

Sometimes, Ariel, your absence is killing me.

For Amy and Caleb lived amid a constant stream of friends of every origin and every color who worshiped every type of god and expressed themselves in every type of foreign idiom. Among this crowd who turned up unexpectedly and sampled the goulash of an evening, once the children were asleep, Andy and Alice were the only ones who terrified Rosélie. Andy and Alice were a couple of African-Americans: Andy, obstetrician in the same hospital as Caleb, and Alice, a law professor at a prestigious white university.

Come now, the term Black American went out years ago. So did Afro-American. As for the word "Negro," it is no longer pronounced. The Negro doesn't exist.

The looks Andy and Alice cast at Rosélie thrust her back into insignificance. Oh, she was a painter, was she? With very little talent, judging by the picture *The Sea at Montauk* that Amy and Caleb, out of pure paternalism, had hung in the middle of their living room.

A child could do as well.

Or me.

They then insisted on calling her Rosalind, so different from Rosélie, and never apologized.

Stephen would faithfully go and fetch Rosélie of an evening for he didn't like her taking the subway after eight at night. He was far from sharing her infatuation for the Cohens. Even though there had been no further quarrel of epic proportions with any member of the family, his presence always caused a certain embarrassment. In his opinion, Amy and Caleb belonged to that most dangerous of species, the right-thinkers. Their conversation resembled a digest of the newspapers they devoured, like priests consumed by their breviaries. They never had a personal opinion on art or literature. They expressed admiration for the plays, films, musical comedies, and art exhibitions they were supposed to admire. In politics, they were so careful not to hurt anyone, they agreed with all sides.

"Listen to them," he sneered. "What a wonderful world we live in! Especially for the Arabs, blacks, Palestinians, Israelis, Indians, Pakistanis, Afghans, and Iraqis."

Stephen had bought a station wagon off a colleague leaving for Australia, which was too big, three times too heavy, and guzzled too much unleaded gas. He hardly drove it, having failed to interest Rosélie in the surrounding natural splendors. Niagara Falls, water, water everywhere!

On the other hand, I'd like to visit the Grand Canyon and throw myself into the void like Thelma and Louise.

Rosélie loved the drive back home at night. They would take up their position in a slow procession of cars, as if they were following a hearse, and cross the bridge. Facing them, Manhattan opened up like a scene from an opera, ablaze with lights, where the skyscrapers represented the divas and portly tenors, painted and dressed in their shiny, frazzled costumes. Sometimes they would stop in a bustling restaurant where everyone was yelling at the top of their voices. Then they would go and listen to jazz in a basement club, squeezed up against each other, experiencing the same vibrations. Unexpectedly, the music conjured up the image of Ariel. The pain assumed the sounds of the muffled trumpet.

One evening Amy insisted they stay for dinner. It was Hanukkah, the Jewish Festival of Lights. She had cooked a traditional meal of latkes and brisket in gravy. After they lit the menorah, a few friends sat down informally around the table in the dining room. Among them were the inevitable Andy and Alice.

The first half of the meal was monopolized by Andy in a solo performance. He showered his listeners with anecdotes at which he was usually the first and only one to roar with laughter. Example: Invited to a Hasidic wedding, something quite unprecedented, he met one of his patients, whose eight children he had delivered. As he held out his hand to shake hers, she had lowered her eyes and murmured: "I'm sorry, Doctor. I don't touch men!"

Are you laughing?

The second half was monopolized by Andy and Alice in a duo. The previous summer they had made a trip to Nigeria, a pilgrimage, in fact, for they had both been in the Peace Corps there fifteen years earlier and had fallen in love with each other. The Peace Corps, ah! What an esteemed organization that brings modernity to Africa absolutely free of charge!

Really? I heard just the opposite. Some see in it the hand of the CIA.

During this second visit, their host had been no other than Wole Soyinka, the renowned writer, who had gone to great lengths to get the Americans to boycott his country. Nigeria, it should be recalled, although birthplace of the first African Nobel Prize winner, proved to be a dunce when it came to democracy. Andy and Alice described in length the prevailing incompetence, chaos, and corruption. No importance was placed on human life. The wonderful poet Ken Saro-Wiwa and eight members of his party had been hanged. Political rivals died a suspicious death in prison. Tribunals ordered adulterous women to be stoned, for women are the first victims of violence by their governments.

There are no dictatorships without sexism. Example: the Taliban and Afghan women.

Rosélie didn't have time to meditate on such a negative vision of Mother Africa before Stephen took advantage of a brief pause in the monologues. He straightaway deplored the violence of black gangs in the United States. His words fell like stones dropped into the depths of a crevasse by a clumsy spelunker. The guests forgot to ask for seconds of the latkes. In a deathly silence, Stephen totaled up the number of blacks in high-security prisons and on death row, accused of murder, rape, and armed robbery, black criminals whose faces were splashed across TV screens.

"You're forgetting they're not all guilty," retorted Andy, choking with anger. "American justice is so inhuman, it crushes the weak and the poor! Those who can afford to pay lawyers with their fat bank accounts are declared innocent. Whereas the others—"

"Even if these blacks appear guilty, and that's the impression the police, the media, and the government want to give, they are, in fact, victims," interrupted Alice impetuously. "Victims of the iniquity of the American social system."

"Inhuman justice for the weak! Iniquitous social system!" repeated Stephen, with a fake naive expression. "American democracy is full of flaws!"

Andy and Alice agreed.

"So," continued Stephen. "If I were an African-American, instead of meddling in the rest of the world's affairs, I would sweep in front of my own door."

Thereupon, he excused himself from dessert and, amid a deathly silence, headed for the door, dragging Rosélie with him. Once outside in the garden, he doubled up laughing. He was still laughing behind the wheel.

"Did you see their faces? The truth always produces the same effect."

This episode, however, did not sound the death knell between Rosélie and Amy, as very well might have been the case. See the trouble with Fina.

It merely provided them with a new topic for discussion during their tête-à-têtes in the park.

"Admit he was rude," Amy concluded. "Admit it. He was at the limit of racism. After you left, Alice cried, she is so sensitive. To make such a speech like that about African-Americans and their unending struggle."

Rosélie tried to defend Stephen. Far from denigrating the glorious struggles of the past, and perhaps of the present, he was preaching for a little humility. He would like Andy and Alice to stop sermonizing, coming from a community who have been left out of the American dream, in which, moreover, nobody believes any longer.

Without admitting it, Rosélie was somewhat proud of Stephen. He had refused to be a mere onlooker, which she had so often contented to be. He had refused to be invisible and forced the Other to see him for what he is worth.

From that day on Alice and Andy treated Rosélie with somber compassion and no longer spoke to her. A sister who stays with a Caucasian of the most dangerous sort can only be pitied. Was it masochism? Certainly not! She was a living example of Mayotte Capécia's complex of lactification, so magnificently denounced by Fanon. Him again!

"She is asking for nothing, demanding nothing, except for a little whiteness in her life."

Stephen, the subject of so much disapproval, felt no remorse. However, he thought it wiser not to set foot again at Amy and Caleb's. When he came to fetch Rosélie, he would sound his horn in front of the garden gate or send Mario to get her. Mario was an illegal immigrant. No job, however thankless, deterred him. He worked as a driver for Stephen, walked the Dalmatians for the second-floor tenants, washed the windows of the apartment on the fourth floor, and took the twins on the eighth to school. He also helped the old couple on the tenth to piss and bought them their ground beef, the only food their toothless mouths could eat. You didn't dare whisper to him that his physique of a Greek god could have got him a less exhausting and more lucrative type of job.

Caleb took a liking for his curly head and dark eyes. He found him a job as a security guard. Mario therefore left Manhattan to the annoyance of all those whom he had helped. Henceforth, dressed in a heavy leather jacket, wearing a flat cap, and armed with a revolver that didn't suit his gentle disposition, he monitored the comings and goings at the hospital and kept the undesirables at a distance.

At the start of the summer, Andy and Alice emerged from their silence and invited Rosélie to exhibit at an arts festival organized by an African-American association. Once she had got over her initial surprise, she realized that these good shepherds hadn't lost hope of bringing their lost sheep back to the fold, in other words returning her to the Holy of Holies, the Race. What surprised her even more was that she was delighted by the invitation. Like a pariah suddenly invited to the master's table. Like a condemned person suddenly pardoned and brought back to the company of the righteous.

She therefore turned a deaf ear to Stephen's warnings. It was not just a question of exhibiting a few paintings, he recalled. In addition, each artist had to explain his work, his sources of inspiration, and his technique. Was she prepared for that, she who had so much trouble expressing herself? Piqued, Rosélie spent the night scribbling page after page.

The festival took place at Medgar Evers College. Situated in the very heart of Brooklyn, this imposing edifice, proudly named after a martyr, appeared to be one of the last bastions of that African-American grandeur so ignored on American soil. The president and board of directors, however, regretted there were so few native-born Americans, and far too many Caribbeans and Africans without a hyphen. The college now attracted first and second generations, born from successive waves of immigration, for whom racism, high tuition fees, and the lack of adequate training would have prevented them from studying elsewhere. There were also a great many white skins, the Latinos, often similar, alas, to the Caucasians. The corridors echoed more with the sounds of Spanish and Creole than those of Ebonics.

On that particular day, a crowd was streaming toward the

college. And Rosélie in a daze thought she recognized tens of Aunt Lénas, Aunt Yaëlles, cousins, and uncles; so true seemed the saying, which everyone mistakenly thinks is racist, that all blacks look alike. In the yard a circle of curious on-lookers were crowded around gigantic sculptures arranged close to the fountains. However hard she elbowed, she was unable to get a closer look. Alice and Andy had in fact men-tioned an African-American sculptor who was taking blacks and whites alike by surprise.

She followed the crowd heading toward an amphitheater. It was on the way there that she was gripped by terror and al-most turned tail.

Was she in her place, she who colluded with the oppres-sor?

Sleeping with the enemy.

Unfortunately, a hostess dressed with a headscarf fit for a Senegalese *drianke* and a boubou in rich brocade, seeing her hesitate, dragged her to the podium with the heavy hand of a revolutionary guard leading an aristocrat to the scaffold.

The panel was composed of six artists: three men and three women. Equality *oblige*. Scheduled for 9:00 a.m., the dis-cussion began around eleven, as they had to wait for a tech-nician to set up the microphones. The ten minutes allotted to each speaker was not respected, since each participant complained louder than the other about the difficulties of being a creator in a materialistic world, thirsting for con-sumerism and threatened by globalization. The most vehe-ment—and also the longest—was the moviemaker. The black public was no longer what it used to be, he hammered out. It no longer encouraged its creators. It had taken a liking for sex, visual effects, and violence, white values that had corrupted it. As a result, the wonderful stories that made up the heritage of the black people, those stories transmitted from mouth to mouth, were destined to perish. These diatribes together with the earlier delays and the rigors of alphabetical order had disastrous consequences. When Rosélie's turn came, just before Anthony Turley's, the other panelists had left, and the auditorium strewn with paper cups and litter was virtually deserted. Amid general indifference, Rosélie churned out the paper she had taken so much trouble over. Moreover, she got the impression that the few people left did not understand a word she was saying because of her accent.

"How about lunch?" he proposed.

Anthony Turley could boast of an impeccable pedigree. His family, originally from Alabama, tired of dying from hunger on land gone to waste practically ever since the South had been defeated, had left for Detroit. There they had found themselves as poor as before, but this time deprived of air and light, and imprisoned in the urban ghetto. The men, embittered, beat their women and raped their prepubescent daughters. He was the fruit of one of these family dramas. His mother, raped at the age of twelve by her uncle, had committed suicide in despair shortly after his birth. He had been raised by his grandmother, gone crazy from the brutality and abuse of numerous common-law husbands. Anthony had grown up on food stamps, spent vacations at summer camps for underprivileged children, and got through his studies with the help of scholarships for needy gifted children. In spite of all that, his entire personality radiated a gallant charm and an impression of joyful strength. You could guess the little boy and teenager he had been, tripping over corpses on the sidewalk and determined against all odds to get the most out of life, as he hummed his way along. He wouldn't have been out of place on a basketball team, for he was well over six feet tall. Not an ounce of fat. Nothing but muscle. His head shaved, as shiny as a mirror, a mischievous gold loop in his left ear, and an easy laugh with the accents of a clarinet.

They crossed the yard, forcing their way through the crowd still gathered in front of the sculptures.

"Have you seen my work?" he asked. "I was very surprised to be invited to this festival. I hadn't got much attention until *The New York Times* wrote a few lines about me, and now things are starting to change."

A helping hand, that's what I need! Who will give me a helping hand? To bring me out of the shadows where I am foundering. The wings of an artist need to be caressed by the light, otherwise they fold and wither like stumps.

There's an unexpected charm about this neighborhood. They crossed a majestic avenue. Then he guided her through a maze of streets filled with little girls showing their chocolate-colored legs as they jumped rope, little boys running across imaginary baseball fields and old folk clutching walkers, and finally, they reached a restaurant called Nature. Yes, kids often took him for Michael Jordan and asked for an autograph. But once they had deciphered his signature, they went away disappointed. Sometimes young girls insisted on taking their photo with him. They often accepted a rendezvous. When he told them his real name they would shout insults at him as if he had wanted to cheat them. One of them had even tried to sue him.

Anthony had invented a substance that was a mixture of clay, resin, melted metal, ground glass with shards of flint and quartz, baked in an oven at a very high temperature. He used it to sculpt animals and creatures of his imagination, trees, and plants. Never humans.

He changed his tone of voice and became serious.

"I listened carefully to what you said . . ."

What did I say? Rosélie had merely repeated Ariel's theory: Art-is-the-only-language-that-can-be-shared-on-the-surface-of-the-planet and blah, blah, blah. Nothing very original.

"I don't agree at all on what you said about nationality, especially race. Aren't you proud to be black?"

Me? Proud?

I'd like to be a Hindu princess combing her long hair from a window in the palace. The prince passes by on horseback and tramples on this billowing stream that flows into the forest.

He took offense.

"Don't you ever feel bitter when you think of all the evil they have done us?"

My good friend, I'm an egoist. I am more concerned about the failure of my present than the wounds of our past.

"I'm not talking about the past. They're still doing us so much harm."

They're not alone. They are joined by a cohort of those who wear the same skin color as ours.

He lost his temper.

"Don't you think it's time for us to take our revenge?"

Revenge? Revenge is not for me. I fear I would never succeed, since I'm in the category of losers.

"That's why I never sculpt humans. I create a world where they and their brutality, their craving for discovering, conquering, and dominating don't exist. A world without Adam and Eve and their descendants of ruffians."

Rosélie livened up. But this world without perpetrators, and therefore without victims, is basically no different from the one I dream of. Without race. Without class. Without borders.

"Utopia!" he said severely, shrugging his shoulders. "Come back to earth."

Then, quite illogically, looking straight into her eyes, he took her hands and asked sweetly, but solemnly:

"When can you visit my studio? Be my guest. It's situated in the very middle of the Detroit ghetto. I bet you've never seen anything like it. It's like a war zone. Sometimes junkies scrounge a few dollars off me. Just to get a fix. My best friend Joe got twenty years for a rape he didn't commit. In the end, his DNA saved him. He didn't harbor any grudge. Allah came to him in jail and now he's a fervent disciple. His dream is to convert me."

There was an aura of immense seduction about him. How tempting to imagine oneself naked, screwed between his massive thighs!

No! Never again! Rosélie firmly shook her head. They would not see each other again!

And yet Rosélie and Anthony Turley saw each other a few weeks later at an exhibition on the Dogons of Mali. Ever since Marcel Griaule spent the night at Sanga over seventy years ago, the Dogons rank number one in the hit parade of African peoples. To what can we attribute this fascination? Whatever the explanation, the Soho Museum had re-created the famous cliffs at Bandiagara and shipped by plane three emaciated old men, exact replicas of Ogotemmeli; apart from the fact that their guns had not gone off in their faces while shooting at a porcupine, their eyes were still intact and "their brown tunics, drawn at the seams, were frayed by wear like an old battle flag." The exhibition curator was explaining to a group of visitors the metaphysics and cosmogony of the Dogons, as rich as Hesiod's, when Anthony and Rosélie bumped into each other in front of a "household mask." They exchanged that loaded look tinged with longing of those who had wanted to go to bed together and hadn't, then awkwardly shook hands. She could make out the surprise at the back of his eyes.

What the hell are you doing with this white guy?

If only he knew the truth! She almost burst into tears.

"What a stud! How did you meet him?" Stephen asked in surprise.

FOURTEEN

Fiela, we are on the fifth day of your trial and you still haven't said a word. Public opinion is mounting against you. The experts have made their reports. How could they possibly assess you? You haven't opened your mouth. They maintain, however, you are sane of mind. Apparently you are of above-average intelligence. It's true at the mission school you carried off all the first prizes. Very early on, however, you had to abandon your studies. You who liked to read. At age fourteen the nuns found you work. As a domestic. The Afrikaner woman who employed you took a dislike to you, said you were a sly little thing. It's true you confided in no one, since no one was interested in you. I know what that feels like. What's the use of talking if nobody listens? It's like a writer whom nobody reads. In the end, he gives up writing.

Rosélie escorted her patient to the street.

> *Patient No. 7*
> *Joseph Léma*
> *Age: 61*
> *Nationality: Congolese*
> *No profession*

In actual fact, Joseph Léma was a former musician. In his country, at a time when he was intoxicated by fame and believed himself to be untouchable, he had composed an opera, *Where Have All the Gazelles Gone?* A genuine masterpiece, wrote the specialists, a combination of rock and traditional rhythms. In it he had dared criticize the dictatorship of the single party. The response had been swift. In the predawn hours, exactly at the time when gazelles go to drink, a band of henchmen had snatched him from the arms of his new mistress. He had then broken rocks for eight years in a camp up north, famished, humiliated, and beaten every day. He owed his salvation to the president's eldest son, who had murdered his father by sprinkling a colorless, odorless, tasteless poison, as dangerous as curare, in his groundnut stew. This reprehensible deed, denounced by the international community, except for the United States, who backed the son, that is, the murderer, in the name of democracy, had at least one happy consequence: thousands of political prisoners were released from jail, something Amnesty International had never managed to do. Hiding out in Cape Town, where his wife and three of his concubines had followed him, Joseph was not only homesick, he was also crippled with pain. At times he could neither stand nor sit. Other times he was unable to walk. Nevertheless, Rosélie believed that his weekly visits—he didn't miss a single one—were above all caused by the need to chew over the past. Every time she listened to him she was amazed. Who was the naive person who claimed that life is a long, slow-rolling river? On the contrary, life is a raging torrent, embedded with rapids, strewn with pitfalls. She watched him hobble back up the street, stiff as a poker, squeezing his butt as if he had a case of diarrhea.

On that particular morning, like a student slipping past

her teacher's watchful eye, she escaped from Dido. She decided to walk across Cape Town. Measure its pulse by the sound of its arteries. Breathe in the stench of its markets, the fragrance of its gardens, and the salty smell of the wharfs. She had seldom experienced such happiness, since she had never dared walk on her own. Even Stephen, who was far from timid, advised her against it.

She walked down Orange Avenue and crossed the Company's Gardens, reveling in the scarlet splendor of the canna lilies and the ragged, motley crowd of junkies, jobless, homeless, beggars, and pickpockets looking for a gullible victim to rob.

Fiela's trial was getting people so worked up that as a precaution the courthouse, a massive brownstone, typically Dutch construction, had been cordoned off. Only the lawyers, witnesses, and journalists were seen going up and down the steps. Behind a police line, idle onlookers were stamping with impatience. At one street corner, television cameras had been set up and journalists were aiming their microphones.

"What's your opinion about the case?"

"I think it's terrible!"

"And what else?"

"Terrible, terrible! It puts our country to shame."

People have really nothing to say!

About twenty fanatics were waving banners to bring back the death penalty. Some people never miss an opportunity! Members of a sect, blacks and whites united in the same madness, dressed in identical flowing robes, predicted the end of the world. Here, they believed, were the first unnatural acts announced in the Scriptures.

"And men shall go into the caves of the rocks and into the holes of the earth, from before the terror of the Lord and from the glory of his majesty when he ariseth to shake mightily the earth."

Others, more learned, jargoned in Latin.

Nos timemus diem judicii
Quia mali et nobis conscii.

Some crafty devils were selling portraits of Fiela they had sketched during the hearings, hinting at horns above her forehead. Although the argument for cannibalism had been more or less ruled out, there was no doubt Fiela had indulged in satanic rites on Adriaan's body. The prosecuting attorney had called in neighbors who maintained exactly the opposite of what the preceding witnesses had said. Fiela terrified them. She never smiled. She had never given birth. Her breasts contained a bile that soiled her clothes during her diabolical suckling. Instead of intestines, her belly writhed with snakes. In the graveyards she parleyed with the dead. She took in wild beasts and trained them to do evil. A raven with wings the color of soot followed her wherever she went, faithful as a dog.

Rosélie bought a pile of newspapers and settled down in the back of a café. The *Cape Tribune, The Herald,* and *The Guardian* ceaselessly maintained that Fiela was a witch. There was nothing new in that! Haven't women always been accused of witchcraft? Ever since the Middle Ages in Europe.

Fiela had deceived everybody by playing the model wife and stepmother. Only *The Times* took the trouble to report on the accuser, Julian, the other side of the triangle. Its version was explosive. Burning with an incestuous love for Fiela, who hadn't reciprocated, Julian had murdered his father, and out of revenge put the blame on his stepmother.

Bravo! Only a Greek tragedy can offer such a web of intrigue.

The peaceful atmosphere in the café was soon interrupted by two nutcases, ready to come to blows because of Fiela. Rosélie wisely asked for the check.

For no particular reason, she headed for the Threepenny Opera. She hadn't been back since her fruitless visit almost a month ago. Like everyone else, Mrs. Hillster had her nose in the newspapers. Going her own sweet way, she had formed her own opinion, radically different from the editorials. According to her, it was a case of legitimate defense. Fiela had discovered a terrible secret concerning Adriaan and murdered him. What secret? What can cause a wife to murder her husband?

Don't tell me it's adultery!

Rosélie got the strange impression Mrs. Hillster was giving her a shifty look and was speaking about *her*. It was as if Rosélie was discovering for the first time this frosty powdered face whose razor-thin lips dripped Revlon-red. A strange gleam danced in her mauve-colored eyes. It was as if a spitefulness had been released, up till then hidden under the smiles and polite small talk. Mrs. Hillster had launched into the tale of a husband who kept a woman in Cape Town, another in Jo'burg, a third in Bloemfontein, and a fourth in Maputo. Here he was known under such and such a name, over there under another, and elsewhere even a third. It must be said to his credit, however, that in each home he showered his many wives with equal tenderness and consideration, and their joy knew no bounds.

After all, isn't that the main point? thought Rosélie. Why try and unmask the face others are hiding from us?

Misfortune comes from knowing the truth.

Fortunately, she kept her uncalled-for thoughts to herself. Mrs. Hillster continued to condemn these women, who are blind to the facts and do not deserve to be called victims. There are certain telltale signs in a couple: the smell of perfume on a jacket lapel, a reluctance to make love, contradictions, and incoherent stories.

"Something like that could never have happened to me," she maintained. "Simon could never have pulled the wool over my eyes. I've got a sixth sense."

Rosélie felt increasingly ill at ease. She was being targeted, she was sure of it.

Mrs. Hillster finally changed the subject. She couldn't find a serious buyer for her villa and shop. Nothing was selling in Cape Town, whose reputation got worse by the day. And then people preferred the coast.

Although she felt distraught, Rosélie couldn't help noticing the presence of a young coloured sales assistant, with a mane of hair like Absalom was said to have. Beneath this ragged frieze, his face was the very picture of vice and brutality, despite a certain animal charm. A perfect contrast with the angelic features of Bishupal. Had he already left for England?

"Oh no! He sent me this friend Archie because he's ill," Mrs. Hillster replied, with a painful look. "He's been ill now for some time and refuses to see a doctor. I'm very concerned about him for he's like a son to me. He's so sensitive, so intelligent."

Stephen too maintained that Bishupal was an exceptional boy. He had given him novels and then poetry to read. Bishupal had adored Keats and the odes, especially "Ode to a Nightingale."

> *My heart aches and a drowsy numbness pains*
> *My sense, as though of hemlock I had drunk,*
> *Or emptied some dull opiate to the drains.*

Not surprising. It's the one everyone likes!

As for Rosélie, she was incapable of giving an opinion on his intellectual qualities. Whenever she was around, Bishupal's mouth opened and shut in silence like a carp's. Dido treated him like a leper and never let him inside the house. He would stand waiting for Stephen to come back in front of his office. When standing got to be too much, he would crouch on his heels like a snake charmer. Only the rattlesnake was missing.

After a while Rosélie, feeling hurt, took her leave. Mrs. Hillster used to revolve around Stephen like the earth around the sun. Now she seemed suddenly to be turning her back on him, even rising up in arms against him.

Back home, a letter was waiting for her.

Short, scribbled on cream-colored stationery from the Royal Orchid Sheraton in Johannesburg (three hundred dollars per night). Faustin informed her that, God be praised, he had finally obtained his nomination. As a result, he had to go straight to Rome to sign his contract and make urgent administrative arrangements. He had no time to come back to Cape Town to say good-bye. But he was expecting her in Washington as soon as possible.

"Don't worry. Raymond will take care of everything."

Rosélie was hurting.

Given her state of mind, she was quite convinced that this missive was a way of breaking up without him getting his hands dirtied. It never occurred to her that Faustin had perhaps so little intuition, so little consideration of who she was and what her life was like that he was sure a word or sign from him would send her running to meet him wherever he was.

So, except for Ariel, the men in her life, Salama Salama, Stephen, and now Faustin, had ditched her in one way or another without further ado. What was wrong with her to arouse such offhand behavior? She looked back on the episodes of her life she had preferred to forget. All those wounds infecting under the scab!

Salama Salama, the original wound.

Surrounded by admirers, Salama Salama had flashed the smile of a star sitting on the terrace of the Maheu café in Paris. Not only did he have the dreadlocks of Bob Marley, but his exceptional talent set him apart, dazzling his growing number of fans. He had given a long whistle of approval when Rosélie sat down at a nearby table, holding a Dalloz law manual to give her a sense of composure and not idle her time away smoking menthol cigarettes and lapping up the air on the boulevard. Her love life had been meager up till then, that we know. One or two cousins, the son of a good friend of Rose's. Few kisses, nothing but platitudes. Suddenly she found herself wanted, desired, and treasured. She hadn't heeded the warnings:

"My dear, be careful. Africa's a wicked stepmother."

"You'll end up waiting for happiness."

She had followed him to N'Dossou, where his family had welcomed her with open arms, his mother even finding that she looked like the reincarnation of her young sister, carried away by typhoid fever. Not surprising. The legend, one of those legends close family ties beget about their family tree, had it that their ancestor came from Guadeloupe. At the beginning of the eighteenth century, Sylvestre Urbain d'Amélie, a merchant from Nantes, owner of a plantation at Grippon, Petit-Bourg, and warehouses at La Pointe, together with Eusèbe, his Creole slave, born on the plantation, old enough to be his son, but in actual fact his lover—at that time people had no morals, not like today—had anchored off N'Dossou to load a cargo of precious red timber. Many a book has been written about the red timber of Brazil. But N'Dossou's was just as good. When Eusèbe got lost in the forest, Sylvestre, after weeks of fruitless searching and half crazed with grief, reluctantly gave the order to his crew to depart. He never got over Eusèbe's disappearance and died the following year clutching to his heart a locket with Eusèbe's portrait painted by Dino Russetti, the Florentine who had settled in Guadeloupe in 1704. Eusèbe, however, was not dead. He had been picked up by the Pygmies, who had taught him their music and how to hunt elephants. Unfortunately, the great trees, the lianas, the miasmas, and insects were anathema to him. Born on an island, he was a lover of water. Together with the wife they gave him, he reached the estuary of the Adzope River, where he founded a family. Ever since that day, the Urbain-Amélies—with Eusèbe the particle "de" disappeared— considered themselves apart, not quite natives, yet not quite foreigners either. They had always colluded with the colonizer whose language they practiced. The men, often hardened sailors, brought back with them girls picked up in faraway ports. Back in N'Dossou, these women mingled their customs with that of the tribe, and that's how things came to be. Thus Salama Salama's grandmother Lina, on his father's side, came from the Cape Verde islands, from a whorehouse in Mindelo. Apart from French, the Urbain-Amélies spoke Portuguese, Cantonese, which they got from Yang-Li, a Chinese great-great-grandmother, and N'Dossou's one hundred and three national languages.

Most people found Rosélie somber, withdrawn, quick to retire to her apartment when there was a visit, and not at all polyglot, since she only spoke French-French. She didn't cook, didn't do the washing, didn't iron, and especially didn't give birth. But since Salama Salama couldn't bear them criticizing her, they kept their thoughts to themselves.

Rosélie could very well have been an example of that reprehensible feminine blindness denounced by Mrs. Hillster. She had never suspected the wedding plans of a companion who for six years had laid his head beside her on the same pillow. How could she have done? Salama Salama penetrated her, made himself at home, and took his pleasure with her several times a night. He asked her opinion on everything. On the lyrics of his songs, for instance, which as a rule he wrote in French. A journalist from the BBC reproached him in no uncertain terms:

"Isn't French a colonial language?"

What is a colonial language? I speak what I am. I am what I speak. I speak therefore I am. I am therefore I speak. Et cetera.

Salama Salama's answer irritated him considerably.

"The French language belongs to me. My ancestors stole it from the whites like Prometheus stealing fire. Unfortunately, they were incapable of setting light to the French-speaking world from one end to the other."

In fact, whereas Rosélie and Stephen agreed about everything, there was nothing but points of friction between Salama Salama and Rosélie, except for the hashish they smoked together, of which Rosélie had trouble breaking the habit. First of all, he blamed her painting. It was a rival. He couldn't bear her devoting so much time to it, locked up days on end in her studio she had installed at the bottom of the compound between the washhouse and the storeroom. What's more, everyone poked fun at it. Servants fetching rice or dried fish for the meals would burst out laughing or make the sign of the cross, depending on their temperament, when they caught sight of the paintings. Second, she loathed his music, reggae music. However hard he tried to get her to listen to the undisputed master, Bob Marley, or read to her illuminating comments on the subject, she stuck to her guns. Finally, he adored children and she didn't. He begged her.

Did she want his father, the man who had produced fifteen sons and as many daughters, to think he was impotent? His younger brothers, the oldest of whom were already taking their first communion, to disrespect him?

When Rosélie, crushed as if the sky had fallen on her head, left the compound, Salama Salama's mother had wept a lot. The reincarnation of her little sister was leaving. What sacrifice would hold her back? Alemanthia, her witch doctor from Benin, advised her to kill a white heifer with three ginger-haired stars marked on its forehead.

They unearthed and sacrificed this rare animal. But Alemanthia lost face, for Rosélie never came back. After that frightful interlude at Ferbène, she had met Stephen, whom she thought would be her savior. She had been wrong about that too, since he had abandoned her to the hands of Faustin, who in turn had deserted her.

Rosélie was lost in these hardly cheering thoughts when Dido came up to inform her that Raymond was waiting for her on the patio.

Raymond, buttoned up as usual in a double-breasted business suit of a dark cloth, looked out of place, like a night bird under the sun. But that afternoon he wore a radiant smile that clashed with his funereal dress. A positive thinker, he interpreted Faustin's letter as a commitment, a promise he was bound to keep. Without wasting time, as he had been told to do, he had every intention of taking care of everything. While he settled into an armchair and spread out his leaflets, she asked him:

"What exactly does Faustin's nomination consist of?"

"I believe he is going to be in charge of the CRTA," he replied vaguely, as if he considered the question pointless.

"What's that?"

"A branch of the FAO, I think, whose director is a child-hood friend of his."

"What does CRTA mean?"

"Center for Research in Tropical Agriculture. You know that Faustin is an agronomist?"

Then he got down to basics.

"Do you want to stop off in Paris for a few days? Women always want to stop over in Paris."

Women? When Raymond talked of women, Rosélie didn't know whether she was included in the species. She was not sure she saw herself as one of those whimsical creatures with uncontrollable and inexplicable desires, prepared to spend a fortune on Fashion Fair makeup, lingerie, and perfumes.

Paris? Now, there's a city that has never taken to me, never celebrated me. Our strained relations go back a long way. To please Elie I had enrolled at the law school, a cold cavern built of freestone in the shadow of the Panthéon, where I shivered with boredom. As a result, I would sit for hours in the cafés of the Latin Quarter, smoking Gauloises like a chimney; the marijuana came later. Afterward I would walk down to the banks of the Seine to purify my lungs. I ended up making friends with a bookseller specializing in colonial photographs.

Algeria: Negro with a Fan.

New Guinea: A Head Hunter.

Ivory Coast: Missionaries and Their Choirboys.

He was the one who sold me a reproduction of a woodcut by André Thevet dated 1522: *Tupinamba Cannibal Indians at a Feast.*

I've always been fascinated by cannibals.

I also bought a photo of twenty or so Guadeloupean women landing at Ellis Island in April 1932. This talisman has followed me everywhere. Braver than me, my ancestors, all alone, without a man by their side. What America were they going to discover? Dressed in their traditional Creole costumes and madras headties, they smile gallantly at the camera.

"Do you know Washington?" Raymond asked.

Washington's the anti–New York, a city in black and white, compartmentalized, segregated, and racist. Even Stephen couldn't invent a theory to absolve it. The search for a manuscript had taken them there one weekend. On leaving the Library of Congress, they had ventured into the black neighborhood around the Capitol, where a driver had knowingly tried to knock them over. At a bus stop some youths had heckled them with obscene gestures and threatening language. In fright they had taken refuge in a white neighborhood with one of Stephen's friends, a specialist of Milton, whose wife was from Ethiopia. They had lunch surrounded by suitcases. Tired of the neighbors' snubs and the insults suffered by the children at school, the wife was preparing to go back to Addis Ababa.

Mother, tell me where I should live and where I should die.

It's true that living with Faustin, she would be spared

such misfortune. First of all, they would have a car. They would live in the wealthy African-American district, whose houses ape the Caucasians' in munificence and ostentation. The Gold Coast, they call it. They would have a chauffeur for the Mercedes, a gardener for the azaleas, and a cook for the barbecues. Faustin would never be at home, always at a meeting, a conference, or on a trip abroad. She would be buzzing with activity. She would belong to a cine club. Oh, not Euzhan Palcy again! Today we are showing *Time Regained*, a film by Raoul Ruiz.

Marcel Proust versus Joseph Zobel. That'll take some doing!

She would also belong to a book club. Nothing trivial! This week we are reading *Oran, langue morte* by Assia Djebar. Subject for discussion: women and violence.

Painting would become a hobby. Out of pure coquetry she would show her canvases to close friends, who would politely scold her: "Why did you ever stop? You could have had a brilliant career!"

Can you see me, Fiela, in that sort of life?

Yet, despite the mockery, part of her began to dream of what she would never possess. Material well-being. Self-confidence. Peace of mind.

Oh, to leave Cape Town, to leave this country ravaged by violence and disease. To start one's life all over again like making up a bed after a bad night's sleep. The frightening thing is that you can never start life over again. Unhappiness, like happiness, is a habit formed at birth and impossible to break.

Dido came out of the kitchen to sit in the sun with them.

Dido and Raymond were the best of friends. Both crazy about the same music. Both dreaming of an aseptic Africa, without garbage, vermin, or germs, where the carrier of the AIDS virus would meet the same fate as the tsetse fly. For the same reasons as Raymond, Dido was ecstatic. She had conveniently forgotten her reservations and warnings of the earlier days, elated by her friend's lucky star. In short, Dido and Raymond were like overjoyed parents who had given up hope for a daughter way past her prime. As a result, anger inside Rosélie built up, swelled, and exploded, as deadly as the atomic bomb dropped on Nagasaki.

"I have," she burst out, "no intention of following Faustin to Washington, D.C."

Raymond paid no attention to this outburst. We all know how women like to put on airs and graces and proclaim the opposite of what they think. But Dido pounced on Rosélie, like a mother scolding her daughter.

"What on earth are you talking about?"

Rosélie was not used to confronting Dido, nor anyone else for that matter. This time, however, she persisted.

"I have said it over and over again. I will not leave Stephen alone here."

Dido looked around her, stared at Raymond to call him as a witness, then thundered:

"And I will not let you sacrifice yourself for . . . for nothing."

"For nothing?" exclaimed Rosélie, appalled.

Like Fina, Dido too was betraying her, reducing her sacred duty to childishness.

"Yes, for nothing!" yelled Dido.

We can only imagine what would have happened then if Deogratias, his daughter Hosannah, his wife, Sylvaine, and Bienheureux, their newborn baby, hadn't arrived to pay Rosélie a courtesy visit, according to African custom. There is no way of predicting what irreparable words would have been exchanged. Instead of guessing what might have been, let us describe the scene that actually occurred. Bienheureux, thus named since his father read the Beatitudes every day, a lovely baby, aged four months and weighing thirteen pounds, was handed round while Rosélie, Dido, and Raymond pronounced those inane phrases babies tend to inspire.

"My God, he's so cute!"

"He looks just like his papa and maman."

"Give Auntie a smile, little man."

Instead of which, Bienheureux began to cry. Sylvaine stuffed a breast in his mouth. Bienheureux gorged himself with milk, burped, and coughed up. Sylvaine wiped his mouth. Raymond, who had raised six children, showered her with advice. Dido too. After a while Dido went back to her kitchen. Raymond took his leave. A silence set in, since Sylvaine, Deogratias, and Rosélie had nothing to say to each other. After a reasonable duration Sylvaine said they had to go. They lived in Langa. The way back in an overcrowded bus would take forever. Once the young woman and her two children had left, Deogratias went into the garage to change his day uniform for his night uniform: a pair of padded khaki pants, a thick turtleneck pullover, and a woolen bonnet pulled down to his eyes. It was still too early to take up his position beneath the traveler's tree. He leaned against the front gate, staring out at the street, greeting the other night watchmen arriving to take up their stations in the neighboring gardens. Most of them were French-speaking Africans, eating the stale bread of exile, having lost their land, their language, and their customs, and trying their hand at the harsh sonorities of a foreign idiom.

FIFTEEN

The proverb maintains: "The absent are always in the wrong." The dead, absent for eternity, haven't a chance to prove themselves right. Rosélie tossed and turned in bed. After Raymond left, she had gone into the kitchen, where Dido had calmed down. Her day now over, Dido too had changed clothes, endeavoring to resume the look of a woman of independent means. A dressmaker in Mitchell Plains, with the help of American catalogs, had made her a dark red pantsuit with wide lapels. Like Deogratias, she wore a woolen bonnet, but hers was elegantly crocheted. She was still a handsome woman who hadn't given up looking for a companion. Up till now she had been more or less faithful to the memory of her late husband. But old age, which was creeping up fast, frightened her. She had set her heart on Paul, a coloured widower whose wife, a cousin of hers, she had taken care of before she died of cancer. She was not put off by his shortness or shyness. She had high hopes and paid no attention to the judicious advice of her sisters.

"Be gentler, less sure of yourself. Men are scared of women who wear the pants."

She kissed Rosélie, then was gone, slamming the door like that of a closet where the skeletons could sleep in peace.

Dominique first of all. Then Fina. Ariel. Simone and her

husband. Amy and Caleb. Alice and Andy. Olu Ogundipe. Mrs. Hillster. Rosélie made the roll call of those who had criticized Stephen as if summoning them to a tribunal. What were they accusing him of? Of hiding something, of being a despot, an insensitive, domineering manipulator, a racist even? All these accusations that drew a picture as sketchy as a police profile led her nevertheless to call into question their entire life together.

She got up and shivered in her nightdress for the air was cold. She hurriedly slipped on some clothes, and without switching on the light, she ran down the black mouth of the stairs. Deogratias had taken up his position on the patio, flooded in light by the streetlamp opposite. Muffled up in his padded quilt, he was snoring as usual and didn't budge as she walked past, just as he hadn't budged on that fatal evening a few months earlier. She went and pressed her nose against the bars on the front gate and looked around her.

What had happened that night?

Stephen had turned the key in the lock. The gate had creaked open in the silence. He had walked down the street. Two tomcats, back arched, had scampered round his feet, meowing and chasing each other. Left and right, the houses were silent. Everything slept except for the night watchmen, wrapped up like mummies on their folding chairs, their Zulu spears within hand's reach. One of them had greeted him, while thinking to himself what a crazy idea to be out and about at such an hour.

"Good evening, boss!"

Stephen hadn't replied, which was unusual. He loved chatting to complete strangers to exercise his powers of attraction. Those who knew him admired his simplicity. In actual fact, Stephen was a child, perhaps because he hadn't had a childhood. That evening, his mind was elsewhere. He was probably thinking of his book on Yeats. He was not happy with the table of contents or his first chapter. Perhaps too he was thinking of something else. What? She would never know.

But perhaps the night watchman had not been surprised at all. Boss was used to wandering about in the middle of the night like a blood-sucking *soukouyan*. Sometimes he would go and drink a late-night beer at Ernie's. The barman knew him well, for he was out of place among the young crowd. Yes, he was always alone. No, he never spoke to anyone. He would drink his Coors, pay, and leave.

In the Van der Haaks' garden the scent of a frangipani hung heavy in the air, its fragrance accentuated by the night. Stephen had turned left onto the avenue. The storefronts were plunged in darkness, shutters lowered, neon lights extinguished. He had walked toward the lighted entrance of the Pick 'n Pay, open twenty-four hours. Seated on the sidewalk, wearing those same woolen bonnets pulled down to their eyebrows, a group of hoodlums on the lookout for mischief had watched him. A beggar, rolled up in his ragged blanket, had woken up to hold out his hand. The Pick 'n Pay was practically deserted. A few night owls were buying bottles of Coca-Cola and bags of peanuts. At this time of night, for security reasons, only one cash register was open. The blond girl in her striped overall uniform was chatting with one of the security guards, who was standing tall beside her for protection. When Rosélie approached, they turned and stared at her with an unfriendly look. She clearly discerned that fear which blacks, whatever they do, instill in whites: "Watch out for the Kaffir! What does she want?"

Yes, what did she want from them? To question them?

"Excuse me. Were you here on the night of February seventeenth? What exactly did you see?"

"Me, I know nothing about it. I was nowhere near here. At the time I was working at a Pick 'n Pay in Newlands. Nothing like here, believe me. A district of rich white folks. Private militia everywhere. Order. Discipline. No drug addicts quarreling over their magic powder. No squabbling drunkards. No homeless sleeping on the sidewalk."

Realizing she was looking ridiculous, Rosélie beat a retreat.

What had happened that night?

Two scenarios were possible.

One of the hoodlums had approached him while the others artfully encircled him. Stephen was not the sort to hand over his wallet without a fight, even if it didn't contain very much. He had put up a struggle. So they shot him. They were about to rob him when the security guards came running, brandishing their guns. It was then they had scampered off.

Or else, Lewis Sithole's version, which was slowly worming its way into her mind. Someone was waiting for him, leaning against the wall, close to the entrance of the supermarket. Someone he knew. Who had the power to drag him out on a bitterly cold night, far from his thoughts on Yeats, at seventeen minutes past midnight. They had first talked quietly together, then they had quarreled. The other person had pulled out his revolver.

She didn't know whom to turn to. Questions galloped around in her head like wooden horses on a carousel.

She walked back up Kloof Street, a black lake floating with pockets of light.

In detective stories, amateurs often play at being sleuths and pride themselves on solving the mystery. How do they go about it? They draw up a list of suspects, interrogate those who knew the victim, compare statements and photos. Through the ramblings of his mother, Rosélie had gathered that Stephen had been a typical, obedient little boy and teenager. She knew full well that beneath his quiet facade he hated Verberie and was deeply affected by the separation of his mother and father, by the impression that neither of them loved him. Some parents fight for the possession of a child. Not those two. They reached an agreement about him, the same way they did about the house on St. Nicholas Road, the furniture, and the old Vauxhall.

Reading University has kept no memory of him. No professor was struck by the promise of his future talent. A few photos of a performance of *The Seagull* show him as Konstantin Gavrilovich Treplev, nothing remarkable, effeminate like young Englishmen often are. Likewise the university at Aix-en-Provence has few memories of him. Some students recall he liked hiking and was a great nature lover. He would gather plants for his herb garden.

There was no premonition of the brilliant researcher, hotly fought over on university campuses, envied as a colleague, worshiped as a professor. Rosélie realized she would have to inquire elsewhere. Her sources would only give her the official picture, the obituaries and hagiographic articles of the *Cape Tribune.* She would have to explore the shadowy zones. She would have to discover what had excited him in London apart from the theater, once he realized the stage would never be within his reach. She was so used to admiring him that she had difficulty imagining him with Andrew, auditioning unsuccessfully among dozens of other boys and girls.

"Thank you very much. We'll write to you. Next!" the examiners would scowl.

She had no idea whom he had flirted with or whom he had desired. He seemed to emerge from the famous London fog in a sudden halo of light. She hadn't the slightest idea of what his life in N'Dossou had been like before she moved in with her two metal trunks, her canvases, and her *lenbe.* She knew that at one time he had taken in Fumio, who had left behind pictures of his mother and two sisters and the boxes of makeup he used to parody the Kabuki actors in his famous one-man show. Since then, like all rebels, Fumio had settled down and no longer did full frontals. Thanks to his father's connections, he had been appointed director of the Japanese Institute in Rabat. Stephen and he kept up a correspondence, never missing a birthday or Christmas card. Rosélie had never bothered her mind about it. Now she had to imagine what interested Stephen when he was not with her. Amateur theatricals.

Chris Nkosi.

The name seemed to loom up all of a sudden. Yet she realized that ever since her first visit to the Steve Biko High School, during the rehearsal for *A Midsummer Night's Dream,* the boy had caught her attention. His name had remained lurking in the folds of her memory, ready to emerge into broad daylight at the slightest call.

The tenth grade had been rehearsing at the Civic Center for Community Action. It was a kind of hangar where Arté had organized a book fair selling hundreds of copies of *Harry Potter and the Sorcerer's Stone*, as well as a hip-hop festival. The teenagers were laboriously stumbling over Shakespeare's lines. Except for Chris Nkosi, alias Puck, who sailed over his text, scaling new heights:

> *Through the forest have I gone,*
> *But Athenian found I none,*
> *On whose eyes I might approve*
> *This flower's force in stirring love.*

He was handsome and arrogant, probably from receiving constant compliments. He wore his dreadlocks like a wig. She bitterly regretted not having asked Olu for his address. The very next morning she would go back to the school to get some answers out of him.

Once she had made this decision, a sense of serenity enfolded her, like a sick person who has long hesitated, then resigned herself to undergo an operation. Either she will die. Or her life will be spared. In either case, the suffering will stop.

She decided to go home.

The last noisy groups of customers were leaving Ernie's and the remaining few restaurants still open. This district of Cape Town used to be out of bounds to blacks. In order to have access you needed a pass. Judging by the looks that bored into her, her presence was still out of place and a threat even today. If they had guns, these young people would use them. In all impunity. Justice would acquit them like it acquitted the four police officers who assassinated Amadou Diallo in New York. Legitimate defense. A black man is always guilty.

But of what?

Of being black, of course!

Precisely, a group was standing at a street corner.

She became scared, turned her back, and almost began to run; then got hold of herself and walked back up the street. When she arrived level with them, she confronted them. A crowd of youngsters, almost teenagers. Squeezed into leather jackets. The boys wore their hair in a crew cut; the girls in a ponytail. Harmless. Their minds were on other things. The boys thinking how best to persuade the girls to come back to their place, and the girls wondering if it was still worth hanging on to what remained of their virginity.

As Stephen used to lament, once again she was making a song and dance about nothing.

She reached Faure Street.

She resolutely pushed open the door to Stephen's study. This was the second time she had entered since he died. While he was alive, she hadn't gone in very much either. Neither had Dido, who, with broom and vacuum cleaner, complained bitterly that she was kept out. She flipped the switch and the light flooded the paintings, the books packed against the walls, the sagging armchair, the heavy desk and its disparate ornaments: a Tiffany lamp, a miniature globe, and a stone paperweight from Mbégou. It was as if the room, motionless and silent, were waiting for its owner to return. As if Stephen's restless personality were still palpitating. It was here he worked for hours on end amid a din of jazz turned up full volume—which always amazed Rosélie—where he read and watched his beloved opera videos. Rosélie had always felt that this part of his life rejected her. That she was not welcome. The attention diverted to her wretched self distracted him from higher preoccupations. She had none of the qualities to rival James Joyce, Seamus Heaney, or Synge. For the very first time she wondered what other interests, perhaps even less noble, absorbed him.

You don't improvise being a voyeur, however. It's not like an old pair of jeans you slip on whenever you want to. It has to be ingrained.

She was no sooner inside than a deep malaise gripped her. It seemed she was committing an indiscretion. That Stephen would come in at any minute and ask her, amused: "What are you looking for?"

Yes, what was she looking for?

An icy cape settled around her shoulders. She was ashamed of herself. She was no better than a grave robber. She knew Stephen threw his keys into a Mexican pot on the window ledge. But when she was at the point of opening the drawers, she lost her nerve. The bunch of keys slipped from her hands and rolled onto the carpet. She quickly switched off the light and dashed outside.

She sat for a moment in the garden. Not a sound. In the distance a few cars rattled up the avenue. She went back up to the haven of her bedroom, put on her nightdress again, and went back to bed. The bed was cold. Cold and empty. She thought of Faustin and burst into tears, not knowing whether she missed him or Stephen more.

Rosélie seldom cried. Tears are a luxury that only children and the spoiled can afford. They know that a sympathetic hand is always there to dry them. She hadn't cried when Salama Salama cheated on her. She hadn't cried when she stood in front of her mother's body, eyelids finally closed, guarded by candles at the bottom of Doratour the undertaker's monstrous casket. She hadn't cried when Stephen died.

There hadn't been a wake. Rough handled back from the morgue midmorning by mindless coffin bearers, the heavy oak casket had been laid to rest in the middle of the living room, gradually smothered in wreaths from the university, schools, neighbors, and anonymous sympathizers. Around noon, they no longer knew where to put them. They were piled up in scented heaps just about anywhere. Emotions were running high in the rooms on the ground floor and in the garden, where people—mostly whites, but also some blacks—students, musicians, and artists who had known and loved Stephen, were praying side by side.

Nkosi Sikelei Afrika.

Yes God, bless this country. Forgive it the terrible things that go on here!

The head of the funeral cortege reached the church while the end of it was still filing past the Mount Nelson Hotel. Many of the mourners remained outside in front of the church before setting off for the cemetery.

There was a crowd too for Rose's funeral. But it was different in her case. With its merciful scythe death had cut short the years of suffering and exclusion. As for Stephen, it had been shockingly unjust, striking down a man, still young in years, talented and beloved by all. On each occasion, Rosélie walked behind the coffin with a mechanical stride, not a tear in her eye and a face so bone dry it was as if she had no feelings. Consequently, nobody took pity on her.

That night, however, she cried. With tears that welled up from a never-ending source deep within her. It was like the rain on certain days during the rainy season when it begins in the predawn hours, slows down in the evening only to pour even harder in the darkness stretching to infinity, and continues until morning. The rivers then overflow their bed and the whole island smells of mud and mustiness. This constant patter of rain finally sent her to sleep with a dream. Or rather a succession of dreams, nightmares in fact, one after the other, exterior day, exterior night, like sequences in a film without words or music.

It was daylight. Was she in Guadeloupe? Or in Cape Town? The crowd was gone. The cemetery was empty. The raging sun was heating the great steel plate of the ocean. At intervals, birds of prey swooped out of the sky onto their quarry, visible only to them through the molten metal. She was looking for a grave. Her mother's? Stephen's? But however much she walked up and down the paths, turning right, then left, she couldn't find it. Suddenly, everything around her disappeared. She was lost in a desert of sand and dunes. Nothing but dunes. Nothing but sand. Nothing but sand. Nothing but dunes. Overhead, the calotte of sky was shrinking and the raving maniac in its middle continued to pound even harder.

It was night. She was lost in a forest as dense as N'Dossou's. Not a single hut. Only tree trunks, eaten by moss and epiphytes, their branches smothered in moving creepers like the arms of a giant. Suddenly, the trunks got closer and closer. They squeezed and crushed her while the boa vines wrapped themselves around her body.

It was daylight. The footpath wound through the grass, which promptly parted in front of her. Nature reigned supreme, everything in its place. The sun way up above, pouring down its usual dose of molten lead. The cottony white clouds, stuck to the blue by the heat. On the horizon, the rigid, triangular-shaped mountains. Suddenly the path turned at a right angle. A farm stood out against a quadrilateral of gnarled vines, planted at regular intervals like crosses. Closer to her was a cornfield. A woman was waiting, angular in her black dress, leaning against the tin siding of the main building. When Rosélie walked up, the woman turned her head and Rosélie recognized her. It was Fiela!

Fiela was wearing an open-neck blouse, as if she were going to the guillotine. Her tiny slit eyes and her face, with its triangular-shaped cheekbones, betrayed no sign of fright. No sign of remorse either. In actual fact, no feeling. It was one of those impenetrable faces that disconcert ordinary people. Rosélie thought she was seeing her twin sister, separated from her at birth and found again fifty years later, like in a bad film.

She went up to her and murmured:

"Why did you do it?"

Fiela stared at her and said reproachfully:

"You're asking *me*? You're asking *me*?"

The sounds that came out of her mouth were guttural, very low, and startling like those of an instrument out of tune.

"I did it for you! For you!"

Thereupon Rosélie woke up, soaked in sweat, her night-dress stuck to her back like in one of her childhood fevers.

The moon shamelessly displayed her belly of a pregnant woman.

SIXTEEN

When she showed up again in his office, Olu Ogundipe had that worried look of someone who has sighted a hurricane looming on the horizon. Yet Rosélie had nothing threatening about her. Instead she was rather shattered and slumped into an armchair. Around her on the walls, all of Olu's beloved heroes stared down at her fixedly. Always the same reproach. What had *she* done for the Race?

"What have you come to give me this time?" Olu said mockingly, not at all hostile. "Another computer?"

She didn't answer, tortured by a sudden urge to burst into tears. He was quick to see it and took an even softer stand.

"I was about to leave. My wife isn't too well, it's her allergies, I have to go and pick up my older children from school. Would you like to come with me? We can have tea at my place."

She hesitated, and once again he poked fun at her.

"You're a pretty woman. But this isn't a trap. We know how to behave. Do we frighten you?"

Telling him that she hadn't always been the mistress of a white man and that her first partner had been an African would serve no purpose. The stereotypes about Antillean women die hard. They are supposed to hate and despise Black Skins. Rosélie hadn't the energy to put up a fight and she let him talk away.

"I know the Caribbean. I lived for three years in Kingston and came up against all sorts of humiliations. I've nothing against my in-laws. Admirable people. But Cheryl's family and friends accused her of soiling her sheets with a nigger, black like me. If we ourselves don't like our color, how can we blame the whites for not liking it?"

All this time he was signing a dozen letters with a majestic flourish.

They went out and crossed the deserted recreation yards that echoed with students' voices from every classroom, chanting lessons and singing a cappella. The sounds merged and composed an unexpected and appealing polyphony.

Olu got onto his favorite subject of conversation: the future of South Africa.

"You'd think Césaire had this country in mind when he wrote *The Tragedy of King Christophe*. Do you remember? 'So here we are at the bottom of the ditch! The very bottom of the ditch! I'm talking of a spectacular ascent!' I think it's the most wonderful piece of theater. What do you think?"

Rosélie had only read *Notebook of a Return to My Native Land* by Césaire, which Salama Salama recited by heart. He dreamed of putting it to rap, cleverly beating out the lines:

"Get lost I said you cop face, you pig face, get lost, I hate the flunkies of order and the cockchafers of hope. Go away bad grigri, bedbug of a monklet."

In the end, the fear of sacrilege stopped him.

Without being disheartened by so much ignorance, Olu continued.

"Give us a few more years and we'll be the leaders of Africa! I'm not talking only in economic terms, gross national product, gross domestic product, but in terms of culture."

Art and culture are necessary compensations for the misfortune of our lives. (Once again.)

They reached the car. The ageless Nissan uttered a series of coughs and started up. The cheerful aspect of the school, a Catholic day school, made it look out of place in the general landscape. Olu's older children turned out to be three kids of an unexpected coffee color ranging from nine to twelve years. They spontaneously held up their cheeks for Rosélie to kiss and she was filled with emotion by such a gesture. It was as if they, the children, absolved her and were giving her back the place the adults had excluded her from.

Olu lived in Esperanza, a district still under construction on the outskirts of Cape Town. Neither township nor residential suburb. Its inhabitants belonged to the laboring middle class trying to emerge from the ashes of apartheid. His villa, like all the others, was surrounded by a concentration camp–type wall, topped by thick rows of barbed wire. And behind, you could hear the barking of hounds, straining furiously on their chains.

"Gangs operate around here," he explained. "Loafers and good-for-nothings who don't want to do a day's work. Let's not close our eyes, there's a lot to be done. I'll quote once more *The Tragedy of King Christophe*: We are 'schoolteachers brandishing a ruler in the face of a nation of dunces!' "

A nation of dunces? Did Césaire say that? Not a very nice remark!

Three other small boys, again coffee colored, ranging this time from four to six years, were playing in a patch of garden. They broke off to hurl themselves on their father with Sioux-like yells, then, in a charming ensemble, held up their warm cheeks for Rosélie, who, this time, almost burst into tears. The living room looked like Olu's office, but more chaotic. The leather sofa and three armchairs were streaked with scratch marks, the Moroccan rug lay crooked. The same dusty photos. In their frames the great men, now dust to dust, struck a sorry pose. Okay, they left behind their books. But who reads them? What is their legacy?

Nobody reads anymore. Everyone watches American sitcoms on television.

My favorite: *Sex and the City.*

Olu was proud of a set of snapshots placed on top of the inevitable piano in petty bourgeois interiors, between the inevitable bunch of artificial flowers.

"You see," he said, priding himself, "that's Césaire and me at Saint-Pierre in Martinique. This is Césaire and Cheryl. He liked her a lot. And here we are all three of us, Césaire, Cheryl, and me, at Le Diamant. Behind us the famous rock. Do you know Martinique?"

Rosélie shook her head. In the Caribbean she only knew Kingston, Jamaica, where she had gone with Salama Salama to a reggae festival. She didn't remember much about this paradise turned hell on earth under the combined effects of crack and ganja. They had been advised to stay in their suite at the Sheraton because of the violence. She had lived in a cloud of smoke and only went out to lie by the pool in the shape of a peanut. When Salama Salama wasn't around, a barman from the Dominican Republic served her *trujillos,* an explosive mixture of rum, lemon, cane syrup, and tomato juice with a dash of Marie Brizard, while leering at her breasts. According to Salama Salama, his concert, which she hadn't attended, had been a triumph.

"I've been to Trinidad, Montserrat, Antigua, and Barbados," he bragged again. "Haiti is my favorite island. The most African, the only one of its kind, you could say. That's where I really felt at home. You know what the Haitians call a man, whatever his color? A Nègre. The day will come when Noirisme, that theory they've so distorted, will be rehabilitated."

Then he disappeared to look after his wife, leaving Rosélie faced with a lukewarm glass of Lipton teabags served up by a domestic in none-too-clean overalls. Large families live in an atmosphere of disorder created by the children—toys lying about on the rugs, teatime remains left on the table, and a constant noise of squabbling, tears, and cries, things that stab at the heart of the lonely. Sitting in this unattractive room where the windows covered by a grid of solid bars let in little light, Rosélie had never felt so vulnerable. She was reminded of the tribe she had grown up in, on days spent at the beach with aunts, uncles, and cousins. It required half a dozen cars to transport everyone, dozens of hampers to carry all the food, and at least three iceboxes for the drinks. Rose, of course, didn't accompany them. No question of undressing in public ever since a little nephew had compared her in a fit of laughter to Bibendum, the Michelin Man. But Elie was there, trim and muscular, swimming agilely in his striped swimming trunks.

What was she doing in Cape Town among people with whom she had nothing in common? Their language seared her tongue. The taste of their cooking insulted her palate. Their music was no music to her ears. Everything was foreign to her. Suddenly, she couldn't understand herself. Her faithfulness to Stephen's memory and her intention to remain at his side seemed absurd. Mrs. Hillster was right: "The dead are always alone."

After a while, Olu reappeared and announced:

"Cheryl would like you to stay for dinner."

Rosélie refused straightaway. She didn't want to intrude. She just wanted Chris Nkosi's address. A mask of hostility immediately covered Olu's face.

"Why? What do you want to know?" he asked.

Rosélie hesitated. What *did* she want to know?

"He was a good, hardworking boy," Olu continued. "Quiet and obedient, until the honorable doctor, your husband, came and filled his head with stupid and dangerous ideas about the theater. Afterward, he liked to think himself as an *artist*. We didn't know what to do with him. He almost failed his exams. He wanted to leave the country. Go to London. Did he have any money? Was he forgetting his color? He'd become a filthy immigrant, parked in a slum, the prey of skinheads. Who knows if he wouldn't end up in jail? Or else convert to Islam and become a terrorist."

It was obviously a joke. Rosélie gave a faint smile.

"It was in England I met Cheryl," he continued. "That's where we got married. I know what I'm talking about. What city is more racist than London? Its reputation as a multicultural paradise is an invention of intellectuals like Salman Rushdie, who, besides, emigrated to the United States."

"I'd like to have a talk with Chris Nkosi," pleaded Rosélie, who, despite the meandering conversation, had not forgotten the purpose of her visit.

"Talk about what?" he shouted angrily. "Leave him alone, for goodness' sake! He's deserved it."

A worried look flared up at the back of his eyes. But she looked so unhappy that he sighed, went into his study, and came out grudgingly brandishing a piece of paper.

Chris Nkosi,
Govan Mbeki Primary School,
116, Govan Mbeki Street,
Hermanus, CO

"His wife's pregnant," he announced as if it were something important. "By this time, she might have given birth."

Thereupon he dived back into his study. In short, if for Olu, Stephen's bad influence boiled down to encouraging Chris, then it wasn't anything very serious. In N'Dossou, a class of twelfth-graders had made a name for themselves performing brilliantly *The Importance of Being Earnest* on the occasion of the twenty-third birthday of the president's fifth wife. (He had repudiated the first three. The fourth, who had opened a center for handicapped children and a maternity clinic, died in childbirth and was christened the African Evita Perón, the Holy Mother of the Nation. Way out in the bush, a thousand workers labored on the construction of a basilica in her honor that was to rival St. Peter's and Yamassoukro's in Côte d'Ivoire.) Some jealous folk had criticized this Westerner, this Stephen Stewart, in *L'Unité,* the single party's single rag. In their opinion, staging *The Importance of Being Earnest* was not along the lines of Authenticity, but rather those of Alienation. Rosélie felt oddly reassured, without, however, admitting what she had feared.

She was deep in these troubling thoughts when Cheryl Ogundipe, draped in a black kimono and wearing a somewhat doleful expression, emerged from her bedroom.

O Love, you are a mischief maker. You're rightly depicted as a blind god. You pounce without distinction on your prey and light the fires of passion.

Looking at Cheryl, even the keen eye of a Caribbean, apt at distinguishing the most subtle shades of color, would have hesitated. You could have mistaken her for a Scandinavian, given her fawn-colored torsade, her eyes the color of seawater, and her Cleopatra nose. She had a face studded with freckles. As if she had looked at the boiling sun of her native island through a sieve.

Rosélie reproached herself for being so surprised. Such contradictions are frequent. The brain, the heart, and sex, each goes its own way. Olu's brain had followed the path of black activism. His heart and sex had led him into the trap of a mixed marriage. For Cheryl was the daughter of a white Jamaican Creole, descended from planters who had lost all their possessions, and an Irish mother whose family had never had any.

Outside the Caribbean, islands and continents drift to and fro. Borders lose their meaning. Differences become blurred. Languages no longer matter. Guadeloupe, Martinique, Haiti, Jamaica, and Cuba fit into one another like pieces of a jigsaw puzzle finally put together again. Immediately the conversation between these two Caribbean women took on an intimate tone.

"Olu says you don't want to go home to Guadeloupe?" Cheryl inquired.

She too said "go home." Go home to the island like going back into your mother's womb. The unfortunate part is that once you're expelled you can never go back. Go back and curl up. Nobody has ever seen a newborn baby turn back into a fetus. The umbilical cord is cut. The placenta buried. We have to walk bent double, but walk even so till the end of life.

"In some respect I can understand you. I swore I would never set foot again in Jamaica. When I was little I suffered agony. Because of our color, my brothers, my sisters, and me, the "guava whites" as you say in Guadeloupe, we were excluded. There was no place for us in the country of the Maroons. Twenty years later I return with a black husband. They find him too black. They make fun of his accent. They call him "alien." But you can't be serious about staying here. However much I adored Nigeria—we lived in Ibadan, I buried my firstborn and gave birth to two of my sons there, then there was the vitality, the music, and exuberance—this place makes me sick. It's as if a shroud is covering it and underneath there is nothing but dead bodies. What's more, if things go on as they are, AIDS will kill off all the blacks and the epidemic will have succeeded where the Afrikaners failed. That's what causes all my allergies. It's psychosomatic. Unfortunately, Olu will stay here until we're both dead. He's waiting. He's hoping, day after day, for a nomination."

Him too! Oh, these nominations, nominations for what, nominations for where, they are the aspiration of those whom revolutions and regime changes have passed by.

They're as slippery as an eel. Lucky are those who can catch one.

Two of the youngest children came in crying the never-ending tears of childhood. Cheryl patiently calmed them down and sent them back to their games.

"Yes, I had a daughter once, the first and only one," she continued. "I carried her for eleven months. She clung to me, she didn't want to let go. When finally the doctors extricated her from my womb with their forceps, she was dead. I too thought I was going to die. Ever since, I've had only boys. Why haven't you had any children? It's children, and children alone, who can brighten up our sad lives."

Did I brighten up my parents' lives? Decidedly not.

"Didn't you want to have children?" Cheryl insisted.

It's much too long a story. Let's just say that first of all I didn't want to be a mother. Then motherhood didn't want me when perhaps I wanted it. Sometimes, I confess, I've dreamed of a son who would be both brother and lover. But I didn't come here to talk about myself.

"Do you know Chris Nkosi?"

"Perhaps," Cheryl replied with a shrug of the shoulders. "As if we don't have enough on our hands with our own children, Olu takes care of all sorts of young people. He runs I don't know how many associations. Boys and girls come and go at all hours of the day, sleeping, eating, and drinking. One of them, a handicapped teenager, stayed here for over a year. Olu stood up for him. Apparently his family thought he brought bad luck and his own mother wanted to kill him. In the end, I lose interest."

The somewhat frugal dinner that followed was filled with

babbling, while ketchup and glasses of Coca-Cola spilled over the tablecloth, fortunately made of plastic. Cheryl reigned over everything with a gentleness that reminded Rosélie of Amy and Cousin Altagras. Some women make the decision to be a mother, nothing else, and stick to it. They close their ears to all the sirens of so-called success.

In the meantime, Olu carried on spouting vacuously.

Once the dinner was over and they had drunk the lemongrass tea, Cheryl and Rosélie promised to see each other again. A promise they would probably not keep, given the way their lives went in opposite directions. Olu offered to drive Rosélie back to Faure Street if she accepted to stop by the church of St. John the Divine in Guguletu, where he ran a choir on behalf of the unflagging Arte. As long as the mouth is filled with songs to the glory of God, it is not smoking marijuana!

In spite of its grandiose name, the church of St. John the Divine was a modest building of clay and straw. Inside there were rows of rough wooden benches. A poorly decorated high altar. It was revered throughout the country because the funerals of a number of ANC members assassinated by the police had been held there. It was from his humble pulpit that bishop Koos Modupe, as feisty as Desmond Tutu, even though he didn't win the Nobel Prize—you know what I think about prizes—had given his famous sermon, shamelessly plagiarizing Martin Luther King, Jr.'s "I have a dream."

All the Holy Joes look alike. At the back of the main nave, two nuns, as skinny as rakes, their nonexistent breasts flattened further by their navy blue serge wimples, kept thirty or so boys and girls at arm's length, while a third, who was obese, beat out the rhythm perched on a platform. An invisible fourth was playing the organ way up in the rafters.

The choir was splendid.

From the throats of these gangly, ill-dressed teenagers, marred by malnutrition and deprivation, came celestial voices, the mystery of the language adding to the poetic power of the chant. Rosélie, who hadn't set foot inside a church since Stephen's funeral, knelt down, reliving the wonders of her childhood: Midnight Mass, Easter, and the Crowning of the Virgin Mary, all those ceremonies whose magic memory occasionally haunted her. She would have liked to lose herself in prayer like Rose, like the women in her family. She would have asked God for strength and courage in the trial she knew was looming like a huge black cloud over her head.

If the guidebooks call Hermanus the "whale capital" of South Africa, it is with good reason. Countless tourists can prove it. Standing in the right place on the cliffs, they have sighted with their own two eyes the humps of these beloved mammals piercing the metallic surface of the ocean. Many of them too have seen with their own two eyes whales, pregnant and heavier still, hastening toward the shore to deliver the fruit hidden in their swollen flanks. Sometimes they die before reaching the sheltered bays and their corpses float on the ocean waters like gigantic rubbery balloons. There is even a whale crier in Hermanus, dressed like a lighthouse keeper, who struts around in season with a loudspeaker through which he yells the latest sightings.

Hermanus lies seventy miles east of Cape Town. It takes

about ninety minutes along the N2. But Papa Koumbaya insisted on driving the scenic route through Gordon's Bay to show Rosélie the splendid views. Add to that the way he crept along, and you can understand why it took three hours to drive a relatively short distance. Then they crawled along streets uniformly lined with souvenir shops and fish restaurants, congested with cars, buses, and pedestrians. In short, the morning was almost over when the Thunderbird drove into the black township. Finally it stopped in front of the Govan Mbeki School, even more forbidding in appearance than the Steve Biko High School. Behind a wall topped with broken glass and the inevitable rows of barbed wire, a rectangle of yellow prefabricated buildings lined a recreation yard, as bare as a monkey's behind. In a stifling room a young woman was typing on a typewriter that would have fetched a fortune in an antique shop. She did not even trouble to look up with her answer.

"Chris? He's teaching. Come back at noon."

It was half past eleven. Rosélie went back to the sidewalk and agreed to meet Papa Koumbaya later on in the center of town in front of the Paradise Ice Cream Parlor.

The black township of Hermanus was a jumble of small houses, shacks, and huts built from bits of corrugated iron, wooden planks, bunches of straw, wattle, dried mud and bricks, everything the ingenuity of misfortune can scrape together. Here, like in Khayelitsha, there was not a single flower, bush, or tree. A bare, reddish earth. As if Nature balks at growing anything green around shacks. Rosélie didn't dare venture far from the school. What sort of a welcome would she get if she explored these alleyways? She was so used to hostility she imagined the inhabitants would come out on their doorsteps, yelling at her to go home, hurling insults, even stones. But didn't she look like an intruder, even a spy, standing there in front of this walled enclosure?

After some time that seemed an eternity to Rosélie, the students filed out in a disciplined, orderly fashion, whereas boys and girls the world over jump for joy, whoop, and let off steam once school is out. The teachers followed somberly, carrying their briefcases. The same story of pitiful wages, poor housing, and no future was written all over their faces, obvious to anyone who knew how to read. Chris Nkosi looked younger, less handsome, and thinner in his crumpled, shabby clothes. He had shaved his dreadlocks, and his face, now exposed, appeared morose and unsmiling. Nothing like the conceited, confident Puck she remembered leaping over the stage. Before she had even made a move, he had recognized her and made straight for her.

"You? What are you doing here?" he asked savagely.

"I came to see you," she stammered.

"To see me? Why?" he asked, just as infuriated.

She didn't reply, stifled by his ferociousness. He grabbed her roughly by the arm and dragged her away.

"We can't stay here. Everyone's looking at us. Let's go to my place."

They set off into a maze of alleyways. As they delved deeper into this poverty, it was the cleanliness that was so amazing. For we always associate poverty with filth. Here, there wasn't a single garbage heap. Not one animal dropping. Not a single piece of litter on what served as a sidewalk. Chris walked so fast, without any consideration for her, that she was out of breath, running like a child to catch up with him. Finally they arrived in front of two shacks separated by a narrow passage that led to a kind of tenant's yard, also kept meticulously clean. The ground was covered with a mixture of gravel and white sand. Kitchen utensils were drying in the open. Dazzling lines of ragged washing were waving in the breeze. Chris pushed open a door into a living room that was about as dark and sparsely furnished as you get, and shouted:

"Brenda!"

A very young woman appeared, almost a teenager, in her last stages of pregnancy, shuffling along with a huge belly and heavy legs. He hurled a few words at her in their language and she turned and headed for the door like a frightened animal, without a glance at Rosélie.

"What have you come for?" he asked again.

Feeling weak, she collapsed into the only armchair and tried to regain her calm.

"I've come to give you Stephen's computer."

He frowned as if he had heard a bad joke.

"What do you expect me to do with a computer? We don't even have electricity in the district. They've been promising it for over a year. But we're still waiting for it."

She couldn't find anything to say.

"We're in South Africa here, you know," he sneered. "Not in America."

"I'm not American," she protested. "I'm from Guadeloupe. A country poorer than yours."

Was she hoping to move him? He gestured in a way that signified he didn't care whether she came from Mars, then repeated:

"What are you here for? What do you want from me?"

She didn't know what to say. She could no longer understand why she was here.

"Your uncle told me you quarreled with Stephen," she stammered.

"And so what?" he asked roughly.

Discouraged, she got up. This conversation was getting them nowhere. She headed for the door, mumbling an apology for having disturbed him for no reason, when he called out to her.

"You've probably just realized that your Stephen was a bastard, haven't you? Not at all the liberal, role model of a professor, benefactor of the young, whom everyone adored. A bastard!"

She turned round to face him, and with the determination of someone who wants to know, she quietly asked:

"Why are you saying that? What did he do to you?"

"Me?" he repeated.

There was silence. Suddenly he began to yell. He was not that far removed from the disproportionate tantrums of childhood. With a distorted face, he became unrecognizable.

"He was a liar and a manipulator. He promised me the world. That he'd get me a scholarship to study in London. He said he had connections at the Royal Academy of Dramatic Art. I'd become an actor. I'd be another Paul Robeson. Better than Laurence Fishburne. I believed him. I believed him. Whereas, in actual fact . . ."

He collapsed onto the table, whimpering like a baby. She went over and placed a hand on his shoulder. He started.

"Don't touch me!"

He sobbed for a long time while she stood motionless behind his back. He finally got hold of himself and methodically wiped his eyes, his cheeks, and his entire face. Then he stood up, jostling her almost, and coldly declared:

"I didn't kill him, if that's what you want to know. Besides, the police have already questioned me. At the time of his death I was in Hermanus, at Tanikazi's, a neighborhood bar, playing darts. Twenty people can testify to the fact. Then I went home. Brenda and I made love. She can testify to that too."

He stared at her spitefully.

"Someone else had the courage to do it, someone about whom he cared fuck-all like me. If I knew his name I'd give him a medal, a medal for doing good."

"If you hate him so much," she asked, amazed she could keep her calm in spite of these provocations, "why did you cry at his funeral?"

"Why?"

He looked around him, distraught, started to cry again, this time silently, and his distress moved her more than his rage. After a while he stammered:

"I was remembering the time when . . ."

"What?"

She had screamed. It was too painful, she now had proof, she was not the only one Stephen belonged to. Others possessed images and memories she could not share. Without answering, he wiped his face again in the same methodical way. She stood just a few steps away, close enough to touch him, breathing in his smell, a pleasant smell of cheap eau de cologne and tobacco. He stared at her with dark, piercing eyes through a forest of eyelashes curled from his tears. He looked so young. He could have been her nephew. Or rather the son Salama Salama so persistently demanded, the son she at times had wanted. A wave of pity tinged with tenderness welled up inside her and surged toward him.

This truce made her grow bolder, and very quietly she ventured:

"What exactly was there between you two?"

He fluttered his eyelids like someone aroused from his sleep.

"What was there between us two?" he repeated. "What do you mean?"

She was already frightened and ashamed of her question. He looked at her again.

"What do you think there was between us?" he said in a childish tone of voice.

He laughed stupidly.

"You're crazy! There was nothing between us. I adored him because he was my teacher. He taught me everything."

Wasn't that what she wanted to hear? Without insisting further, she walked out.

Brenda seemed to be waiting for her in the yard. With a smile she motioned to her to come over. Rosélie had trouble understanding. But Brenda insisted. Surprised, Rosélie obeyed and followed her into a room. A narrow shop. A girl was standing behind the counter leafing through an old illustrated magazine. Just about everywhere bunches of flowers were heaped on the ground, in front of the door, on tables, shelves, and window ledges, as round as suns, as rigid as ginger lilies, cut out from recycled cans of Ovomaltine, Nestlé's condensed milk, Lazzarro coffee, Mozart cocoa, Del Monte tomato paste, Baci di Dama biscuits, Gustoro olive oil, and drums of motor

oil, gas, and paraffin. The effect was stupefying. The humble
room had become a petrified magic garden. The old dream
of alchemists seemed to have come true. A hand had trans-
muted base matter and changed it into gold.

"Madam, buy?" Brenda articulated with difficulty.

Worried, quite rightly, at not being understood, she immediately forced a bunch into Rosélie's hands.

"Did you make these?" Rosélie asked.

Brenda nodded and proudly handed her a business card
that looked like the ones she had had printed for herself.

> *On your visit to Hermanus,*
> *Don't miss Brenda's Garden*
> *No. 17. Lane 3. Alley A.*

So she's an artist too. In her fashion. Wasn't she teaching
her a lesson? A lesson of courage. Her flowers were born in
the heart of the ghetto, in the midst of poverty, at the heart
of life's ugliness. Filled with admiration, Rosélie looked at
her. Despite her drawn features, covered with the heavy mask
of pregnancy, she was pretty. If it hadn't been for her belly,
you would have mistaken her for a small boy. The inevitable
shaved head. The high cheekbones. A slightly curled upper
lip revealing pearly-white teeth. At the end of her slender
arms, her hands were surprisingly strong, with nimble fingers. Hands made to deliver beauty under any circumstance.
If only Rosélie could have communicated with her instead of
being content with smiles and superficial gestures. She had
the feeling they were standing on either side of a river or on
a harbor wharf watching a ship leave, separated by the inex-

orable space of the ocean. Just in case, she scribbled down her address and telephone number and explained that she too was a painter. If Brenda came to Cape Town, would she come and see her studio? Did she understand what she was saying? She nodded reassuringly and mumbled a few incomprehensible phrases. Then, with the graceful simplicity of a child, she kissed her. Rosélie was expecting anything but that. What did that kiss mean? Was it a customary gesture of politeness, the way Olu's children had kissed her? It couldn't possibly be a symbol? The symbol of her reintegration!

When she emerged from the yard, a bus crowded with tourists was bumping down the lane. AFRICULTURAL TOURS was painted in gigantic letters on its side. Them again! It was their latest invention. The Ministry of Tourism had understood that what the privileged from the North want when they travel to Southern shores does not boil down to sun, sea, and safaris, guaranteed to include zebras and giraffes. As for the lions, they're asleep. Can't you see them over there? They also need thrills and chills, a new version of *panem et circenses,* a gut-wrenching retrospective scare.

Look, ladies and gentlemen, take a good look! Yes, you can take pictures with your digital cameras. It was on this exact spot that ten little niggers were shot during one of the ghetto's most violent revolts. Their blood has irrigated the soil that has nurtured these wonderful flowers Brenda is giving you today.

Brenda's Garden.

There was something in it for everybody. Brenda managed to make ends meet. The tourists satisfied their conscience and their curiosity.

SEVENTEEN

Flowers! Rosélie's house was overflowing with them. Roses of every color. Gladioli. Irises. Arum lilies, anthuriums, and birds-of-paradise. An unexpected branch of mauve cineraria gave a pastoral touch. They must have cost a fortune. Delivered that morning by Interflora, they gave the room a slightly suffocating, formal atmosphere, reminiscent of Stephen's funeral. They came with a message. Faustin informed her he was leaving for six months to supervise a tea-growing experiment in Indonesia. As a result, his move to Washington had been postponed.

What a lot of trouble he was going to! She had already understood.

In spite of these bland thoughts, her heart was in pieces. She went into the kitchen, where Dido was holding a mirror and putting the finishing touches on her makeup. While dabbing her cheeks with a bisque-colored powder, she glanced at Rosélie.

"Come with me," she proposed, seeing her expression. "It'll do you good."

Rosélie had good reason to distrust Dido's propositions. But anything was better than staying on her own on such an evening.

"Where are you going?" she asked.

"To Hildebrand's wedding, Emma's little sister," Dido

replied, now thickly layering her eyelids with mauve. "Besides, you were invited, but you've forgotten."

They took the bus, packed as usual. Any other crowd would have had a quiet laugh at this tall coloured woman, daubed like a carnival puppet with her heavy, showy jewels. But not this one. People got on, got off, stood up, sat down, silent and glum, without even turning their heads. Even the children, obediently holding their mother's hand and looking like miniature adults, already had a funereal expression.

The wedding reception was being held in the section III village hall, the residential area of Mitchell Plains, the one modeled closest to a white district. In spite of its barbed wire, it was almost pleasant, with streets lined with leafy parasol trees. The hall had a rather welcoming aspect. At the entrance, hefty private security guards rigorously checked identity cards. It was not unusual for criminals to mix brazenly with the guests and rob them at gunpoint as the night wore on. The previous week, in the very middle of the Holiday Inn at Rondebosch, a white middle-class suburb, the wedding guests had been robbed, the women stripped of their jewelry and the men their wallets. A hothead who had tried to intervene had been shot dead in cold blood in front of everyone.

The wedding couple had gone to great lengths. The rotunda that could accommodate five hundred people had been repainted. Bunches of pink and white lilies bloomed in vases and amphoras. Multicolored lights twinkled beside Chinese lanterns. The buffet table, presided over by liveried waiters, hired for the occasion from Pepper and Vanilla, Cape Town's most famous white caterer, was awash with food: piles of fruit, mangoes, papayas, grapes, mountains of cakes, salads, slices of avocado, *gambas* as big as your forearm, cuts of fresh and smoked salmon, chicken cooked in papillote, grilled meat, saffron rice, and whole roasted suckling pigs, whose combination of natural juices and spices emitted a suffocating smell that made Rosélie feel sick. Then there was the choice of vintage champagne, planter's punch, sangria, scotch, and fizzy drinks. Dressed in red and wearing matching bandannas, the popular Prophets were playing on a stage at a deafening volume to the delight of the youngsters, who were already swaying their hips to the beat.

Two lives could not have been more different than those of Emma and Hildebrand, sisters nevertheless. Same father, same mother, as they used to say in N'Dossou. Like two life stories written by novelists of opposite temperaments. Whereas Emma suffered misfortune after misfortune, as we have described previously, Hildebrand was living a fairy tale. Having left school without even her primary school diploma, she had nevertheless found a job as an orderly in a private clinic. All day long, she cleaned and disinfected three floors of wards, changed piles of sheets and towels, and served meal trays to patients, unrewarding and exhausting work that she carried out with a smile, because nowadays what matters is to find a job. Anywhere, anyhow, and at whatever price. Four of her brothers were unemployed without benefits. It was then that the young Dr. Fredrik Vreedehoek, trained in London, had appeared to check the temperature of one of his patients. On seeing Hildebrand, demurely preoccupied with her cleaning products, his own temperature had risen dangerously. Three days later, he moved in with her. Five months later, he married her.

Coloured marriages are a complex business. It's not just a matter of class and education, like everywhere else. Bourgeois with bourgeois. Graduates with graduates. Inheritances from parents or grandparents. Life insurance. Bank accounts. A plot of ground to build a house or a weekend cottage. In addition, it's a question of skin color. The golden rule is not to marry anyone darker than yourself. If Hildebrand had been dark-skinned, Fredrik Vreedehoek would never have dreamed of slipping a wedding ring on her finger. Although heavily melanized over time, her family descended from Jan, who in November 1679 had set foot in Cape Town as head of the Dutch East India Company. Before he died, Jan had legitimized his fifty-eight illegitimate children with one sweep of his pen, and given his name to the Malagasy slave who for thirty years had groaned under his two hundred or so pounds without ever forgetting to call him *baas* at the moment of orgasm. But Hildebrand's hair waved the color of a cornfield. Her complexion had the hue of maple syrup. Any prejudice against her melted under the glow of so much blondeness, which, failing family jewels or property, she would pass on to the child already showing up under her lace dress. However, it had been tacitly agreed that once the wedding festivities were over, the Vreedehoeks would cut all ties to this family, light-skinned perhaps, but without a penny. This left a bitter taste of mourning over the wedding celebrations. Hildebrand's eyes filled with tears at the thought of never again embracing her beloved mama and papa, her brothers, sisters, young nephews, and Judith, her favorite niece. Her mother, rigged out in a puce-colored two-piece suit with leg-of-mutton sleeves, greeted the congratulations like condolences. As for Emma, she openly sobbed on Dido's shoulder, overwhelmed by a new reason to hate life. She had raised Hildebrand and now, alas, she was going to lose her.

Dido dragged Rosélie to a table already occupied by some cousins and their teenage daughter, who was looking longingly at the dancers she wasn't allowed to join. She wore patent-leather Mary Janes and a dress of white lace. Her hair was rolled into ringlets that danced black and shiny down her neck. Her mother boasted to anyone within hearing distance that she looked like Halle Berry.

"I wonder why they chose that band," groused the father. "They're only playing rap. Isn't our music good enough for them?"

There then followed a discussion on the merits of iscathamiya, South African jazz, mbaqanga, and kwaito, which were head and shoulders above African-American music, that dared compete with them on their home territory. Besides, South African music was head and shoulders above every type of music. Dido was of the same opinion. Nobody could touch Hugh Masekela or Miriam Makeba!

What could you expect? She stuck with the artists of her generation.

"Not to mention gospel!" added the man. "Nobody can beat us."

Whatever the African-Americans might think, they are only novices in the genre. Rigged out in ludicrous chasubles, they sway to and fro, shouting in their churches, whereas everyone knows shouting isn't singing. Once again, listening to these affirmations of vibrant chauvinism, Rosélie felt empty-handed. Nothing in her culture made her want to fight tooth and nail for it.

Pity I'm not Haitian! In that case, I wouldn't know what to choose.

Ayiti péyi mwen!

Carimi.

Perhaps she dreamed the world would be one because of her own destitution? Did it betray a desire to align everybody on the same tabula rasa as herself? She had lost her parents and her land, loved strangers who did not speak her language—besides, did she have a language?—and pitched her tent in hostile landscapes. Faustin joked about it sometimes.

"You're like a nomad. Your roof's the sky above your head."

Aren't we all nomads? Isn't it the fault of this wretched, topsy-turvy century in which we live? At the age of twenty-six my mother could make up her mind and say: "I shall never leave Guadeloupe again!"

Even if I'd wanted to I could never have imitated her.

Faustin! Dido had enthused over his flowers and took his procrastination at face value.

"It's better that way," she declared. "It'll soon be summer in America. I hear it's suffocating in Washington. You'll arrive for the autumn, the loveliest season."

Why had Faustin set his heart on her? Wounds heal when you're twenty. They infect and fester indefinitely at fifty. Women who are paid by the job exist too. Cape Town's full of them, hanging round the streetlamps on the waterfront. The authorities, who hunt them down, claim these depraved women come from Madagascar, not South Africa.

Whores always come from somewhere else!

Faustin had set his sights on her, she who was already so fragile, so infirm. You don't shoot at an ambulance. She was forgetting the pleasure he gave her, the impression she had of regaining her youth, of starting life over again, and at times she thought she hated him.

Gradually the atmosphere changed. The veneer of good manners cracked, and the guests, despite their elegant surroundings, sunk into vulgarity. With the help of alcohol and good food, voices grew louder, shrill, and quarrelsome. Tongues were loosened. The women criticized the callous Vreedehoeks, who were forgetting that white folk had despised them as well. The men, shrugging off such gossip, attacked the government. It was the whites who were profiting from the new regime. The whites and Kaffirs. Not the coloureds. The world no longer considered the whites as pariahs. They could travel, do business, and get rich. The Kaffirs' wildest dreams were coming true. Thanks to special programs, they were invading the universities. Soon the country would be flooded with Kaffir doctors, lawyers, and engineers with degrees!

Rosélie was the friend of a relative, so she was treated like family. Everyone knew the terrible ordeal she was recovering from. Another dirty trick by the Kaffirs! They'll ruin South Africa just like they've ruined the rest of Africa. Corruption, coups d'état and civil wars are their progeny of misfortune. But their sympathy was expressed in Afrikaans, a language that Rosélie, little gifted for languages, could not understand. So despite the smiles, she felt terribly isolated.

It was then, as she gazed around the room, she thought

she recognized Bishupal. Yes, it was him, flanked by Archie, the young coloured guy who had replaced him at Mrs. Hillster's. Apparently recovered, he was standing somber and indifferent at the edge of the dance floor, as if he were oblivious to the commotion around him. When their eyes met, she smiled at him. He immediately turned away and, grabbing his friend's arm, was quickly lost in the crowd. Rosélie didn't know what to think. What had gotten into him?

Hadn't he recognized her?

Suddenly the lights dimmed. In the midst of shouts and applause, a female singer and a guitarist walked onto the stage.

"Rebecca! Rebecca!" screamed the guests.

Rebecca gave a gracious wave of the hand, then in a pleasantly husky voice began to sing a popular song that everyone seemed to know, since they sang the refrain in chorus: "Buyani, buyani."

What will my life be like if I stay here? Rosélie wondered lucidly.

A powerful desire unfurled, flapped like a sail in the wind, and dragged her along. Blood, they say, is thicker than water. The Thibaudins would have to accept her and silence their reproaches. Even the prodigal son was embraced by his father: "Bring forth quickly the best robe, and put it on him; and put a ring on his hand, and shoes on his feet; and bring the fatted calf and kill it, and let us eat and make merry; for this my son was dead and is alive again; he was lost and is found."

She wouldn't go and bury herself in the hills at Barbotteau. She had always preferred the city, its life and energy.

She would go and live in La Pointe, in the house on the rue du Commandant Mortenol where she had grown up, among her childhood memories. In the living room, the photo of her first communion. On the Klein piano where she had practiced her scales. In the library on the first floor, the books that had bored her to tears but which Rose made her read for her general knowledge. Next door, her bedroom and the chaste, single bed where her recalcitrant body had experienced its first teenage desires. The mirror where she had gazed at her own reflection, dreaming of a magic wand that would transform her. Would she have the courage to enter Rose's room? On the dressing table, the three porcelain cups painted with Japanese ladies and their ebony chignons were covered in a layer of dust. Next to them, a souvenir from Paris: a glass ball in which the dome of Sacré Coeur peeked through the snowflakes. An hourglass congealing time. All these trite trinkets that had outlived their owner.

The very next morning after her arrival, she would get up at four to go to dawn mass. The bells would ring out in the cool of the morning and the bigoted churchgoers would stream to the cathedral like flies to a puddle of cane syrup. Every day she would take communion. Every Sunday she would visit Rose's grave, her arms loaded with flowers that would warm the coldness of the marble.

"She must have loved her mother so much!" people would wonder. "So surprising after what happened."

But what had happened? Nothing very much when you think about it. Everyone knows each of us kills the one she loves.

The coward does it with a kiss
The brave man with a sword.

Once her act was over, Rebecca bowed and left the stage amid the cheers. The lights came on again and the hubbub of conversation resumed.

"She's our greatest singer," the man boasted.

"Nobody comes close to Hugh Masekela!" Dido flung back at him.

A woman dared contradict him.

"Hugh Masekela? Old hat!"

The discussion almost turned nasty. Fortunately, a new band started up. Old-timers who began to strike up the old, familiar tunes. Dancers poured onto the floor. Dido grabbed Paul's arm, the widower she was after, willowy and melancholic, who seemed frightened by her vitality. Rosélie stayed alone behind her drink.

Yes, there's something appealing about those songs whose words we cannot understand, something that speaks to us deep down. We can give them wings, embroider them with flowers and stars, and color them however we want. I've always preferred sitting down to listen to music. I've never known how to dance. Neither did you, Fiela. My reputation followed me throughout my teenage years: "She's hopeless at jamming," the boys would whisper in contempt. For years I was a wallflower, like you, watching my cousins perform boisterous dancing moves with their partners.

When the music stopped, the dancers surged back to their seats, Dido delighted at having smooched with her widower. At that moment, Bishupal, still flanked with Archie, loomed up at their table. They formed an odd couple: Bishupal, handsome and melancholic like an archangel driven from paradise, and pretty-boy Archie with an evil streak. On seeing them, tongues began to wag. Shame on them! Those two with their vice and wickedness had gone to live with Archie's mother, the widow Anna van Emmeling. The poor woman had no idea two boys could make love together and, deeply shocked, she had run to her confessor. Ever since, she had been immersed in novenas. She couldn't sleep a wink at night while the two demons got drunk, copulated, and quarreled.

Oblivious to this gossip, Bishupal gave Rosélie a piercing look, then without a word, a smile, or a blink, he turned round and, dragging Archie with him, disappeared into the crowd.

Despite the liters of Plaisir de Merle ingurgitated and the late hour they had come home—even then Dido hadn't gone to bed and sat up all night watching Keanu Reeves in *Sweet November*, lamenting his solitude on film and her own in real life—the sun hadn't opened its eyes when Dido dashed into Rosélie's room to announce the news.

The verdict was splashed all over the front page of the *Cape Tribune*.

Fiela had been sentenced to just fifteen years in prison. Naturally, the counsel for the prosecution had asked for life, deploring between the lines that capital punishment had been abolished along with apartheid. Only the ultimate punishment would have fit the horror of the crime. But the jurors hadn't agreed with him. The two lawyers requisitioned for the job, those pink-skinned, fair-haired youngsters whom everyone took for a pair of nincompoops, had accomplished wonders. Halfway through the trial they had skillfully changed tactics. They had called to the bar a load of witnesses from goodness knows where! One man swore he had seen Adriaan more than once blind drunk at some ungodly hour. A woman testified he had exposed himself to her eight-year-old daughter on a secluded path. One of his colleagues at the Vineyard Hotel complained he fondled her breasts and buttocks at the slightest opportunity. Another claimed he organized secret poker games in a corner of the hotel kitchen. In short, the picture of a model father and upstanding husband, a regular churchgoer, singing the Psalms loud and true, endured a setback. The two pink-skinned, fair-haired youngsters whom everyone took for a pair of nincompoops had introduced a doubt. That's all it needs in justice, a serious doubt! Suddenly Adriaan was suspected of having led a double, even a triple or quadruple life. Obviously, public opinion protested, convinced that Fiela was guilty. An angry crowd surrounded the courthouse, demanding an eye for an eye and a tooth for a tooth. Kill the murderess. Cut her into little pieces like she had done to poor Adriaan.

There was a photo too with the article in the *Tribune*. Standing between her guards, a great gawk of a woman, like me, an enigmatic face, like me, preparing to add her name to the already long list of mad women and witches. Nobody would ever know the truth. Fiela hadn't said a word during the ten days of her trial. She hadn't betrayed her joy on hearing her sentence. She hadn't thanked her saviors. In short, she took her secret with her into jail.

Fiela, Fiela, during all this time I was so preoccupied with my own tormented life I neglected you. You at least know the path mapped out in front of you. It seems as if I'm on the brink of a precipice where I shall fall and never climb back up. Tell me. You can tell me everything. Why did you kill Adriaan? What was his crime? You forgave him the first time when he gave Martha, the little neighbor, a belly. What was worse about this new crime? Did your lawyers hint at the truth? What was he hiding from you again and again, that you finally found out?

Rosélie cut short Dido's recriminations she had already heard so many times about the barbarity of the country ever since the Kaffirs had come to power, and extricated herself from the sofa bed. Joseph Lema's consultation was at eleven o'clock on Faure Street. The buses took forever, so she would just have time to stop over on Strand Street. She didn't know what she was hoping for from Inspector Sithole. To talk. To talk about Fiela. To talk about Stephen too. Both stories were now muddled in her head.

Where does mine begin? Where does his end?

But Inspector Sithole was not at the police station, where there reigned an atmosphere of utter pandemonium. Black offenders, black and white police officers. Offenders and police officers, their brutal, vicious faces identical, as if good and evil, order and disorder, justice and injustice were one and the same thing. Probably through close contact they ended up looking like each other. A white officer, his face covered with acne, though he was long past the age of this juvenile scourge, his upper lip bristling with a führerlike mustache, as fat as Lewis Sithole was willowy, was sitting at his

desk. Frowning, he put Rosélie through a formal interrogation—Name–Address–Profession–Purpose of Visit—before informing her:

"Sithole has lost his wife. He's left for KwaZulu-Natal.
He'll be back tomorrow or the day after."

As she was about to leave, he stopped her with the same
old song, uttered in that indefinable tone of voice that was
both reassuring and threatening:

"It's often said that the police don't do anything. But it's
not true. We are not idle, and we always end up discovering
the truth."

Once outside, Rosélie walked in the direction of the
Threepenny Opera without realizing it. It was as if her body
were obeying orders from her brain without her knowing it.

Bishupal's incomprehensible rudeness obsessed her.
Never very communicative or smiling, at least he was polite.
One evening, tired of seeing him crouched in front of
Stephen's study, she had brought him a chair and a glass of
Coca-Cola, which he had accepted.

At this time of day the shopkeepers were still washing
down the sidewalks. The homeless had cleared off, leaving
behind their empty wine bottles, open cans of food, piles of
old rags, and litter. Fiela's much too light a sentence was on
everyone's lips. The way justice worked, in ten years she
would be as free as a bird, free to reduce another innocent
body to shreds.

She could see from the entrance that there was no trace of
Bishupal or Archie at the Threepenny Opera. Sitting on a stool,
a blond girl was leafing through a magazine. Some white customers were rummaging through the opera shelves, some

blacks through world music. Mrs. Hillster looked more ravaged than ever. With her hooked nose and her beady eyes between wrinkled eyelids, she looked more and more like the wicked fairy, or rather the picture we have of the wicked fairy, since, should we forget, she is a fictional character. Mrs. Hillster must have been the only person not to be shocked by the jury's clemency toward Fiela. She had other things on her mind.

"I can't find a serious buyer either for the house or the shop," she complained. "An African embassy made an offer for the house. But I don't trust them. You know what I mean, don't you?"

Of course! It's a well-known fact the African embassies are broke and leave nothing but debts behind them, in Washington as well as Paris. But Rosélie wasn't here to discuss African embassies.

"It so happens I met Bishupal yesterday at a wedding and he refused to say hello to me."

At the mention of his name, Mrs. Hillster looked like a stunned boxer after receiving a punch in the stomach. Her eyes filled with tears.

"Bishupal doesn't work here any longer," she stammered.

"Since when?"

The words couldn't get out quick enough.

"The boy I cherished like my own son is an ungrateful wretch. Since he sent me this good-for-nothing Archie, who knows nothing about anything except hip-hop, confusing Verdi with Rossini and Callas with Elisabeth Schwarzkopf, not anyone can work with music, you have to have some background, he smoked joints, and what's more he was unbearable, insolent, always on the phone, I called Bishupal to know when he was coming back. Nothing unusual about that, was there? But he was so rude, telling me he wasn't my slave and that I was a filthy colonialist like all the rest! Me, me? That I'd exploited him like all the others! Me, me? After everything I did for him, ever since the day Stephen introduced him to me."

"It was Stephen who introduced him to you?" Rosélie asked in dismay.

"Oh, you didn't know?" Mrs. Hillster exclaimed, a gleam flickering at the back of her eyes. "Bishupal was a messenger boy at the Nepalese embassy. They fired him, I don't know why exactly, and Stephen, who liked nothing better than playing the Good Samaritan, flew to his rescue. He brought him here, paid for his correspondence courses with his own money, and found him a studio apartment."

That was just like Stephen, overly generous, always surrounded by all sorts of protégés, students, young artists, poets, painters, and sculptors. But Mrs. Hillster dispensed her information with venom, visibly relishing the meaning that might be implied.

"He ended up screaming at me that he would never set foot here again, neither he nor Archie! What's more, he was about to leave this lousy country for England. I'm not surprised at what you're telling me, he always hated you."

Me? Why?

But Rosélie didn't ask the question out loud and fled.

In her absence, Joseph Léma, feeling at home in his surroundings, had undressed. Uncovering his bony shoulders, he had lain down on the couch in the consulting room. He had already commented on Fiela's trial to Dido, who had offered him a cup of coffee. He was now ready to expose his point of view to Rosélie. South Africa was a very strange country. Its philosophy of reconciliation and forgiveness following the crimes of apartheid was most irritating. Fiela deserved nothing better than a public execution. It would put some sense in the heads of women who wanted nothing better than to imitate her and sink their teeth into their husbands. Nigeria was setting the example by stoning adulterous women.

Rosélie did not discuss matters further. Once again, she had other things on her mind.

EIGHTEEN

After a sleepless night interspersed with dreams no sooner forgotten than the memory of their horror lingered on, Rosélie went down to her studio. When she opened the windows, the sky stretched colorless and dismal. A cloth knotted tight above the city. A bitter wind lashed her face. In the murky half-light of dawn, the backyards emerged, cluttered with an odd assortment of garden tools, hosepipes, and pressure-cleaning equipment. She closed up again the shuttered windows and sat down on the sofa reserved for visitors without a glance at her gloomy canvases, like dejected daughters ignored by their mother.

Don't we mean anything to you? they asked her in silence. You seem to forget we are the blood that gives you strength, the blood that pumps your heart, your arms and legs. If you stop painting, you'll stop living. When are you coming back to us?

Soon, soon. I have to sweep in front of my own door, as they say in Guadeloupe. In other words, I have to sort myself out.

She clasped her head between her hands in a theatrical gesture. If she went and knocked on Widow van Emmeling's door, Bishupal would be obliged to see her and answer her questions, like all the others she had interrogated. But what would she ask him? Her knees gave way and her thoughts recoiled. She remembered her visit to Hermanus, Chris Nkosi and his puerile look: "You're crazy!"

He must have sniggered behind her back. Poked fun at her. Like Bishupal would poke fun at her. Like everyone else.

Like everyone else?

As if she were fleeing some kind of danger, such as a hurricane drawing inexorably closer to the shore, she dashed out of the studio and bolted down the stairs. While she ran down the stairs, the wail of a police siren heading for a police station with a van full of crooks beat time with her steps. Too bad for those who had been robbed, raped, and murdered under cover of night. Nobody suffered as much as she did who had lost everything. She ended up near the traveler's tree. In the meager light of day, Deogratias, still cramped in his night uniform, was sipping a root tea he had brought in a thermos. The Gospel according to St. Luke was wide open in front of him. He looked up from his reading and said in surprise:

"Up already?"

She managed to stammer a reply and went into Stephen's study. It was like stepping into a pharaoh's tomb. Treasures lay in the shadows within hand's reach, irresistible temptations for robber voyeurs. But she didn't switch on the light or pull up the shades. Nothing interested her. She didn't try to force the locks, open the drawers, or check the computer, sitting silent, pale, guarding its secrets. She simply sat down in the armchair that Stephen had used so many times, where his body had left its imprint on the leather seat. She laid her hands flat on the wood, recalling those years she had always thought were happy. Stephen and she never quarreled. She let him decide everything, arrange everything, and solve everything. In his opinion, he did what he thought best. From their very first meeting in the Saigon bar, the roles had been cast and had never changed. He was the lifeguard. She was the drowning swimmer. He was the surgeon. She was the heart patient. A bond of gratitude echoed that of love.

She relived those years. New York, Tokyo, Cape Town. Until that final night, which had brought it all to a grating and incongruous end. All those years laden with happy memories, seldom important or noteworthy, which put end to end made up a successful union. Successful? For the first time she dared scrutinize this word like a jeweler hunting for a flaw in a diamond. Soon tears streamed down her cheeks.

What was she crying for? She had to agree with Inspector Sithole's idea that Stephen's death was not the work of young junkies short on crack. It was not a routine incident for journalists out of a job. The gratuitous violence of modern times had nothing to do with the matter. A nauseous truth was lurking, like a baby swaddled in dirty diapers.

As for Stephen, deep down inside her, in that part where the light of truth never ventures, she had to admit that she had always known who he was. Moreover, on the first day, hadn't he warned her, quite casually, in his offhand, playful manner?

"I never accost women. They scare me too much."

She had simply chosen to ignore the evidence. Blessed are those who have two eyes and see nothing. *Sa zyé pa ka vwè, kyiè pa ka fè mal*, says the Guadeloupean proverb. She had refused to pay the terrible price of lucidity.

So what was suddenly weighing on her? Why was she filled with a feeling of revolt, a feeling she had been duped? At this point in her thoughts, she clumsily tried to be ironic.

No Simone de Beauvoir expressions, please! But irony didn't help. She hurt even more.

"Your Stephen is *de la mierda*!" Fina had screamed.

"You're sacrificing yourself for nothing," Dido had said, going one step further.

Who should she be crying for?

In fact, should she be crying?

It was Dido who interrupted all these thoughts with her tray of coffee and the *Cape Tribune*. On the front page, Fiela, who was en route to the high-security prison in Pretoria, once reserved for the most recalcitrant political prisoners, had been replaced by another woman, white this time, united in the same madness and wickedness. Once again the righteous would be scandalized. This woman had drowned all five of her children, the youngest being only a few months old, in the family bathtub.

Rosélie cut short Dido's fulminations with a wave of the hand, drew a cup to her lips, drank a sip of the scalding liquid, then asked, very quietly:

"You knew, didn't you?"

Immediately Dido's expression clouded over. As if she had been waiting for this question for days. Like a night moth imprisoned by mistake in an attic, her gaze frantically fluttered around the room, then came and settled on Rosélie.

"What did I know?" she asked.

"Stephen," Rosélie simply murmured.

All Dido's affection welled up in her eyes, which suddenly sparkled with tears. She hesitated, then stammered:

"Yes, I knew. Like everyone else. But what about you? When did you know?"

Thereupon Rosélie burst out crying, sobbing noisily.

"You never mentioned it," Dido went on vehemently. "So I never dared bring it up. It was beyond me. I was in agony. I said to myself she must know. So she accepts it? Can one accept something like that?"

Rosélie poured herself a second cup and very slowly said:

"Deep down, I knew. From the very beginning. Accept it? I don't know whether I accepted it. I refused to admit the truth so that I wouldn't have to make up my mind."

There! I've said it.

Halfway through that gloomy morning, Rosélie sitting on the patio, shattered, mulling over every moment of her life in a new light, Dido rattling her pans in the kitchen as if to allay any suspicions, Inspector Lewis Sithole walked in, obviously finished with mourning his wife and back to his usual workaday face. He was accompanied by two white officers, bundled up in their uniforms, a juvenile version of Laurel and Hardy. Rosélie said how sorry she was. But he shrugged his shoulders.

"We didn't live together. She lived near Pietermaritzburg with our two sons since she could never get used to Cape Town. We never got on together during or after apartheid."

He went on without blinking.

"I have a search warrant. We would like to search your husband's study."

Rosélie couldn't believe her ears. It was something straight out of a detective story. Agathie Christie or Chester Himes? *The Murder of Roger Ackroyd* or *A Rage in Harlem?* He motioned to his stooges.

"Go ahead, guys!"

Without further ado, Laurel and Hardy dived into the study.

Am I dreaming? A Spanish writer wrote: "Life is a dream." So yes, I think I am dreaming. I'm going to wake up nestled against Rose's ample breasts, the taste of her milk in my mouth, the warm smell of her skin in my nostrils. I can't believe this is happening to me. What have I done to deserve such agony? What am I paying for?

The same crime again and again. There is no forgiveness for daughterly assassins.

Underneath his professional countenance, Inspector Lewis Sithole was ill at ease. His wily-tomcat mask was cracked in places and an embarrassed compassion showed through. By force of circumstance he had become Rosélie's friend and suffered in his role as tormentor.

"Everything is falling into place," he said. "Yesterday we arrested Bishupal Limbu for the burglary of the Threepenny Opera last February, a week after your husband was murdered. However hard Mrs. Hillster swore blind he was innocent, we didn't believe her. Ever since, we have had him under surveillance. We knew that sooner or later he'd make a wrong move. And we were right. Not only did he quit his job and begin living it up, but he bought two plane tickets to London, two round-trips as required by the immigration authorities, one for himself, one for his friend, a certain Archie Kronje, and he paid for them in cash. South African Airways informed us immediately. He was unable to explain where the money came from. He said it came from his savings. From what he earned! We checked it out."

Here he stopped so that Rosélie could no doubt compliment him on his flair. As she remained stunned, motionless, almost devoid of thought, he went on.

"We know that your husband got him a visa for the U.K. This was not the case for Mr. Kronje, who has never left the country. Mr. Limbu sent a telegram, then another, to a certain Andrew Spire, who had changed his phone number for some unknown reason, to ask him to vouch for his friend's visa. The post office sent us copies both times."

"Andrew!" Rosélie exclaimed, aghast, the tournure of a diabolical coalition suddenly emerging in front of her eyes.

"Do you know him?"

The tone was unmistakably that of an affirmation and not a question.

"Yes!" she stammered. "He's . . . he was my husband's best friend. We spent every summer for almost twenty years with him in Wimbledon."

Inspector Lewis Sithole leaned forward, closer, almost touching, and Rosélie could smell his wholesome breath, a mixture of tobacco and breath freshener.

"And that's where the plot thickens, and we have to deal with the second case, much more serious, concerning your husband's murder. You can help us by answering two questions. First of all, in your opinion, how did Bishupal Limbu come to know Mr. Spire?"

Rosélie's heart had slowed down to such a point she thought it had died. She managed to stammer out:

"Stephen had enrolled Bishupal in a correspondence course in London. Perhaps he had asked Andrew to help him."

"Perhaps. Secondly, do you know whether Mr. Spire was thinking of giving him a room in the event Bishupal emigrated to England?"

"I have no idea," Rosélie replied in agony.

Inspector Lewis Sithole thought for a while, then resumed his account.

"Despite Mr. Limbu's insistence, reassuring him that Archie Kronje was a protégé of your late husband's, like himself, Mr. Spire seemed to have got suspicious. He did not answer either of the telegrams. So Mr. Limbu went to the cybercafé on Strand Street and sent him a series of urgent e-mails, of which we have a copy. Still no answer. In your opinion, why did Mr. Spire choose to remain silent?"

I have absolutely no idea. Once again, Inspector, who is leading the investigation? You or me?

"Since we have no authority to interrogate Mr. Spire, we have asked our colleagues at Scotland Yard to do it for us, and we are waiting for their answer. We want to know the exact relationship between Mr. Limbu and Mr. Spire, how they came to know each other, and whether there had been a prior agreement between the two that Mr. Spire had finally broken."

What agreement?

"It is possible that on the advice of your husband, Mr. Spire had promised to put Mr. Limbu up, and even help him financially to settle in England."

All that didn't make sense. Stephen was far from being naive. How could he possibly advise an individual with no qualifications whatsoever to emigrate to England? At that moment, one of the officers, Laurel, emerged in the study doorway and declared in a whining tone:

"Boss, there's over a hundred videos here!"

"Leave them where they are!" the Inspector ordered. "There's no point looking at them, they won't give us any clues."

No, it's only Verdi. Unless you like the trumpets in *Aïda*!

"And what about the computer? And the diskettes?" Laurel insisted.

"Take them away!" Lewis Sithole shouted without hesitation.

Laurel disappeared once again inside the room. Followed by a heavy silence.

"Don't you think," the Inspector started up again, "that Mr. Spire suspected Bishupal Limbu of being implicated in the murder of your husband, and consequently wanted nothing more to do with him?"

How could he suspect anything seven thousand miles away, knowing nothing about Bishupal or the terrible events in February? I was the one who informed him. Breaking with his usual reserve, his coldness toward her, Andrew had immediately offered her a plane ticket to come to England. She could stay with him as long as she wanted. For a while she had toyed with the idea, given her state of mind.

But to get back to the subject, any murderer acts for a motive. What motive did Bishupal have for attacking Stephen? What fool kills the goose with the golden egg?

The Inspector's mask cracked completely and the fraternal face hidden underneath emerged. Nevertheless, he didn't mince his words.

"Your husband had a liaison with Mr. Limbu for over two years. It would seem he did not keep his word, especially about settling in England. Hence the constant quarreling. My theory is that one evening in February one of these quarrels, particularly violent, ended the way we know."

I'm sorry, Inspector, some people call imagination the mother of invention.

"I'm not inventing anything," he went on gravely. "Everything I'm telling you has been verified. I must admit we haven't found the murder weapon, despite our searches at Mr. Limbu's. He lived in a studio apartment in Green Point. You remember that telephone call to your husband at seventeen past midnight?"

Rosélie, crushed, didn't remember a thing.

"We interrogated the neighbors," Lewis Sithole continued. "They knew your husband, he was a regular visitor, and they can testify to the almost daily quarrels that disturbed their peace. Plus the music, plus the drugs."

Drugs? And what else? It was Stephen who cured me of my marijuana habit. He advocated its liberalization, but he hadn't smoked a single joint for eighteen years.

"A few weeks before your husband's death," the Inspector continued, "the tenants sent a petition to Kroeger and Co., the proprietors of the building. They demanded Mr. Limbu's departure. They won their claim and in May Mr. Limbu was evicted. He took refuge in Mitchell Plains with the mother of his new friend, Mr. Kronje."

His new friend? Nobody in fact seemed to mourn Stephen very long! Me! Bishupal!

The Inspector shook his head.

"Bishupal Limbu and Archie Kronje were in a relationship about a year before Mr. Stewart died. They met playing football, their favorite pastime. They immediately became inseparable and Archie moved into Green Point. Apparently, your husband took it very badly. The couple's quarrels became a three-sided slugfest."

Who are we talking about? The man I lived with for twenty years, whom I thought my savior, whom I always admired and respected? The man in whom I had complete trust? Stephen mixed up with two boys, crudely fighting over possession of one of them!

"It's a tragic case of jealousy, the details of which are not yet clear," Lewis Sithole concluded.

A sordid affair, that's what it is!

At that moment, loaded with their loot, Laurel and Hardy came out of the study. The Inspector stood up and, in a tone that was meant to be reassuring, asserted:

"I believe Mr. Limbu will soon confess. He's a very sensitive individual. Not like that little thug Kronje, whom we've arrested several times for burglary and drug dealing but have had to release each time for lack of evidence."

Oh yes! Bishupal was considered by one and all to be an exceptional individual!

"Believe me," Inspector Lewis Sithole said, "he won't be able to keep it secret for long. Then this nightmare will be over for you."

Over? It's only just beginning. All my memories, all my convictions have been shaken to the core as if by a hurricane. The peasant emerges from his hut, miraculously intact, and no longer recognizes his surroundings. He walks among a field of ruins. Here, there were trees, guava, lychee, and hog plum. There, banana groves. Now everything is torn up and gone. The earth lies belly-up. The roots slither like snakes.

Despite appearances, my life resembles Rose's. All women's lives are alike: victimized, humiliated, or, failing that, abandoned. Simply, unlike Elie and so many others, Stephen had done it with elegance.

> *The coward does it with a kiss*
> *The brave man with a sword.*

Dido appeared among the bougainvillea, carefully balancing a cup filled with a steaming liquid.

"Drink!" she ordered. "This will make you feel better. It's an herb tea made with shoots from an Egyptian fig tree and Madagascar violet petals."

She would have done better to drink her potion herself, she seemed so exhausted, red-eyed and swollen eyelids. Rosélie obeyed feeling the welcoming warmth of the brew spread throughout her numb body. Dido sat down opposite her and stammered:

"Are you angry with me?"

About what? I'm simply angry with myself, for being a coward.

Dido began to cry.

"You seemed to put so much trust in him."

Yes, I was trusting, happy, in my own way! Some people assert that happiness is never anything but an illusion. So why be angry with Stephen? He gave me that illusion for twenty years.

Stroking Dido's hand, which lay on her knee, Rosélie gave the order:

"Let's not talk about it anymore."

For the moment, grief and revolt were boiling inside her. The time had not yet come when she would be able to reexamine her life impassively, like rereading a book whose pages you have turned over too quickly and failed to understand. Like listening to music again that contains a leitmotif you hadn't heard the first time. When would this salvation begin to dawn? All she could see in front of her was a quagmire of pain to be crossed.

"I think I'm going to leave," she murmured. "Nothing's keeping me here any longer."

She had made up her mind at that very moment while she was talking. What was the point in fact of staying in Cape Town, playing the vestal virgin in a desecrated temple? Her position was not only improper but ridiculous.

To go home!

After the infinity of the ocean the plane flies over the mangrove, bristling with white birds, the cattle egrets. The crowd of unruly passengers jump to their feet before the plane has come to a complete standstill, despite instructions from the flight attendants. I have never seen the new airport of glass and concrete designed to handle the increasing number of planes. That's progress for you. Unfortunately, the island has recently been given over to all sorts of violence. They are holding up the Ecomax supermarkets. The backpacker tourists are at a loss as to where to buy their packets of cooked ham. They are fleeing this paradise, so different from what they were promised. Where are the madras headscarves and ties of the crowds who used to wave farewell to the ocean steamships? Where are the *doudous* with their shiny hair?

Masked men carrying sawed-off shotguns have replaced them. As a result, the airline companies are folding their wings. The hotels are shutting up shop.

Aunt Léna is waiting for me at the airport. She looks more and more like Queen Mary, to the extent that a mulatto woman from Guadeloupe, a sort of Indian half-caste, can look like English nobility. Her hair, always carefully waved around the ears, is white, completely white. What's more, she no longer drives. She sold Papa Doudou's Citroën DS 19 ages ago. She's an old lady now, a dowager. She has called on the services of a great-nephew in charge of communications with a big company in Jarry who "returned home" last year and got lucky finding a job on an island with 35 percent unemployed. He has a mustard-colored Twingo, absolutely horrible, like all French cars; apparently it's easier to park. He's looking at me as if I landed from Mars. You can read what he's thinking: I don't believe it! That's her?

Once again Dido burst into tears.

"If you leave, if you leave me, I'll be all alone."

"Come now," Rosélie attempted to joke, "you'll have Paul as a consolation."

Dido cried even harder.

"Paul! Didn't you hear he's just moved in with Gabriella?"

Gabriella was a cousin of hers, a widow as well, mother of three. She too was taller than Paul and had wide hips. But her smile and hazel eyes had kept the demureness of her younger years. Her voice was gentle and she spoke with her eyes lowered. In short, she was the complete opposite of Dido. Her sisters had warned her: women should never wear the pants.

NINETEEN

It was in Papa Koumbaya's car, shortly before they arrived at Lievland, that they heard the news. Dido was dozing in a corner. Rosélie's thoughts were roaming sadly around Stephen: Did he love me? During all these years, was he putting on an act? And why? Papa Koumbaya was droning on about life in the men's hostels. He was just at the point in the story when he would grab his dick and get the sperm frothing when Sun FM suddenly interrupted the jerky rhythm of a rap song to announce the tragedy.

Fiela had cut her wrists with the handle of a spoon she had filed like a dagger. Taken immediately to the prison infirmary, she had never come round. Her body had been returned to Julian.

Rosélie at once was terror-stricken and guilt-ridden.

Fiela, Fiela, in the debacle of my life, forgive me, I forgot about you. I too, I abandoned you. Yet you seemed no longer to need me. In the end, you won. Tell me. Why did you insist on such a punishment when the jury had decided otherwise? Did you think you were guilty? Or did you no longer have the heart to live?

Like me.

Rosélie had kept her word. She hadn't set foot in Lievland since Jan died.

She was going back this weekend because Dido had in-

sisted. Sofie had suddenly fallen ill. The doctor, far from op-
timistic, believed she had only a few days left. She was no
longer eating. She complained of suffocating. At times her
breathing would stop, and she lay inert, her cheeks and lips
turned blue.

At Lievland, the tourists kept coming. Coaches lined up
in the parking lot and released chattering crowds, prepared
to admire everything, to take pictures of everything, the vineyards, the ring of mountains, the homestead and its furnishings. Dido and Rosélie went up to the de Louws' private
apartment. Sofie had been carried from the child's cot she
had slept in for years to the canopied bed in the middle of
the room, which faced the coromandel ebony wardrobe from
Batavia that Jan had stared at until his final hour. Her body
was swallowed up by the bed. The bed itself was swallowed up
by the room, whose floor was tiled in black and white and resembled a small craft on the immensity of the ocean.

Rosélie went over to her.

It was as if Sofie were on the other side of our world,
going by her gaze, dimmed blue between her wrinkled eyelids. So much like Rose's in her patience and determination.
She was waiting for her son.

That's how mothers are. They can't believe in the ingratitude and thoughtlessness of their children.

The morning went by in a strange atmosphere. The sunlight poured into the room, playfully caressing the funereal
checkerboard of the tiles. Through the windows could be
heard the cries of the tourists, some Swedes this time. They
were ambling in the fields, holding one another by the waist
and posing for photos. Outside was lively and joyful. Inside,

reverence and dread to greet death. Dido and Elsie were reading the Psalms in a low voice. Rosélie relentlessly massaged the white, ice-cold body, so white, whiter than the pillow, the sheets, or the eiderdown. Under the pressure of her hands the blood flowed, but merely produced a glimmer of warmth here and there, like a bonfire that is constantly dying. Although her hands were steady, out of habit, her mind was in a state of confusion. Chaos. Her thoughts were as tangled as a skein of wool: Rose, Sofie, Stephen, Faustin, and Fiela were spinning round and round in her head.

Sometimes, childhood memories surfaced.

Rose's bedroom in La Pointe. The wide-open window showed a cutout of the sky. In the middle stood the bell tower of the church of Massabielle, as clear as on a photo, crouching on its hill, housing the miraculous Virgin Mary for the adoration of the faithful. The last time the statue had been carried through the island she had made cripples walk again while a deaf-mute from birth had begun to shout "manman" at the very sight of her. Rose, who at the time weighed 250 pounds on her scales and was a tight fit in her rocking chair, was balancing her on her thighs, rolls of fat squeezed between the wooden armrests. Wheezing passionately, she asked:

"Who do you prefer? Your papa or your maman?"

Rosélie didn't hesitate and docilely gave the hoped-for answer:

"My maman."

Then Rose showered her with kisses.

At other times Stephen took the place of Rose. The decor had changed. The sun was shining, remote and cold.

They were in New York. The bay windows looked out onto the glistening Hudson and the high-rises of New Jersey. Stephen was sitting cross-legged on the bed in his jogging outfit, his hair in his eyes.

"Out of all your lovers, which one did you prefer?" he asked.

"Out of all my lovers!" she protested. "There were not that many, you know full well."

The civil servants in N'Dossou didn't count. Oh no! My private life is hardly material for a pornographic novel. Neither *Confessions of O* nor *Emmanuelle* nor *The Sexual Life of Catherine M.* nor *Perverse Tales* by Régine Deforges. The voyeurs wouldn't lose their sight spying on me. I kept my virginity until I was nineteen, a venerable age, even in my time. I've never been to an orgy or had multiple partners. I've never fornicated in a public place such as a museum, an elevator, or a church. Never been sodomized. For me, sex has never been a feat or a performance. It has always simply rhymed with love. That's why I wouldn't know if one black is better than two, three, or four whites. I've never compared my men.

"Even so," Stephen insisted. "Which one did you prefer?"

Here again there was no hesitation.

"You, of course!"

Then he showered her with kisses.

Was he lying then?

Fiela, wherever you are now, you must know. Just one word of consolation. Did he love me? Had he always put on an act? Is it possible to put on an act for twenty years? And why?

Then it was Faustin's turn. In her life Faustin had symbolized one of those children conceived at the last minute, a latecomer, a *krazi a bòyò*. They give immense happiness to their forty-year-old mothers.

I can do it! My husband can do it. I took my insides to be a bundle of dry, wiry ligaments and his sex a stick of dead wood. What a mistake! Together we created life.

Toward the end of the morning, the tourist buses moved off to other vineyards. Soon a flow of private cars replaced them. Friends and relatives of the de Louws, attracted by the smell of death, that inimitable smell, sadly nodded their heads and remarked:

"Well, Sofie didn't survive Jan for very long. A few weeks ago we were gathered in this very same place for a similar painful event. It's as if the couple is tied to an umbilical cord, stronger than the ties uniting mother and child. As if he couldn't bear to be separated from her."

We shouldn't be duped by the good-natured expression, the self-conscious countenance, and the unassuming dress of these farmers and their wives. They had composed the silent cohorts, the pillars of apartheid, throughout the country. Each in his own manner had paved the way for Afrikanerdom once the ties with England had been severed. They had often occupied regional postings in the Party. Dido, who knew them all by their first names, introduced them to her friend Rosélie, clairvoyant, magician, capable of performing miracles. As a result, they bowed to her out of superstitious respect. As for Rosélie, she was fighting her malaise. She hadn't forgotten Jan's last look. Consequently, she braced herself for the insults and contempt that lay behind every eye.

If Stephen had been there, she would have been treated to one of his tirades.

"What are you afraid of? What are you going to invent now? They are preoccupied by the same fears that haunt every human. The same fears as yours. Fear of death, fear of life, fear of the known, and fear of the unknown. Of the foreseeable and the unforeseeable. Must we constantly blame people for what they once were? Must we forever hold it against the English, the Americans, the French, the white Creoles in Guadeloupe, and the *békés* in Martinique for the crimes of their slaveholding ancestors? We must move forward."

Stephen was unfair. She didn't deserve these reproaches. She wouldn't have asked for anything better than to make peace with everyone, to live free and die. Was it her fault if the other camp wouldn't lay down their weapons? They could never forget the Good Old Days, and despite the passing of time, their prejudices remained intact.

Whatever we do, the world is like badly ironed laundry, impossible to get the creases out.

Around noon, the prayers stopped. The room of the dying woman emptied, with everyone's thoughts on getting something to eat. In the courtyard the women lit stoves and began preparing *braais*. The men opened cans of beer, and despite the nearness of death, the homestead's courtyard was as festive as a fairground. While devouring their lamb chops, friends and relatives were making dire predictions. How frail Sofie seemed! Three times in a few hours her breathing had stopped, then started up again in fits and starts with a persistent death rattle. Would she survive until Willem arrived? In other words, until the following afternoon? Rosélie gained everyone's esteem by asserting that Sofie would live as long as was necessary. Her gift at clairvoyance, however, surprised nobody. The Kaffirs, everyone knows, make excellent sorcerers.

Halfway through lunch the new parish priest, Father Roehmer, a small, sickly man, climbed out of his four-wheel drive. He was giving Sofie Holy Communion, as he did every day. Despite his fragile appearance, Father Roehmer had survived nine years in a high-security prison, accused of being a Communist in a cassock, a KGB agent, and a supporter of the ANC. He appeared not to harbor any bitterness over his past suffering and humiliation. He smiled, shook hands, and patted his former enemies on the back. An old friend of Dido's, he went up to Rosélie as if she were a longtime acquaintance and said in a familiar tone of voice:

"Dido tells me you're leaving us. When are you going?"

She had no idea. In fact, she had vaguely noted the address of a few estate agencies and even more vaguely sorted through her personal belongings and made an inventory of the furniture she hoped to sell. Suddenly the thought of saying farewell to Cape Town was heartrending. She realized that, unbeknownst to her, ties were binding her to this city, ties she had never formed with any other place. Even that of her birthplace. Liberated as if by magic from her fears, she would walk through the streets drinking in the arrogant, enigmatic beauty that was so special.

In the morning, she would walk as far as the wharf for Robben Island when the sea opened its bleary eyes, muffled in gray like the sky. The sun hesitated on its path: was it expected to climb up there once again with the little strength it had left? She had no inclination to mix with the crowd of tourists already lining up for the ferries, shivering in their anoraks. She waited for the light to slowly dawn and the day to change as she strolled through the harbor. She never tired of this sight. The whole world was here. Japanese, Brazilians, and Liberians, as black as Niggers of the *Narcissus*, were washing down the decks of their rust buckets. Americans, Australians, and Scandinavians with mops of flax-colored hair were preparing to sail out to sea. Next to the catamarans, birds eager to take flight, balancing on the crest of the waves, idle passersby were admiring a fore-and-aft rigged schooner from the pioneering age of navigation.

Silently, dusk fell.

The mountains glowed red before turning blue and melted into the surrounding darkness. Without warning the penumbra became umbra. One by one the visitors withdrew, leaving only Father Roehmer and the cronies of death, never tired of trotting out psalms and litanies. Dido handed round cups of very strong coffee flavored with cardamom, which revived people's spirits. Prayers were replaced by talk. The subject turned to Fiela. Some thought that the priests of her parish should refuse to give her remains a religious burial. Others, including Father Roehmer, objected. In this country where the Truth and Reconciliation Commission had pardoned unimaginable torture and heinous crimes, why should Fiela not be forgiven? This caused a heated debate. One can only compare what is comparable. Can one compare the guilt of an individual with the collective guilt of the supporters of a political regime?

Incapable of expressing an opinion, Rosélie slipped outside.

The courtyard of the homestead was bathed in darkness. The trees, bushes, and even the flower beds had taken on disturbing shapes. The old superstitions of her childhood resurfaced and she began to run clip-clopping over the flagstones, arousing echoes of the three-legged horse of the Bèt à Man Hibè.

Standing rigid in the dark, Stephen, Faustin, and Fiela were waiting for her beside her bed.

The night was long.

Willem's taxi arrived earlier than expected. At noon, whereas they were expecting him in the early afternoon. When he entered the room, blond and weather-beaten by the sun, the smell of wide-open spaces in the folds of his clothes, Sofie uttered a sigh as if something had come undone inside her. Staring wide-eyed, she examined him from head to foot so as to engrave his image for eternity. Then she closed her eyelids while a mask of peace settled over her face.

Eternal peace.

TWENTY

At six forty-five the sound of the telephone ringing drew Rosélie from her bed. It was Inspector Lewis Sithole.

He did not apologize for calling so early, for he had an excellent reason. As he had predicted two days earlier, Bishupal had decided to squeal, as they say. Mrs. Hillster was right, he wouldn't have hurt a fly. Even less Stephen. It wasn't him. It was Archie Kronje. It was an incredible story. Archie had got it into his head to blackmail Stephen. He had asked him therefore to bring three thousand U.S. dollars in cash and to meet him in front of the Pick 'n Pay. But he misjudged him. Stephen had in fact gone to the appointed meeting empty-handed, in a fighting mood and threatening to inform the police of his drug dealing. The quarrel had turned vicious and Archie had fired. The murder weapon apparently was at his poor mother's, wrapped in a towel hidden under a pile of sheets.

Fiela, Fiela, you have shown me the way. To be done with life. Living is a bitter potion, a purgative, a calomel I can no longer swallow.

For days on end Rosélie abandoned her consultations and remained in her room, virtually from morning to night and night to morning, lying prostrate on her bed. Despite the increasingly bitter cold, she kept the windows wide open in order to counter the feeling of suffocation that was creeping over her. She never closed her eyes. On a clear night she could count the stars, which twinkled for hours on end, then suddenly were snuffed out like candles on a birthday cake. The moon was the last to disappear, swaying on its swing until dawn. But when the nights were ink-black, she would watch the air slowly whiten, the sky turn gray, and the silhouette of Table Mountain loom up, pachydermatous, like an elephant emerging from the bushes. First of all, only the natural elements of the decor came to light: the clouds, the pines, and the rocks. Then the humans appeared. The first tourists took up their positions around the cable-car station. A new day was dawning.

Andy Warhol said that we would all be famous for fifteen minutes of our lives.

Rosélie had not foreseen that the *Cape Tribune, The Observer,* and other dailies and weeklies would snatch up her story so that thousands of readers who had never heard of her could relish it. That photos of Stephen, Bishupal, Archie, and her—my God, what do I look like, am I really so ugly?— would be splashed over the front pages. Admittedly, the details were juicy.

The honorable professor of literature, the specialist of Joyce and Seamus Heaney who was writing a critical study of Yeats and had made a name for himself in college theater productions, murdered a few months earlier, was in fact leading a double life. No doubt about it, nowhere is safe nowadays, and the university's no better than the church. After the pedophile priests and bishops, here are the professors slumming it. My God, whom can we trust our children with? What do these false mentors teach them? Vice, nothing less. The papers reeled off fictionalized biographies of Stephen. They had readers believe that this admired, respected, and celebrated professor had secretly accumulated a series of dirty tricks. In Africa, his well-placed connections had got him out of a tight corner. But in New York, where love is a many splendored thing, a minor had filed a lawsuit and Stephen had had to leave to flee a prison sentence.

These unfortunate circumstances, however, had a positive side to them. The journalists had discovered that the companion of this modern-day Dr. Jekyll and Mr. Hyde, Rosélie Thibaudin, originally from Guadeloupe, a Caribbean island under French domination—some still are, a smattering of islands, two or three pieces of confetti on the ocean—who was totally unaware of her partner's misdemeanors—how blind can you get, women are so stupid—was a painter. Misfortune often works like a magnet. Anxious to get a closer look at this poor dupe, people made a beeline for Faure Street. They hadn't counted on Dido's presence of mind. Thanks to her, the house had become a trap. Not only were they wasting their time—Rosélie was invisible, wrapped in her grief, far from prying eyes—but they weren't allowed to leave until they had visited her studio. Although they had hoped for better, her paintings were so dark, so unattractive, in other words, not at all exotic, they were obliged to dig deep into their pockets. Dido was the one who fixed the price, admittedly depending on the person, and tolerated no excuses. She took her job as manager very seriously. That's how she not only sold two paintings to Bebe Sephuma, attracted like everybody else by the smell of scandal, for her house in Constantia, but also dragged out of her the promise of simultaneous exhibitions, one in Cape Town and the other in Jo'burg. That evening, taking a bowl of soup up to Rosélie, she counted up with satisfaction the day's takings and remarked:

"You see, some good always comes out of evil. It's a law of nature."

Rosélie, who could only see her life in ruins, had trouble making out the contours of good.

She was ashamed and she was hurting.

Sometimes she had the strength to leave her room, leave the bed that everyone had scorned, and climb up to her studio. Her canvases gave her a cool reception.

We are tired of waiting, they complained. We've done nothing to hurt you. Can't you understand that we'll never betray you, like your men have done, one after the other? We'll always be faithful to you.

She tried to explain. Pain and shame had swooped down on her, wreaking havoc on her, obscuring her convictions. She must get control of herself and think things through.

Did she really want to leave Cape Town? To go where? And find what? The indifference of Paris? The emptiness of Guadeloupe? Who was she? Who did she want to be? A painter? A clairvoyant? She invariably ended up losing hope in her wrecked life.

That morning she got dressed very early so as not to keep Papa Koumbaya waiting. Despite Dido's efforts to dissuade her, she had made up her mind to pay Bishupal a visit.

"What do you hope to get out of that little bastard?" Dido fumed. "You'll just hurt yourself even more, that's all."

I hope to understand.

Understand what?

What is there to understand?

Inspector Lewis Sithole, who was now a daily visitor to Faure Street, thought along the same lines.

"She'd do best to put all that behind her," he repeated to Dido, who highly approved.

Behind me? It's a vicious circle: If I haven't understood, even if I can't forget, how can I manage to grin and bear it? And start off again along life's bumpy road.

As unlikely as it may seem to those who know the age-old hatred between blacks and coloureds, Dido and Lewis were having a love affair. Rosélie, in fact, was the culprit. Through drinking endless cups of coffee in the kitchen, lamenting on life's unfathomable machinations, Lewis and Dido had grown closer together. Lewis, who owned a secondhand Toyota, had offered to drive Dido home to Mitchell Plains. First he had stayed for dinner and then the night, when he had performed as well as any other.

Blushing like a virgin, Dido confided in anyone within hearing distance:

"He's not very handsome, but he's got a heart as good as gold."

She was now planning to rent her house and move in with Lewis in an ultramodern apartment block built by the police in False Bay. Her relationship with the Inspector assured her all the papers for free and firsthand knowledge of criminal cases. That's how she learned that Bishupal's defense was proving difficult. Beneath his angelic looks, he had a stubborn streak. He refused to follow the strategy advocated by his lawyer, once again a young fellow officially appointed to the case, but we know now we have to be careful of young lawyers officially appointed to the case. He refused to dissociate himself from Archie or accuse him. On the contrary, he claimed responsibility. He had approved the murder committed by his friend. He had even bought the gun.

The street emerged livid and shivering from the torment of the night. Rosélie was hurt.

How little I count! Whereas I had hit rock bottom, the world hadn't budged. The gingerbread facades of the pastel-colored Victorian houses hadn't moved. The bougainvillea glowed red against the wrought-iron railings. In the gardens the roses continued to perfume the air, which shimmered from their scent.

At the same time, she felt the unwitting exhilaration of being alive.

Floating through the streets, the warm, heady smell of the ocean, like that of tar, tickles my nose. The familiar hand of the wind stings my face.

Already up, armed with secateurs, Mrs. Schipper was inspecting her bushes, branch by branch. As usual, she did not deign turn her head in the direction of Rosélie and the Thunderbird. Had she read the editorials in the newspapers or watched television? Was she informed of the latest details of the tragedy that had been played out on her doorstep? Had she commented on the facts with her relatives and friends?

And what about the domestics arriving for work? And the night watchmen ending their guard duty? Furtive comings and goings. A murmur of respectful greetings.

"*Goeimore!*"

Nobody had shown any sympathy for Rosélie. Deogratias had continued to meditate the Beatitudes and snore as usual. Raymond had stopped visiting, yielding to evidence and reason. Only Dido and Lewis Sithole remained loyal, attentive to her every need.

The latter had given her a flag tree with salmon-colored flowers, which he planted himself at the foot of the traveler's tree.

While awaiting his sentence, Bishupal was being detained at Pollsmoor, a former political prison now reserved for juvenile delinquents. The highway was already congested with all types of gleaming cars, full of people going about their business in the pursuit of money. Papa Koumbaya, who had said nothing when his hero Stephen bit the dust, continued to drone on as usual. She closed her ears. Under her tightly shut eyelids she watched a series of images file past. The worst thing is trying to imagine the unknown. To visualize a truth patched up like a photo torn to pieces and stuck together again.

She understood now why during the last summer vacation Stephen had left her alone in Wimbledon on the pretext of a colloquium on Oscar Wilde at the university of Aberdeen. She remembered how surprised she had been. In the middle of summer? He hadn't even troubled to reply, stuffing his traveling bag determinedly. He had entrusted her to Andrew. In the evening they used to go and watch old films by Luis Buñuel. Since neither of them could cook, they would have a pub dinner. Despite his sullenness and silence, she was convinced he was a friend, whereas his only allegiance was to Stephen.

Pollsmoor Prison comprised an endless number of buildings linked by covered exercise yards. It was a hive of activity humming with police cars, vans, and scooters, and Rosélie had to show the pass Inspector Lewis Sithole had obligingly got for her over a dozen times. She finally found herself in a rectangular visiting room with cream-colored walls. As usual, there were very few whites. Only blacks. Mothers, yet again, recognizable by their tears and their looks of distress, were seated in front of glass partitions. You had to press a button and speak into a kind of ear trumpet. A dozen black and white police officers were pacing up and down, scowling and fingering their guns.

When Bishupal entered, flanked by a guard who shoved him to his seat, Rosélie had trouble recognizing him. He was dressed in oversized striped pajamas. His mane of silk had been ruthlessly shaven and his bare head appeared enormous, the color of old ivory, dappled in black. His emaciated face seemed to be just two huge eyes and he looked like a concentration camp survivor. All that, however, couldn't deprive him entirely of his beauty, grace, and juvenile appeal. Rosélie felt a pang of jealousy.

"Why are you here?" he murmured savagely. "I didn't want to see you. Then I told myself we have to get it over with. I had to come and tell you."

Rosélie realized this was one of the few times she had heard his voice, pleasant, deep-sounding, and slightly nasal. Up till then he had only spoken in monosyllables with her:

"Here!"

"Thanks!"

"Many thanks!"

The perfect employee at the Threepenny Opera. The perfect poet's apprentice. Who was he, in fact?

In its generosity, the *Cape Tribune* had depicted him as a depraved individual. He apparently lost his modest job at the Nepalese embassy because he sold his favors for visas. According to the paper, it was a lucrative business. Although the path to Kathmandu is less traveled nowadays, the rush has gone, but there are still tourists anxious to admire the Bhimsen Tower.

Following that, he is said to have prostituted himself.

Where exactly was the truth? It probably wavered somewhere between these two extremes. Rosélie thought she could read between the lines a story of solitude, naiveté, and dashed hopes.

She had prepared a little speech. But as usual the words disobeyed her. They fled in confusion left and right, and she remained silent, a sob sticking in her throat like a fishbone.

"He never loved you," he said slowly, his eyes sparkling through the glass partition. "Never."

She wasn't expecting such spitefulness, which destroyed everything she had imagined.

"Neither me. Nor anyone else," he continued. "He was only in love with himself. Stephen had no heart."

"And you, did you love him?" she managed to stammer.

"There was a time I worshiped him," he said without any emotion.

He leaned closer to the partition and hammered out between his clenched teeth:

"He got what he deserved. If we had to do it again, we would. Archie had the balls to do it. I lacked the courage."

She heard herself burst into tears. He stared at her with the same coldness, then went on:

"Don't feel sorry for us. There's no point at all feeling sorry for us."

There was silence.

"Even if we get fifteen or twenty years, we'll be thirty-three, thirty-four when we get out. We'll still have a life in front of us."

He threw himself back and cruel-heartedly let out:

"For you it's over with."

The words burned through her.

"Why do you hate me?" she groaned.

He stood up in exasperation and motioned to the guard that the visit was over.

"You're mistaken. I don't hate you. I've no time for you. Don't ever come back."

He walked away, determined, resolute, and yet so helpless, so pathetic in the uniform that was too big for him, that Rosélie was heartbroken.

The interview hadn't lasted five minutes.

Rosélie regained her room and returned to her bed with the window wide open to the chill and din of the city. She had always thought New York a noisy city. Cape Town was even noisier. At times its cacophony deafened her.

How can you possibly take your life when there are no barbiturates at hand? Go into the Pick 'n Pay and look for rat poison on the cleaning shelves? No *Madame Bovary*–type ending. The thought of Emma's atrocious suffering took away all her determination. You cut your wrists like Fiela with a razor blade? She hadn't the courage to do that either. How do you go about it? You lie down and wait for the end fixed by God. That's what Rose did, nailed to her bed, slowly suffocating in her own fat.

Shortly before noon, Dido pushed open the door and announced mysteriously with a strangely overjoyed expression:

"Get dressed. You've got a visit."

A visit? You know full well I don't want to see anybody.

Dido insisted in the same enigmatic way:

"It's not a reporter. It's not a busybody either. He says he's a friend of yours."

A friend? How many friends do I have in this country? In Guadeloupe? In the whole wide world? Nobody loves me. Yet out of curiosity she got up, slipped on some clothes, and went downstairs.

A man was waiting for her in the living room. A white man. Tall, with a slight paunch, a full head of black hair, gray eyes, and tanned cheeks.

Where have I seen him before?

"Don't you recognize me?" He smiled. "My name's Manuel Desprez. But everyone calls me Manolo because I play the guitar in my spare time."

It was like a record she heard for a second time. The memory came back to her. Tea at the Mount Nelson some months ago. Another professor! I hate the lot of them through having frequented them too much. This one teaches in the French Department. But English, French, Oriental Studies, they're all the same. Same arrogance. Same conviction they belong to a superior species. The intellectual species.

I hear there was a major debate on *Café Creole*, a monthly program on Guadeloupe television, about the role of intellectuals. Nobody could come up with an answer and one person dared say they were useless.

But that's another story.

"I didn't come earlier," he explained, "because I was sure you preferred to be alone during all this media fuss. I waited a little while, but you were always on my mind."

His tone seemed sincerely sympathetic. She was so seldom treated to such feelings that Rosélie felt a lump in her throat. She almost burst into tears. He noticed it and clasped her to his chest and his scent of Hugo Boss.

"Have a good cry if you feel like it. In my family they tell me my shoulders are very comforting."

She moved away, grimaced a smile, and stammered that no thank you, she'd be okay.

"Would you like me to take you to Clifton?" he proposed. "I know a place where they serve mussels and an excellent white wine. You'd think you were in Brussels."

That too I've already heard somewhere before. It's awful how men lack imagination.

Okay, let's go to Clifton! She followed him to the door under the approving eye of Dido.

Once again Nature showed its indifference toward man's affliction. Sunlight, radiant but freezing, flooded the streets. The sky was like a silky blue scarf dappled in white and spreading to infinity. The ocean immersed everything with its bitter smell of salt. The highway was still gleaming with cars full of carefree people. How unjust happiness is! Dispensed to some, denied to others. With no explanation.

The Sea Lodge at Clifton was a trendy restaurant for the natives. Few tourists. At this hour it was packed. Every head looked up and Rosélie rediscovered, like a familiar dress mislaid and forgotten, the contempt of a dozen pairs of hostile eyes. A white man with a Kaffir whore. Manuel Desprez seemed not to have noticed and was arguing with a waitress for a table on the terrace. Perhaps he was secretly excited by all these looks? Like Stephen? When they had been seated he took her hand across the table, to the fury of their neighbors.

"What you need is a change of air," he asserted. "To travel. I've been invited to a guitar festival in Cadix. Would you like to come with me?"

She gave no reply, preferring to ask point-blank the same blunt question she had asked Dido.

"Did you know?"

He blushed, and this juvenile flush made him look thirty years younger.

"I suspected," he confessed in a low voice. "Like everyone else. Quite a bit of gossip went round the department. There was a lot of whispering among the students and profs."

That hadn't prevented them from naming Stephen teacher of the year and giving him the complete works of Dollar Brand, knowing his love of jazz. He must be having a good laugh at their hypocrisy where he is now.

But what about me in all this? Wasn't I being the most hypocritical? What did he think of me?

"Stephen loved you immensely, never doubt it," he added awkwardly.

Really? Two days ago, someone well placed to know what he was talking about told me the complete opposite.

"Yes," he insisted. "All those who knew him, who frequented him, knew it. He never stopped talking about you. He was very worried about you. He said you were hypersensitive, a tormented soul. All he wanted was to protect you."

And yet he's the one who finished me off, who killed me. Nothing unusual.

Each man kills the thing he loves.

"Let's go to Cadix," he repeated agreeably. "I'm the perfect traveling companion, discreet and obedient. I'll do everything you want. If you like, I'll just carry your cases for you."

"*Fanm tonbé pa janmin dézespéwé,*" says the song from Guadeloupe. Bishupal, with the impertinence of his young age, was mistaken. The life of a woman is never over. There is always a man to help her continue on her path. Salama Salama had avenged her for the boredom and solitude of her adolescence. Stephen had prevented her from having a nervous breakdown after Salama Salama abandoned her. Faustin had brought her in from the cold after Stephen's death. This Manuel was offering to console her for both Stephen's and Faustin's betrayal. But, in fact, all these providential rescuers were not helping her at all. All they did was distract her from herself. All they did was distract her from what should be the focus of her preoccupations. Her painting. What would her life have been like if in Paris she had not met Salama Salama, who had deafened her with his reggae music? If in N'Dossou she had not met Stephen, wrapped up in Seamus Heaney and Yeats? And Faustin in Cape Town, yearning for his nomination? She would probably have focused on herself. She wouldn't have relegated her painting to the back burner and put her life on the line. She would have fought tooth and nail to perfect it and impose it.

She looked at Manuel Desprez. No doubt this fifty year-old, in good shape, three hours a week at the Equinox health club, an hour's walk every day plus swimming, would make any woman happy in bed and an excellent lover. But she wouldn't go with him to Cadix, prelude to a new affair of the heart or sex or both, which, in the more or less short term, would end in disillusionment. Yet another one. Furthermore, she no longer had the courage to go through everything she had gone through all these years and once again suffer exclusion and incomprehension. The mixed couple is a strong wine for strong constitutions. The fainthearted should abstain.

She had already wasted too much of her time.

Suddenly, she saw her future clearly mapped out for her in a straight line for the remaining years of her life.

Fiela, all things considered, you didn't set an example. You chose to die. But it's not a question of dying. It's a question of living. Clinging to life. Obstinately.

She wouldn't leave Cape Town. Suffering is equivalent to entitlement. She had earned this city. She had made it hers by reversing the journey of her ancestors, dispossessed of Africa, who had seen the isles loom up like a mirage to the fore of Columbus's caravels, the isles where the cane and tobacco of their rebirth would germinate.

I shall no longer wear my heart out with loving. Why don't we pay more attention to love songs and ballads? They hold the truth. When I was small, Rose, who still sang, though in a somewhat strangled voice, had one song she

used to sing constantly. Listening from the cradle, I should
have heeded the words:

> *Ah! N'aimez pas,*
> *N'aimez pas sur cette terre!*
> *Quand l'amour s'en va,*
> *Il ne reste que les pleurs.*
> *(Oh! I beg you not to love / not to love on this earth! /*
> *When love goes / Only tears remain.)*

She looked at Manuel again, his handsome, considerate
face, and said firmly:

"I won't go with you to Cadix. I've never liked traveling. It
was Stephen who forced me and I obeyed. Now I want to do
as I please."

He didn't admit defeat and smiled.

"Then I won't go either. I too am a stay-at-home. I'll come
back and see you, if you let me, and we'll listen to Bach's
cello suites. Do you like Bach?"

After Verdi, Johann Sebastian Bach?

Rosélie dashed up to her studio, taking no notice of Dido
idling on her kitchen doorstep like a madam curious for
news. The windows had remained wide open. The five
o'clock afternoon sun was pouring in, frigid. For those familiar with nuances, however, its glare was tarnished. Darkness
was already lurking like a hungry beast prowling in the background. Gradually, Table Mountain would be defeated by the
shadows of night and it would relinquish its watch over Cape

Town. Then, from just about everywhere—the townships, the shantytowns, and the wastelands stretching to infinity—would emerge the cohorts of frustrated lovers who, unable to possess the city by daylight, took advantage of the night to ravage its body, finally vulnerable, accessible, and prostrate.

Rosélie carefully selected a canvas: forty-three inches by fifty-one. She fixed it to the wall. Grabbing a crayon, her hand drew in rapid, precise strokes a pair of eyes in the very middle. The eyes that had so impressed her. Drooping, half-slit eyes glowing between heavy lids. For those eyes, the surrounding world did not count. Only what boiled inside mattered and that remained a mystery. The entire face would be built around these eyes. Then, one by one, she unscrewed the tubes of paint, choosing the colors she liked: red, black, blue, dark green, and white. She squeezed them against the palm of her hand, spreading their contents onto her palette. She felt the dull sensation of her insides impatiently preparing to give birth. Finally, she approached the square of canvas where that impenetrable gaze held hers, and resolutely, she began to paint.

Fiela, is that you? Is this me? Our two faces have merged.

This time, she knew what her title would be. She had found it even before she had started. It had welled up from deep inside her on the crest of a raging tide: *Cannibal Woman*.

READING GROUP GUIDE
The Story of the Cannibal Woman

SUMMARY

One dark night in Cape Town, Rosélie's husband goes out for a pack of cigarettes and never comes back. Not only is she left with unanswered questions about his violent death but she is also left without any means of support. At the urging of her housekeeper and best friend, the new widow decides to take advantage of the strange gifts she has always possessed and embarks on a career as a clairvoyant. As Rosélie builds a new life for herself and seeks the truth about her husband's murder, acclaimed Carribbean author Maryse Condé crafts a deft exploration of post-apartheid South Africa and a smart, gripping thriller.

The Story of the Cannibal Woman is both contemporary and international, following the lives of an interracial, intercultural couple in New York City, Tokyo, and Cape Town. Maryse Condé is known for her vibrantly lyrical language and fearless, inventive storytelling—she uses both to stunning effect in this magnificently original novel.

DISCUSSION QUESTIONS

1. *The Story of the Cannibal Woman* is told mostly in the third person. However, there is an "I" that abruptly inserts itself

into the story starting in chapter three. Who does this voice belong to? Rosélie? How does the narration evolve and change throughout the novel?

2. Several of Rosélie's friends express concern regarding her relationship with Stephen. How is Rosélie hindered by her marriage and how does she benefit from it?

3. Stephen, known for making strong and often controversial claims, states on page 46 that "the only valid creations in life are those of the imagination." Do you agree with this? How does the novel support and/or contradict this statement?

4. Rosélie's best friend, Dido, does not like Stephen and is often caught giving him hateful stares. In reference to this on page 107, the narrator states that "good friends are always Cassandras." If this is a reference to Cassandra, the clairvoyant in Greek mythology, does that posit Rosélie as a Clytemnestra-type character? And if so, what would this imply about Stephen and the circumstances surrounding his death?

5. The song lyrics on page 110 imply that sex is the answer to despair and unhappiness. Does Rosélie believe this to be true? What about her clients?

6. On page 112 Stephen's computer and cell phone are described as foreign and almost evil. How and why is Rosélie reluctant to engage with technology and the modern world?

7. Racism is a constant theme in the novel. How is racism manifested in Cape Town versus in New York City?

8. Given that Rosélie is a painter and Stephen an English professor, art is important to this story. On page 127 the

narrator notes that Fina "had given up [writing] and made due with a teaching job, which is the opposite of creativity." Is the narrator claiming that the creation of art is a singular and solitary act? Does the novel on the whole support this claim?

9. On page 182 Amy says, "If I'm going to be devoured, I prefer it to be by my children." Who or what devours Rosélie? Herself? Society? Men? Art? How does this relate to the title of the book?

10. Rosélie claims she won't leave South Africa to go to Washington, D.C., because she doesn't want to leave Stephen. Is this the only reason? Why else might she be tethered to Cape Town? In what ways has Rosélie already abandoned Stephen?

ENHANCE YOUR BOOK CLUB EXPERIENCE

1. Give everyone in your book club a copy of Aeschylus's play *Agamemnon*. Compare its macabre elements (cannibalism, murder, blood) to *The Story of the Cannibal Woman*. You can download a free PDF version from the Text Kit website:

   http://www.textkit.com/learn/ID/6/author_id/5/

2. Get your discussion started by serving South African or French wine. Check out *Anthony Dias Blue's Pocket Guide to Wine 2007* (Fireside) for suggestions: *http://www.simonsays.com/content/book.cfm?tab=1&pid=521445*.

3. Research the current race relations in post-apartheid South Africa. Does the novel accurately portray South African society?